The Gregg Press
Science Fiction Series

The Crystal Button
by Chauncey Thomas

The Gregg Press Science Fiction Series

David G. Hartwell, *Editor*
L. W. Currey, *Associate Editor*

The Crystal Button

Or, Adventures of Paul Prognosis in the Forty-Ninth Century

CHAUNCEY THOMAS

With a New Introduction by
ORMOND SEAVEY

GREGG PRESS

A DIVISION OF G. K. HALL & CO., BOSTON, 1975

This is a complete photographic reprint of a work first published in Boston and New York by Houghton, Mifflin and Company in 1891. The trim size of the original edition was $4\frac{5}{8}$ by $6\frac{7}{8}$ inches.

Frontispiece illustration by Richard Powers.

Printed on permanent/durable acid-free paper and bound in the United States of America.

Republished in 1975 by Gregg Press, A Division of G. K. Hall & Co., 70 Lincoln Street, Boston, Massachusetts 02111.

Library of Congress Cataloging in Publication Data

Thomas, Chauncey.
The crystal button.

(The Gregg Press science fiction series)
Reprint of the 1891 ed. published by Houghton Mifflin, Boston.
1. Utopias. I. Title.
HX811 1891.T52   335'.12   75-5642
ISBN 0-8398-2314-2

Introduction

PAUL PROGNOSIS, the dream traveler of *The Crystal Button* finds himself suddenly in the forty-ninth century dressed only in a nightgown. Appearing in public without clothes is one of everybody's most common dream subjects; normally it is an expression of psycho-social anxieties. Besides the disorientation and embarassment, it is quite cold in this dream. Paul Prognosis, however, handles the situation better than most of us could. For one thing, he finds beside him his faithful dog Smudge. (Smudge in fact turns out to be the only bit of untidiness in the highly sanitized world of the future.) Also, he does not shrink from the sight of the architectural beauties around him. Instead he admires. "With eyes of wonder he gazed upon colonnades, triumphal arches, monuments, towers, facades alive with sculptured decorations, and domes like cumulus clouds that wall the horizon. And in the centre of the square rose a white column that pierced the very zenith."

Walking along this much-ornamented avenue are multitudes of handsome people in strange flowing garments. They seem not to notice Paul Prognosis, but seeing them he grows more and more uneasy about his vulnerable appearance. In panic he runs away, down unending streets and avenues, until a brazen gateway opens to him and he finds himself in the warm study of Professor Prosper. There he learns that he is in the city of Tone in the year 4872, exactly 3000 years after the accident in the Charles River that had started his adventure into the future.

Paul Prognosis adjusts to his new surroundings quicker than most travelers in time. In Edward Bellamy's *Looking Backward: 2000-1887,* Julian West is terrified at first to wander the streets of the new Boston, bereft of his fiancee and friends. Hank Morgan in Mark Twain's *A Connecticut Yankee,* surely the most cocksure of time travelers, still has twinges of longing for Puss Flanagan and the niceties of Hartford. Not so Paul Prognosis. Though he has left behind him wife and child, he never betrays a moment's regret. He seems indeed to have forgotten his particular identity back in the nineteenth century. Wonderment is the emotion on which he seems to subsist totally during his stay in the future. And whether examining machinery or society, he always has an eye out for the way things work. As a mechanical engineer, Prognosis has an unerring instinct for order, which he expects to see reflected in the physical universe.

The Author's Preface reveals the sources of this interplay between order and anxiety. He had written the book, he says, as a kind of release of personal tension, when reading itself was insufficient. Obviously a man accustomed to vigorous self-control, the "sloughs of anxiety in which I was otherwise liable to flounder" were neither welcome nor easily subdued. He set about curing those anxieties through a determined effort of imagination.

> A congenial subject was chosen: the material and mechanical possibilities of the future. Here was a field of inquiry limitless, and with scarcely a footprint. Here, the inventor could experiment on the largest scale, with no expense for models or patent-rights, and become completely absorbed in his self-imposed task, with no one to criticise his schemes. The plan worked admirably. An ideal world was thus opened, into which the imagination could enter at any time and wander serenely amid the glittering sights of a wonderland ever new, and with ever shifting scenes.

There is an inescapable note of determination in this proposal. The reiterated passive voice suggests the determined clumsiness of a man of business who knows what he wants and lets no inconvenient self-assertion get in his way.

Chauncey Thomas[1] knew well how confining models and patent-rights could be, since his life had been spent in the ordered world of engineering and design. Born on May 1, 1822, in Maxfield, Maine, he had been apprenticed at fifteen to a carriage making firm in Bangor. There he had shown signs of mechanical talent, becoming through his own efforts the principal bodymaker, an appropriate job for a self-made man. In 1845 he moved on to Boston as a journeyman with the carriage makers Slade & Whiton. He soon was put in charge of all construction. Recalling his early successes, Thomas is engagingly modest. "It would seem that there must have been a great lack of competent mechanics in those days, when one so young as I should be pushed forward into a place of so much responsibility. Looking back, I now believe it was altogether in my favor that I learned my trade in a small place like Bangor, for upon going to Boston I was all eyes, feeling my ignorance, and filled with ambition to know all there was to be known." [2] Like his hero Paul Prognosis he was by temperament an engineer and inventor rather than an entrepreneur. In the 1850s he married and set up business in his own right. By the time Thomas was writing *The Crystal Button,* he had become one of the leading carriage makers in New England. He was not, however, any captain of industry like W. D. Howells' Silas Lapham. The carriage trade was an industry of small manufacturers; Thomas's factory in Boston employed no more than forty workmen in 1880 and mostly built carriages to order. He had attained some prominence within his chosen trade, but he tried to resist the arrogance of the self-made man. "I can not forget the struggle for existence which I had before gaining a firm foothold, but I suppose it was only such as thousands of others have experienced. Still, I take pleasure in thinking that, *while I have often suffered from dealings with others, others have not suffered by their dealings with me.*"[3] Like the faith of his imagined prophet John Costor, this underscored profession is simple to the point of homeliness, but there is no doubt that either belief was firmly held.

Self-made man and carriage manufacturer, Chauncey Thomas would appear a highly unlikely novelist. Yet Thomas had been tempted to artistic creation earlier in his life as well. While with Slade & Whiton he severely injured a knee, putting himself out of work for two years. While recuperating he read avidly in astronomy and mathematics and did considerable drawing. He even considered becoming an artist. Here too his own experience enters into the characterization of Paul Prognosis. In the novel the young mechanical engineer receives a head injury that leaves him in a sort of coma for ten years. During that time his mind is not dormant; he becomes instead a creator of the future, a work of art which he is able later to set down fully on paper.

Thomas was at least serious enough about the novel he had been writing for six to eight years to want it published. As a gesture in that direction he showed the manuscript in 1880 to a literary man of his acquaintance, George Houghton. Thomas knew Houghton as the editor of *The Hub,* a trade magazine of carriage manufacturers, and a friendly correspondence had developed between them. Houghton wrote poetry when he was not hustling up news about the carriage trade; Houghton-Mifflin published two collections of his verse, *Niagara & Other Poems* and *The Legend of St. Olaf's Kirk.* Houghton was politely encouraging to the carriage maker, but Thomas must have developed second thoughts about going further with what had after all been only a diversion. Then in 1888 Edward Bellamy's *Looking Backward: 2000 - 1887* was published and soon created a sensation. Following in its wake were a whole series of refutations and imitations. George Houghton remembered the novel he had looked at almost ten years earlier and volunteered to edit it himself.

As the nineteenth century was coming to a close, it seemed possible to speak of the future almost familiarly. A widespread sense that the present was a period of transition lead figures as diverse as Henry Adams and Jack London into projections about the direction of the future. Edward Bellamy's book sold a million copies and made its author into a political figure as the head of the Nationalist movement. Ignatius Donnelly, a Minnesota populist politician, wrote *Caesar's Column* (1891), a bloody dystopia in which the industrial society of the future explodes in revolution, leaving only an agrarian remnant to escape to Africa and begin again.[4] William Dean Howells, who always labored to be conscious of American social realities, wrote *A Traveler from Altruria* (1894), describing the visit of a utopian, Mr. Homos, to a New England upper class resort. Even Mark Twain's *A Connecticut Yankee in King Arthur's Court* (1889) offers a kind of future in reverse, as the benefits of technology and the modern state are imposed on sixth-century England.

As a work of fiction *Looking Backward* does not stand out from its company in the late nineteenth century, but as a cultural document it is revealing about the generating forces behind this sudden flux of writing. Human nature may or may not be basically good, but it is basically uncomplicated and easily dealt with. Julian West's difficulties in getting a good night's sleep are sufficiently symptomatic of the dilemmas of the present. Social order can be established with a minimum of constraints. Bellamy reorganizes the work force into an "industrial army," but nothing is said of the imposed discipline characteristic of any army. Social institutions, once thrust into the future, tend to dissolve or lose their particularity. The legal system disappears; politics even as a mode of thought disappears; religion is reduced to moral uplift, for which there is nevertheless a vast popular appetite. Bellamy does not try to deal with the "labor question," the term under which he subordinates all the unpleasantness of the present. Rather the "labor question" is somehow transcended; it vanishes upon being looked at in a different light. The American literary culture of the late nineteenth century was powerless to deal with the material realities around it. Addressing an audience afflicted with bad nerves and feminine reticences, writers resorted to transcendance, the native American variety of escape. What could not be looked at would surely go away in time.

Edward Bellamy was a professional writer and therefore immediately absorbed in the enervating business of literary self-deception. He was thus locked into his audience as Chauncey Thomas never was. Thomas was writing for himself. Of course he had read widely enough in current literature to adopt some of its behaviorisms. The silly alliteration of the name "Paul Prognosis" recalls the forced humor of magazine fiction. But his awkward book hints at perceptions beyond anything the slicker Bellamy was capable of.

Contemporary reviewers mostly noted the resemblances between the two books, which are indeed striking though coincidental. Both novels are set in the Boston of the future (in *The Crystal Button* called "Tone," completing a transformation from the "St. Botolph's Town" of the original English Boston). In both novels a genial old scholar with a wife and one daughter shows the young protagonist around; in *Looking Backward* it is Dr. Leete, in *The Crystal Button* Professor Prosper. Like Bellamy's Congress, which meets every five years to make a few minute adjustments, Thomas' Government of Settled Forms is adjusted to a totally static society. The doctrine of John Costor is a blander version of Mr. Barton's sermon in *Looking Backward.* "It is hardly likely that so many people will read the book as read 'Looking Backward,' " the reviewer for the *Overland Monthly* predicted, "and yet they would find it quite as worthy of being read, — perhaps it might have been so, had it been published first, — as it might have been for it was written first." [5] The *Catholic World* reviewer thought *The Crystal Button* better than *Looking Backward.* "There seems to be no good reason why Mr. Thomas's, which is planned on similar lines, should not also sell well — unless because it comes too late before the public. It is pretty nearly as plausible, and in some respects better written, and the story it tells is much superior." [6] Yet the message of John

Costor was no substitute for genuine religion in the eyes of the *Catholic World:*

> For once we must allow ourselves the luxury of truth, although we antedate by thirty centuries its perfect advent as here described, and say that Mr. Thomas is a most depressing prophet. And for a reason not far to seek. The 'truth' of which the 'crystal button' is the symbol is wholly material and social. There is in it not only no vestige of spirituality, but not one glimpse of anything worthy to be esteemed the natural beatitude of rational creatures. It is only the pig that is contented when his belly is full and his pen 'rustles with sufficient straw.' What a comment the whole brood of these forecasting novels unconsciously supply on our Lord's question: 'When the Son of Man cometh, shall He find, think you, faith on the earth?' [7]

The apparent similarities between the two novels were sufficiently striking that Houghton-Mifflin, which had just taken over *Looking Backward* by merging with Ticknor, published letters from both Thomas and George Houghton attesting to the novel's prior conception.

Aside from the coincidence of place, many of the similarities between the two books are simply local versions of generic similarities among all utopias. Sir Thomas More in his *Utopia* (1516) also does away with political process and puts everyone to work. The differences between Thomas and Bellamy are both more subtle and more basic. Bellamy did not set out to be a social reformer; he commented a year after the book was published: "The idea was of a mere literary fantasy, a fairy tale of social felicity. There was no thought of contriving a house which practical men might live in, but merely of hanging in mid-air far out of reach of the sordid and material world of the present, a cloud-palace for an ideal humanity." [8] There is no love interest in *The Crystal Button,* and the carriage maker felt no revulsion from "the sordid and material world of the present." Thomas deliberately sets his scene thirty centuries away rather than a mere 113 years. The revolutionary changes Thomas describes are the product of a gradual evolution away from the experimental age in which he lived. The pyramids in which workers live in Tone are new to Paul Prognosis, but they are a thousand years old. Thomas faces an awkward paradox in the combination of stability and technology: everything must be changed but also permanent.

A millenialist fervor grips Bellamy, in strange contrast with the book's love story. Thomas' book is more a product of the

1870s, a present that could be improved on but was hardly bent on self-destruction. "Unlike most utopian novelists," Vernon L. Parrington, Jr. notes in his study of American utopias, "Thomas does not moralize about the present. The future will be better, he thinks, simply because engineers will have had time to work out a more practical system." [9] Parrington also suggests that much of Thomas's program reflects ideas popular in the 1870s, such as government insurance and currency reform.[10] The dangers Bellamy was to see later in monopoly capitalism were hardly visible to Thomas. When Paul Prognosis awakens after his ten year dream, he finds himself the unconcious founder of a large engine factory. In his bemused postscript he confesses himself unsure whether he prefers the present or the imagined future or which in fact is real. In dreams he still visits Tone. "In spite of Dr. Clarkson's confident assurances to the contrary, I sometimes entertain a suspicion — it can hardly be called a fear, for it is not unpleasant — that the dual life I now lead may some day again melt into one, and that one the world of fancy."

The city of Tone certainly offers special attractions for a mechanical engineer. Bellamy's technological innovations, a sort of radio and a few other things, are more or less cosmetic. For Thomas on the other hand, science and technology are the chief interest. Unlike other utopian theorists of the nineteenth century, his future is a field for experimentation rather than for settlement. Thomas' interest, moreover, is not merely in gadgetry. Much of *The Crystal Button* is devoted to the operations of pure science. Prosper and Prognosis attend a scientific conference; Prognosis visits the Standard Pendulum and Meridian Peak Observatory. Thomas invents a subway system for Tone in which electricity and compressed air are the energy sources for rapid transit. Trains now travel 200 miles per hour, and there are airships which fly at up to forty miles per hour. "A great deal of *The Crystal Button* sounds like pages taken from *The Scientific American.*" [11]

As a builder of landaus, coaches, coupes, and victorias for the Boston gentry, Thomas naturally felt a naive love of the sumptuous. The architecture of Tone is dwelt upon in considerable detail. Parrington compares the Tone architects' use of sunlight and air to that of Frank Lloyd Wright, but form is far from function here.[12] In *The Bostonians* Basil Ransom offers Henry James' acid comment on Harvard's Memorial Hall, a representative piece of Boston self-importance. "He thought there was rather too much brick about it, but it was buttressed, cloistered, turreted, dedicated, superscribed, as he had never seen anything; though it didn't look old, it looked significant; it covered a large area, and it sprang majestic into the winter air."[13] (Memorial Hall was completed in 1874 while Chauncey Thomas was at work on his novel.) Thomas' own principal public monument, the Tower of Peace and Good-will with its triumphal arches, marble and bronze statuary representing allegorical personages, bas-reliefs, spiral galleries and colonnades, is an extrapolation into the forty-ninth century of the magnificence of Thomas' native Boston.

Yet somehow in the midst of this triumphal architecture and technology there are hints of anxieties unresolved. Paul Prognosis first appears dressed only in a nightgown. While the Learned Fellows of the High School of Science are presenting their papers, he discovers that he has suddenly become bald, a symbolic self-mutilation. Through a sort of telephone he hears of another version of himself living in South America. Then the comet Veda appears out of schedule from Professor Prosper's calculations, and the world of perfect order is utterly destroyed. Somehow the hold of the future on Paul Prognosis must be broken in order for him to live again in the present.

Despite two fairly encouraging reviews, *The Crystal Button* never had anything like the popularity of *Looking Backward.* The audience that wished to be reassured about the immediate future did not want to hear about the forty-ninth century and especially not about the end of the world. Thomas' dream future is more of a prelude to the twentieth century, where dream and reality, order and anxiety are inevitably mixed. And like Yeats or Faulkner he finally offers his enchanted time to us, not as an escapist fantasy but as a sustaining delight in the face of dissolution. He may yet be able to visit Tone awake as well as asleep. "Life has many experiences that are less to be desired; and what city of the after-life Death holds in his sacred keeping, I know not. Perchance — who shall say nay? — each one of us is now building his own, even as I have builded Tone." It is a remarkable vision for a Boston carriage maker writing in his spare time.

Ormond Seavey
New York

REFERENCES

1. Chauncey Thomas, author of *The Crystal Button,* should not be confused with another Chauncey Thomas, a Denver-born writer on western subjects. W. J. Burke and Will D. Howe confuse the two in their standard reference work, *American Authors and Books* (rev.ed., New York: Crown Publishers, 1962).

2. "The Hub's Portrait Gallery. Chauncey Thomas. Second Vice-President of the Carriage-Builders' National Association," *The Hub,* 1 February 1880, p. 479.

3. *Ibid.,* p. 480.

4. Jay Martin, *Harvests of Change: American Literature 1865 - 1914* (Englewood Cliffs, N.J.: Prentice-Hall, 1967), pp. 232 - 33.

5. *Overland Monthly,* 18 Second Series (October 1891), 439.

6. *Catholic World,* 52 (March 1891), 935.

7. *Ibid.,* 936.

8. Quoted in Martin, pp. 221 - 22.

9. Vernon L. Parrington, Jr., *American Dreams: A Study of American Utopias* (Providence: Brown University Press, 1947), p. 65.

10. *Ibid.,* p. 67.

11. *Ibid.,* p. 65.

12. *Ibid.,* p. 65.

13. Henry James, *The Bostonians* (New York: Modern Library, 1956), p. 247.

THE CRYSTAL BUTTON

OR, ADVENTURES OF PAUL PROGNOSIS IN THE FORTY-NINTH CENTURY

BY

CHAUNCEY THOMAS

EDITED BY

GEORGE HOUGHTON

BOSTON AND NEW YORK
HOUGHTON, MIFFLIN AND COMPANY
The Riverside Press, Cambridge
1891

The Riverside Press, Cambridge, Mass., U. S. A.
Electrotyped and Printed by H. O. Houghton & Co.

"The assertion that the sole essential quality of God's word is *truth* brings the Eternal Presence into instant communication with every pure spirit." — Rev. NEWTON M. MANN in *A Rational View of the Bible.*

AUTHOR'S PREFACE.

YEARS ago, being unduly engrossed by business cares, the writer became aware that some sort of recreation was an immediate necessity. What should it be? It must be something with force enough to lift me out of the ruts of everyday life, and away from its uncompromising facts, its obstacles to be overcome, and its sloughs of anxiety in which I was otherwise liable to flounder. Reading, both heavy and light, had already served a good turn as a sedative, but this proved too mild treatment as a means of diverting a preoccupied mind.

Heroic measures were finally determined upon in the form of close study, designed as a counter-irritant. A congenial subject was chosen: the material and mechanical possibilities of the future. Here was a field of inquiry limitless, and with scarcely a footprint. Here, the inventor could experiment on the largest scale, with no expense for models or patent-rights, and become completely absorbed in his self-imposed task, with no one to criticise his schemes. The plan worked admirably. An ideal world was thus opened, into which the imagination could enter at any time and wander serenely amid the glittering sights of a wonderland ever new, and with ever shifting scenes.

This agreeable labor occupied many leisure hours between the years 1872 and 1878, within which period the substance of the chapters now gathered together in the form of a connected narrative was gradually committed to paper. Why it was not published at the time of its completion in 1878, and why, at last, it is now offered with some hope that it may tempt the appetite of a certain class of readers, even though already surfeited by imaginative literature, are points that will be fully explained in the accompanying letter by the Editor, on whose shoulders rests much of the responsibility for the appearance of the story at this time and in its present form.

CHAUNCEY THOMAS.

BOSTON, MASS., *March* 3, 1890.

EDITOR'S PREFACE.

OPEN LETTER TO THE PUBLISHERS.

DEAR SIRS: — For three months past, the undersigned has been engaged in the pleasant task of editing, for a Boston gentleman, the manuscript of a novel entitled "The Crystal Button, or Adventures of Paul Prognosis in the Forty-Ninth Century," which may perhaps commend itself as a fitting companion-piece to Mr. Edward Bellamy's "Looking Backward."

Of course, neither author nor editor has any idea that it will rival that remarkable production; but, in many ways, it helps to supplement with details the same general picture of future possibilities that Mr. Bellamy has so skillfully and attractively painted.

Permit me to state briefly that the present imaginative work, of which the accompanying table of contents will give some idea, was written many years ago by the well-known coach-builder of Boston. The thought was to foreshadow the future possibilities of mechanical and material development; and the work of authorship was entered upon as a means of diversion from the cares of business.

The original manuscript, now before me, shows that it was begun in 1872, and that the author wrote the closing page on February 9, 1878. The slight story, now cut in two and used as "Introduction" and "Conclusion," was written somewhat later, but bears no date.

About the year 1880, the author showed me this manuscript, and asked advice whether it was suitable for publication in book form. I read it with great interest, but reported that, in my humble opinion, it needed and well merited somewhat more finish, and also required to be sustained by some sort of narrative. It is to be feared that this report served to shelve it, for I heard nothing more about it until I read Mr. Bellamy's book in August of last year, when its remarkable similarity in general scheme to that of "The Crystal Button" led me to request an opportunity to re-read the latter. As a result of the correspondence that followed, the author expressed willingness to make it public, providing I would undertake the work of rearranging and editing it, which agreeable task is now approaching a finish.

I believe it to be a good book, in every way helpful and stimulating, decidedly practical in many of its suggestions, and covering a great variety of topics that seem to me to appeal to the interests of large classes of readers.

Its chief defect, if such it may be called, is the fact, already stated, that its general scheme so closely resembles that of Mr. Bellamy's book that it would be difficult to convince the public of its priority, — a task I should shrink from undertaking, although I know it to be a fact. It is unfortunate that its scene should likewise be laid in Boston; but there seems no sufficient justification for an editor's attempting to change the locality, especially in view of the danger of complicating numerous references that might easily be made inexplicable.

On the other hand, the author departs from Mr. Bellamy's track by dealing mainly with mechanical and material development, as the table of contents clearly shows; and just here he naturally possesses originality and strength, being one of the ablest mechanics and inventors that the American coach trade has thus far produced. It is only near the close, in the chapters entitled "Law," "Government," and "Money," that he enters Mr. Bellamy's field, and he does so by cross-paths. To the suggestion that the introduction of certain notes in passing might help to emphasize or supplement some of Mr. Bellamy's views, the author has not only prohibited this, but also requested the removal, so far as possible, of everything in his original manuscript that might suggest parallelism with any ideas presented in "Looking Backward," although, at the same time, he expresses general approval of the ideas therein advanced.

In the judgment of the editor, however, the all-important point of the present book is its theory of the simple but effective means by which the world finally attains the high level of the new civilization, which is described through the teachings of a reformer known as John Costor, whose text is ever "Truth! Truth!" It is Costor's emblem, the crystal button, that very fittingly gives the title to the book. Upon this foundation of truth, exerting its benign influence in wholly peaceful ways through the instrumentality of the individual, the family, social life, the arts, the government, and finally through the grand consolidation of all governments, he erects the pillars of his ideal state. Whatever Socialism and Nationalism may or may not accomplish, this lesson of truth-loving and truth-observing is certainly a kind of seed that can hardly fail to produce good fruit, whatever the soil on which it may chance to alight. In this, as you will observe, consists the moral force of the book.

Please pardon the length of this letter, but I feel desirous to do my duty, as far as I am able, in adequately introducing the work to your attention; and, with your permission, it will give me pleasure to submit the manuscript to you as soon as it is completed.

Very respectfully yours,

GEORGE HOUGHTON.

YONKERS, NEW YORK, *February* 10, 1890.

CONTENTS.

PART III. THE CRYSTAL BUTTON.

PART IV. A DAY'S RAMBLE WITH MARCO MORTIMER.

PART V. THE CELESTIAL VISITOR.

PART VI. CONCLUSION.

THE CRYSTAL BUTTON.

PART I.

INTRODUCTION.

CHAPTER I.

Paul Prognosis meets with an Accident.

"MAMMA, is n't it a nice Christmas present? Don't you think papa will like it?"

"I 'm sure he will, dear."

The door-bell gave a sudden sharp alarum that was like a scream. Mrs. Prognosis sprang from her chair. "I suppose," she said, "it 's another telegram asking your father to hurry over to the broken drawbridge. But he must be there by this time. I do wish they would give Paul an hour's rest on this day before Christmas." She went to the door, her daughter following.

"Your pardon, ma'am," spoke up a hoarse voice, "but I 've bad news for you."

"Bad news? Oh, about the broken draw?

I know about that. My husband is at the bridge now, attending to repairs."

"It's another sort of bad news that I'm bringing you, ma'am."

"Another sort? Paul — my husband — what has happened to him? Is he in any trouble? — is he dead? Tell me, man, is Paul Prognosis dead?"

"No, not dead, ma'am; but he's been hurt."

"How? — Where? — At the bridge? I will go with you to him."

"He is coming to you. They are bringing him to you. No, ma'am, you must n't go." He put up his left hand, in which he held his cap, as if to detain her; then dropped it respectfully, and repeated with a pleading voice, while tears trickled down his pockmarked cheeks: "No, no! ma'am, you must n't go. Dr. Clarkson is coming, and he sent me to tell you about it."

"Tell me quickly, then, and tell me the truth."

They stood close together on the trellised doorstoop of the contractor's house, on one of the steep hill-streets in the older part of the city — the slight woman with her earnest, troubled face, to whose skirts clung the shivering child, and the coatless workman, dripping wet, and with particles of ice in his beard and long hair. His right hand was concealed in a handkerchief, and a dark stain gradually spread about its folds, until a scarlet drop fell upon the icy coating of the stoop. But Mrs. Prognosis did not notice this, and the man made no allusion to it. The December wind that whistled through the lattice-work and dead leafage, chasing little whirls of fine snow, was biting cold; but only the child seemed to feel it. "Patty, go indoors, and wait for mamma." The child silently obeyed.

"You see, ma'am, there was an accident at the bridge, where the Boss put in his new patent draw last summer. A schooner, loaded with lumber, got caught by the tide and jammed in, side on, and chocked the draw so that the keeper could n't work her back, and travel was stopped. They sent for the Boss, and he and I — I 'm his foreman, ma'am — were at work down below there, when Jake Cummings, — you know him, perhaps — he 's the draw-keeper, an old fellow with rheumatism, and five children, and the old woman dead a twelvemonth, — he slipped on one of the guys, and pitched head-foremost in among the ice."

"Yes, yes — but my husband?"

"Well, the skipper on the schooner threw a rope to the old man as he drifted past, but he missed it, and went downstream with the current. Then the Boss plunged in and followed him, swimming hand over hand in a way that made the crowd cheer. There they both were, in among the ice-cakes and some floating logs and lumber that had got loose from the schooner; and the Boss soon had hold of Jake, but he could n't seem to make any headway when he turned upstream. When I saw that, in I went too, with Smudge at my heels; and we all brought up in a bunch, with the ice crunching about us, and a small boat from the schooner, that was trying to get at us, shoving the drift against our shoulders. It looked like we had seen our last Christmas, the whole lot of us, dog and all. Well, at last, I — we got him out and aboard the boat."

"Who — who was it you got out?"

"The Boss, ma'am."

"Thank God! and thank you, my friend!"

"And Smudge, too; he ought to be thanked. He stuck to the Boss through it all. As for old Jake, I could n't get at him."

"And my husband did n't succeed in saving him, after all?"

"That I don't know."

"He must have. Paul always succeeds."

"I hope so, ma'am. Smudge went in again after the old man. As for me, I could n't see much after I got aboard the schooner, till Dr. Clarkson poured something hot into me. He will tell us. Here they come."

Without another word the woman ran to meet the approaching file of men, bowed by the weight they bore between them on an improvised stretcher. Every hat came off as she drew near. It was growing dusky now, so she could scarcely distinguish the white face that lay there, but she kissed the cold lips, shivered, and gave a piteous look toward Dr. Clarkson, who only said: "Have courage, Mrs. Prognosis. I think a warm bed is all that is needed." She stooped, and clasped in hers one of the cold hands, that gave no response. In that hand, clenched, while all else hung nerveless, she found a little rag of linen, with a buttonhole, in which clung a small glass button. She thrust this in her bosom, again took the chilly palm in hers, and accompanied the procession of silent men as they mounted the stoop and the front staircase to the south chamber, where a few neighbors gave what assistance they could, under the direction of the doctor, and then quietly retired. Beside the bed sat Smudge, the only spectator.

For the next hour, Dr. Clarkson kept the tearless wife busily employed in doing whatever small tasks he could think of, whether helpful or not, and especially such as related to her child. He saw that she was calm — so calm that a stranger might have misjudged her. But the family physician knew.

Just before midnight, when breathing had been fully restored, he left her, saying: "I find no injury of any kind. He no doubt received a severe blow on the head from the ice or a drifting log, though I do not find even a scalp-wound. What the result will be, I cannot now foretell. But keep up courage, Mrs. Prognosis. I have known your husband many years. He is a strong man, in robust health, with everything in his favor, and I believe he will be spared to you unharmed. Fact is, a man like that we can't very well get along without. Everybody respects him, and the only ones who ever disliked him were a few malcontents who, at one time, imagined they had reason to fear his truth-telling. But some of these very men are now his best friends. There 's that Tom Haggerty, for instance, — he followed in after him with Smudge, and I hardly know which proved the better water-dog. Well, he seems to be perfectly comfortable for the present. To-morrow morning we shall know more about the case. In the mean time I leave him in your care. I can do nothing further to-night, and you can do nothing but watch, wait, and hope. He helped to save old man Cummings like a hero, as he is; and I think he 'll be able to receive thanks in person before the holidays are over. I hope so — I believe so. Good-night."

In the stillness of that night before Christmas, Mary Prognosis thus found herself in her chamber alone with her husband — with him, and yet alone, for, up to this time, he had given no sign of life other than his breathing and a low sigh now and then. Yet still not wholly alone, for in the next room she could also hear the breathing of her child — their child. "O God, spare my child's father!" She knelt beside him, and felt relief as a few tears gushed from her eyes. "This will never do! — I must be strong."

She passed downstairs and locked the doors of the house; listened to the buffets of snow against the windows; went into the child's room and put the little hands under the coverlet; and again returned to her husband's bedside, where the dog still kept patient vigil. The bell in the city-hall boomed the first hour. She looked at the watch that had been taken from the drenched clothing. The hands recorded thirteen minutes past three. That stilled minute-hand must have stopped just there when the crash came. She found the key, and was about to wind it — and then, suddenly changing her mind, shut it in a little jewel case. Reopening the case, she put beside it the glass button, and then turned a key on both.

How cold it was! She spread another blanket

on the bed. As she did so, the sleeper turned himself wearily, opened his eyes and raised them to hers with a confused look, that gradually calmed into a faint smile; and he made a movement with his hand to take hers. Then, with a voice somewhat strange from weakness, he asked, with a pause after each word: "Is — Jake — all — right?"

"Jake is all right, dear."

"Then all 's well. I am very tired. Good-night, darling."

"Good-night."

CHAPTER II.

Paul bids his Wife "Good-night."

FROM the time of that accident on Christmas Eve, Paul Prognosis never spoke an intelligible word, and never showed a sign of recognition of those about him, for a period of ten years. His life was spared, and his general health continued good, but the current of his thought was broken. Was it broken, or merely diverted? Could a man, having the intelligence and training of Paul Prognosis, lose all power of connected thought while the engine of his heart still performed its functions, and his brain, apparently uninjured, continued to receive its full supply of vitalized fluid? Could concussion of the brain mean death to its tissues, while every other part of his body throbbed with vigorous life?

From boyhood, he had displayed a degree of mechanical knowledge that was closely allied to the intuition of a genius. His friends called him such; if he had foes, they probably thought him a "crank," but no one ever heard that term applied to him. The small competency his father left him, he had devoted to gaining instruction in his chosen pursuit. He had next worked in the car-shops, and been gradually promoted until he became master-mechanic, and then mechanical engineer. In every position he occupied, he soon became master of it. The more abstruse the problem presented to him, the greater the pleasure he found in solving it. His inventions were numbered by scores, and many of these were patented ; but he seldom took much further interest in a question he had once answered to his own satisfaction. He would hand the patent-papers to his wife, saying: "Well, Molly, you 're a better hand than I am at keeping things safe and snug. Put this where you can find it, and it may perhaps come handy some rainy day."

Later, he began to be called on by corporations all over the country to act as an expert in matters requiring mechanical keenness, and he finally left the car-shops, to become a contractor on his own account. Thus far, he had not realized the profits he deserved. But his fame was worth a fortune, and he was just beginning to understand how it might be coined. And now, to be struck down in his thirty-fifth year, with the best part of his life before him and everything to live for, — and from no fault of his own, but the reverse, — all who knew him agreed that it was one of those dispensations of Providence that are unintelligible to those who have confidence in divine justice and compassion.

For a time his friends showed active sympathy for him and for the woman who was well-nigh a widow, and also for the daughter who might as well have been fatherless. But the months became years, and calls for sympathy in other directions were many and pressing, and people gradually ceased to remember the Boss's misfortune — all but Dr. Clarkson. Oh! old Jake, he never forgot; but he was too old and too poor to do more than look and speak his sympathy.

And the wife? She hoped against hope until it died in her heart, and then set herself to work to eke out the small quarterly income she received from his annuity, and to give her daughter such training as she knew he would have approved.

So the years slowly wore on, bringing many another Christmas eve and morn, but the man who had been a master among men now looked upon the faces of his nearest and dearest, and knew them not; looked upon the electrical engine which his own hands had made, and which at last began to find work wherever there was work to do, and saw not that it was an engine; gazed from undulled eyes, and with a contented smile upon his lips, but gave no sign of recognition to anything around him. He spoke — spoke often and connectedly, but seldom responsively. "Thank you," he would say to Dr. Clarkson; "your conversation, Professor, interests me exceedingly. I do not think I fully follow you in your description, but the mechanical progress you indicate suggests wonderful development since the plodding steps of inquiry pursued in my day." The Doctor often sought to lead him further when he spoke in this manner; but he would branch off into some irrelevant remark, such as: "Wonderful, indeed! but it precisely fills a need that we felt in the nineteenth century. I see that it means economy of energy as well as of time."

When, in the later years, the Doctor's son Will became a frequent visitor at the house, he always addressed him as Marco, and often appealed to the young man for information in regard to the workings of anything he happened to hold in his hand, seeming to regard it as some mechanical wonder. To his imagination, a waste-basket became a colossal tower; a toy wagon, a railway train; his wife's jewel-box, a mammoth tenement house; or so it seemed to those around him, judging from his fragmentary comments. All faces, all things, were changed to him, but apparently in no way unpleasantly. He took untiring interest in every new object to which his attention was called, and the same object always retained the new guise in which he first viewed it. The same waste-basket was always the same colossal tower. The only living thing that seemed to maintain quite the same relations in his inner as in his outer world, and that he always called correctly by name, was his dog Smudge. Smudge was his constant companion, both in the street and in the house; and the intelligent devotion of the dog was such that Dr. Clarkson was wont to remark that "Smudge evidently lives in dreamland as well as his master. And," he would add, "it must be a pleasant sort of place to live in, for a happier couple of friends you won't find in all Boston."

It was quite clear that the windows of Paul's mental dwelling-place were closely shuttered. But inside those darkened shutters — what was going on there? There was life still there. And why not? If nothing material can be utterly destroyed — not even the delicate fabric of this rice-paper, which burns and leaves no ash — how much less should we expect to see the immaterial blotted out of existence. Was the precious knowledge, so laboriously stored beneath the white dome of Paul's rugged forehead, thus instantaneously annihilated? Might not the swift current of his mental activity, accidentally diverted from its normal confines, have made for itself an underground course, where no eye, however sympathetic, could follow its secret windings? Might not his former projects in the realm of mechanics, and his prophecies that others had considered wild fancies, — might not these, when no longer fettered by limitations of matter and mechanical means, have finally materialized? Might not his *could be* of yesterday have become the *now is?* Might not all possibilities he formerly dreamed have thrown aside their shadowy veils and become realized, in the domain he now occupied, where thought could be continued uninterruptedly and unhindered? Might not the occasional mutterings of his lips, although unintelligible to his hearers, be vague hints from a world unseen and unknown to those around him, yet none the less real to him? So Dr. Clarkson sometimes thought, and so he once told the weeping wife when she confessed to him that all hope had left her. Was it not within reason to consider that last greeting: "Good-night, darling!" a token that life still flickered in the paralyzed brain after the injury, and a prophecy that, under favorable conditions, it might some time flash again and disclose the guest of the darkened chamber once more himself — once more Paul Prognosis, the mechanical expert — with a "Good-morning!" on his lips?

PART II.

A DAY'S RAMBLE WITH PROFESSOR PROSPER.

CHAPTER III.

Paul's Remarkable Introduction to the City of Tone.

"WELL, as my name 's Paul Prognosis, this is a pretty predicament for a respectable citizen of Boston to find himself in, tramping about the streets at day-dawn, and with nothing but a nightgown on. And cold — it is cold! I must get into one of these houses by some means. I wonder where my house is! And where am I? — that 's a still more important question."

He looked about him in search of a doorway that might serve as a haven. To his surprise, he found himself standing in a public square, that was wholly unfamiliar to him, surrounded by buildings vast and magnificent. Everywhere novelty, everywhere order, everywhere beauty! Great structures on every side, aglow with the morning sunshine, appalled him by their majestic proportions; while unbroken vistas of wide avenues, opening up on every side, revealed the extent and grandeur of the city. With eyes of wonder he gazed upon colonnades, triumphal arches, monuments, towers, façades alive with sculptured decorations, and domes like cumulus clouds that wall the horizon. And in the centre of the square rose a white column that pierced the very zenith.

Such harmony and richness of color on every side — was mortal ever before permitted to gaze upon them! such elegance of form, yet apparently so substantial — such graceful and dreamlike proportions throughout all these vast architectural piles!

"This is all very well, but I must find a place where I can dress and warm myself."

Something warm touched his hand. He gave a spring to escape, but the warmth continued — it was the warmth of breath. He looked down, and gave a joyful cry. "Why, Smudge, old fellow! You are indeed a friend in need. You 'll lead me home, won't you?"

But Smudge merely gazed up into his face, and made no movement to lead anywhere.

"I believe, Smudge, that you are lost too. We are both lost. Where have we been, and where have we now come to? Did I lead you, or did you lead me? In any case we 're in trouble now together; and, whatever further happens, we must stand by one another. But this is certainly the most beautiful architectural display I ever saw. If this is Boston, then I 'm no Bostonian. But where, then, can we have got to?"

He involuntarily glanced down to see if the street was paved with gold.

"No, this is not the new Jerusalem."

At this moment his attention was attracted by multitudes of oddly dressed people, who thronged the sidewalks, even brushing against him. Strangely enough, he had not before noticed them; and, still more strangely, his previous obliviousness to their presence did not excite his surprise. It was enough that they were there, and that some one would now be able to afford him shelter.

"But are they men and boys, or men, women, and boys? And if the latter, which are the boys and which the women? They all seem to be dressed very much alike. And how handsome they all are! This one must be a girl. Dear me, what a pretty face! But who ever saw such queer clothes? Yet they are as simple and becoming as they are queer."

These observations renewed the unpleasant remembrance that he himself was in undress uniform, and he gathered his gown about him, crouched within it, and withdrew to an archway.

"I would n't mind exchanging this costume for one just like theirs. What must these people think of me? I shall certainly be arrested if I don't succeed soon in finding my house, or somebody's house."

And he continued to creep along stealthily, vainly trying to hide himself in corners and doorways, while the blaze of day grew steadily brighter, and the populace passed to and fro in increasing numbers. Very strangely, however, no one gave the slightest attention to him. Indeed, they did not seem to notice him any more than if he were an impalpable spirit. But he knew they would, and a terror began to possess him that he would be stoned and beaten. Standing about in this way would never do. He began to run — to run wildly, Smudge bounding beside him, up and down unending streets and avenues, until the breath was well-nigh out of his body, — until a brazen gateway suddenly opened before him without effort on his part, and he darted through it, then up a broad winding staircase, through another open doorway, and found himself, with Smudge at his side, in the midst of a snug library, where the warmth of an open fire cheered his eyes, and where, face to face with him, sat an elderly man at a table littered with papers, occupied with inspecting what appeared to be a small coffee-mill.

CHAPTER IV.

Paul makes the Acquaintance of Professor Prosper.

THE gentleman whom he thus unceremoniously confronted did not notice him at first, and he tried to attract attention by speaking, but not a word could he utter. At length, he laid his hand on the gentleman's shoulder, and with great effort managed to find his voice, though it startled him by its harsh and far-away sound; his words seemed to him to have that strained formality that one hears from a prisoner at the bar, addressing the judge.

"I beg pardon, sir, for this intrusion, which must appear to you wholly unwarrantable, but I have lost my clothes, and do not know where I am. Can you please direct me, sir?"

The old gentleman looked up without any visible surprise — certainly without any appearance of annoyance. He made no reply, but seemed as if waiting to have the question repeated. Paul again made an apology for his appearance, and again humbly asked for assistance in finding his way.

"Why, this is odd," said the gentleman at last, using a strange accent and a language that was not quite familiar to Paul, although he found that he could understand it readily enough, — "you are talking in Old English, and you speak as though you were well acquainted with it. I thought I was the only living man who could do that." Then he added, reflectively: "Poor fellow, he must have escaped from some madhouse. But he speaks Old English remarkably well — better, I admit it — much better than I can."

There suddenly occurred to Paul the similar thought, that he must have entered a retreat of some kind, and that he was now in the presence of one of the patients. But any apprehensions he might otherwise have felt on this account were relieved when the gentleman calmly continued: —

"Yes, I will gladly help you all I can. You say you are lost. Tell me where your home is."

"Where my home is? That 's it," said Paul, brightening, — "where my home is? Yes, yes." He felt his mind wandering a little, as every man's mind is apt to do when he is suddenly relieved from some great anxiety, and then confronted by the simplest possible question of every-day life. "I live on Cedar Avenue, number 201. And if you will be good enough to send for a hack, I can go home at once without troubling you further."

"Strange, very strange!" repeated the old gentleman — "such perfect command both of Old English words and also of old phrase-forms! But, my dear sir, where is Cedar Avenue?"

"Why, don't you know? It's not far from the Common, and is nearly as old as the city."

"I never heard of it, or of the Common you mention; and it can't be in this city, for all our avenues are named systematically, and Cedar is a name that does n't belong to the system."

This was somewhat bewildering. Remembrance of the great city through which he had recently prowled flashed across Paul's mind. It had not seemed like his native city. "Is this not Boston, sir?"

The gentleman again looked at him sharply, without replying; and Paul, who once more began to waver between doubts as to whether he had been transported or whether his questioner was demented, could only find words to add, in a hopeless sort of way: "If I am not in Boston, please tell me where I am, and how I came here, and how I can get away."

"Why, my dear sir, do you not know that you are in the good city of Tone? Such is the fact. You say you live in Boston. Is it possible that you do not realize that the ancient city of Boston, like the ancient language you speak, is merely an historical fact of the remote past? One would think you were a relic strayed from a former age. But allow me to ask you a few questions, and see how far we can understand one another."

"I will try to answer them, sir."

"What year is this?"

"Why, eighteen hundred and seventy-two," answered Paul quickly, glad to be thus led off with an easy one. "You see I have not altogether lost my wits."

"And who is the chief officer of state?"

"Ulysses S. Grant."

"Mention, if you please, some notable persons now living in other parts of the world."

"Well, in England there is Queen Victoria; Emperor William in Germany, Alexander in Russia, and Victor Immanuel in Italy. In France — I have forgotten who is at the head of affairs in France just now, or in Spain either, for they turn so many political somersaults that it is difficult to keep track of affairs in those countries."

"And you say that you live in Boston?"

"Yes," answered Paul, more at ease, and no longer annoyed at his questioner's reiteration, although now convinced that the other was hopelessly beside himself.

"And Boston is where?"

"In the good old Bay State, Massachusetts," said Paul, smiling for the first time.

"Marco!" called out the old gentleman, — "Marco, I wish you would come here for a few moments."

Through the curtains from an adjoining room soon advanced a handsome young fellow, about twenty years old, and an athlete in build, whose fine figure showed to advantage in his simple flowing garments. "This is my young friend Marco. And this is a stranger whose conversation interests me more than I can tell. I wish, Marco, you would look up a few facts for me. Please examine the chronological tables of Blackmole's Ancient History, and see in what year of the Christian Era there was a President of the ancient Republic of Washington, named Grant, — was it not Grant you mentioned?"

"Yes, Ulysses S. Grant."

"This stranger, Marco, who is no doubt a recent inmate of some asylum, but who appears quite harmless and is evidently a person of rare erudition, particularly interests me because he speaks with wonderful fluency and correctness the old English language, on which, as you know, I pride myself. It is of course possible that a demented person, and especially one versed in ancient history, might fancy himself transported to the field of his former researches, and living in the days of Grant and Queen Victoria; but what I now want to do is to see how far he is consistent in his imaginings."

While the old gentleman was thus speaking, Paul watched the young man as he swiftly ran over the pages of the book before him. He also glanced at them; but, to his astonishment, he was unable to decipher a word. They were evidently printed in some kind of shorthand, and the speed with which the searcher pursued his task seemed to indicate that the volume was either perfectly familiar to him, or he was able to catch its contents with lightning glances.

"Well, Professor," said the young man, "there was a President named Grant, who was elected soon after the close of the First Civil War, — the war that resulted in the extinction of negro slavery. He was previously chief in command of the Government forces. That was in Anno Domini 1868. The same Grant was reëlected to the presidency in 1872."

"That must have been about the time when electricity was first introduced as an illuminator."

"I see no mention of electric lighting until a few pages later."

"And how about the enfranchisement of women?"

"That followed not many years afterward; but it is well along in the next century that I find a woman President named."

"Let us see, a moment," commented the Professor. "The present year being Anno Pacis 1372, and adding this to Anno Domini 3500, the Year of Peace, we are now, according to the old style, in the year 4872. Stranger, your friend Grant was President just three thousand years ago. You 've had a good long nap, if you 've been asleep ever since then."

Paul was now so thoroughly confused that he did not try to make any response, beyond a piteous sigh: "What am I to do?"

"Simply make yourself perfectly comfortable, and consider my home yours until further notice. I will see that you are supplied with everything you need."

"Thank you, sir — thank you with all my heart! And my companion here — my dog — can he also remain?"

"Certainly. Well, the most evident need you now have is clothing. Marco, take the necessary measures as to height, girth, and length of leg, and telephone to the East Central warehouse for full costumes — day and evening, and for both house and street."

This having been done, the old gentleman continued: "By the way, I do not yet know your name."

"Paul Prognosis."

"And mine is Prosper, Fellow of the Academy of Sciences — people generally call me 'Professor' for short; and my young friend's name is Marco Mortimer — a rather musical name, is n't it? My daughter likes it so well that she is preparing to link hers to it. Madam Prosper-Mortimer — is n't that a name to be remembered? Marco, you have no need to simulate nervous haste. Your blushes speak your modesty. But there 's the signal from the parcel-delivery tube. Will you please attend to it, Marco? There 's nothing like present duty as a cure for confusion."

In response to this request, the young man opened a circular bronze door in one of the alcoves, and into his arms swiftly dropped a number of compact parcels.

"There," continued the Professor, "I think you 'll find the outfit complete; and Marco will now conduct you to our spare chamber, and afterwards see that you have breakfast. Try and eat a good hearty one, for I propose to give you a walk that will require your best energies. While you are employed upstairs, I will finish my correspondence."

CHAPTER V.

The Expected Advent of a Celestial Visitor.

AFTER an absence of an hour, Paul returned to the library, attired in his new costume and closely followed by Smudge. The latter had a look of surprised wonder, but his master was now quite calm.

"Mr. Prognosis," said the Professor, "as you are our guest, it is only proper for you to know that you may find my mind a little preoccupied by reason of the preparations it is my duty to make in view of the near approach of the great event."

"You refer to your daughter's marriage, I presume."

"Not at all. Why, is it possible? Are n't you aware that we now stand on the threshold with expectant eyes, awaiting the advent of the greatest spectacle in recorded history?"

"I was not aware of it, sir."

"It is to occur just three days from now. You very likely noticed, before you came in, that the streets were crowded with people, although the sun had only just risen. The whole world will be out-of-doors for the next three days, awaiting and discussing the expected event. As for myself, I have already completed nearly all my preparations for the observations I am to make. But, again, you know nothing of this; you do not even know that I am an astronomer, and have direction of the telescopic and photographic work at this station. I have a few errands still to attend to, but you can accompany me, and we can talk as we go along."

"Thank you, sir. Nothing could give me greater pleasure than the walk you propose. But the great event you allude to, may I ask what that is?"

"Just think of it, Marco, — a fellow mortal who apparently has no knowledge of the fact that the Year of Peace 1372 marks an epoch above all epochs in scientific interest! But no doubt, Mr. Prognosis, I shall find you all the more interesting as a companion for this very reason. You will prove an audience such as I probably could not find elsewhere on this globe. You can't help being interested in this most remarkable occurrence, and especially so if your mind has any scientific bent. How is that?"

"I am proud to say that I have made science the special study of my life — that is, the science of mechanics mainly; but no one can search deeply and understandingly into mechanics or any one branch of that study, without acquiring some general knowledge of science and a taste for science generally."

"Very true. And in what branch of mechanics were you mainly interested?"

"In engineering and motive forces. I was among the first to foresee the future possibilities of electricity, and I have received several patents for inventions in that line, which I hope may some time prove valuable to the world as well as to me."

"Indeed, that is interesting. But patents, I must tell you, are among those many things of the remote past that found no place in the world's economy after the Experimental Age was gone. However, we will talk of that some other time. To-day, let us forget that there ever was a yesterday. We will simply look at things as they present themselves to our eyes. We will calmly accept the world as we find it, — I think you will be quite willing to, — and calmly prepare our minds for the great coming."

"But this great coming; what is it?"

"It is a brief call that will be paid our planet by the huge comet Veda, — she never appeared in your Christian Era, — which will pass in review before our very doors."

"Is the end of the world indeed so near at hand?" cried Paul.

"There is no need of anxiety on that score. For centuries past our astronomers have been engaged in their calculations, which are now completed, and with an accuracy that is beyond all question. There can be no collision, there can be no disastrous results. The world has not been slowly builded to its present degree of perfection to be suddenly demolished. Next Sunday morning, shortly before sunrise, the comet will cross our heavens, and the only fear is that she will approach so near that we shall be unable to gaze upon her."

"But the world's tides! The proximity of such vast masses of matter cannot but result in causing another Noah's deluge!"

"Our best scientists think it was this same comet Veda that caused the deluge of which you speak; but the world must then have been enveloped in the tail, which is now deflected from the direct line of its approach; and, in the slight disturbance of all the usual conditions of the solar system, the power of attraction will be exactly compensated, and our tides will scarcely record the event. Moreover, the passage will be brief, and effects of light and heat will be largely neutralized by our enveloping atmosphere. I can assure you, Mr. Prognosis, that you need not fear danger of any kind."

"Of course it would be useless to do so. If the world were to be blotted out of existence in the twinkling of an eye" —

"But I have assured you that it is n't going to be! Neighbor Mars and ourselves agree on this point."

For some reason the astounding intelligence that had just been communicated to Paul did not affect him as strongly as might have been expected. He had already observed and heard so many strange things during the hour just passed, that he was becoming quite prepared and even expectant to hear more; and he had now fully recovered from his preconception that the Professor was insane. By some means, which his mind could not yet compass, and he no longer made any attempt to do so, he found himself amid scenes and circumstances that were wholly new to him; but his training and experience fitted him to appreciate their supreme interest, and he lent himself unreservedly to the pleasant task of observing everything about him. In response to the Professor's last remark, he merely asked: "You speak of 'neighbor Mars' — is it positively known that Mars is inhabited by human beings?"

"Inhabited? Why, certainly. We have had communication with its people for centuries past, and we already know all that can be communicated by signals. We know their customs, and several discoveries of great value were communicated to us by their scientists. We know their history, which dates back much further than our own so far as we possess records. They are much more advanced than we are, and have greater wisdom. They are our teachers in many things. It was partly by means of the lessons they taught us that we were able to reorganize our world on better principles, and make it what it now is — a pleasure-house instead of the workhouse it was in the dark days of which you have been speaking. Why, my dear friend, you have only to look at my scientific journals here, or this, my morning newspaper, to see how invaluable we find our acquaintance with that elder and more comfortable planet, where men grow larger, and live longer, and have a firmer grasp of ideas than we have. Just read this paragraph, for instance."

"But I cannot read this kind of print."

"What? Oh! of course not. That 's founded on a system wholly unknown in your time, but now developed to a degree of perfection that cannot but command your admiration. There are no letters, you will observe, as in the clumsy method by which your Old English was written, but we employ these simple symbols, every one of which flashes a well-rounded idea, so that we are now able to present one of the largest histories of your day in a few-score pages."

"But is n't it difficult to learn? Can your children learn it?"

"Certainly. They are more skillfully taught than in your day, but they study no harder, and they are able to read at about the same age. And when they are once masters of the art, they are able to absorb the complete library of the world's knowledge, which century by century has increased in volume, instead of painfully grasping a small department of knowledge, as even your most highly cultivated men were content to do. How many professors of your acquaintance, who were wise in history or the languages, were also acquainted with the primary chapters of mechanics?"

"Very few, I must confess."

"Well, now, when all men are educated, they are also sufficiently acquainted with the several leading branches of human knowledge, so that the interests of our people are identical and mutual. And please bear in mind also, that we are no longer compelled to waste time in learning what you knew as foreign languages. The language you now hear me speak is the common language that all men speak — that is, all men on this planet. The Martian language is different, and thus far only a few of our professors have learned it. I do not know it myself. That is the only foreign language we come in contact with nowadays. But let me warn you that many people whom we shall meet to-day will set down your speech as foreign. I think they will understand you, but of course not as readily as I do, for I have specially studied your ancient tongue. Whoever you may be, and whatever your other accomplishments may prove, you will be a valuable as well as welcome guest by reason of the many hints you can no doubt give me in my studies in that line."

"I am gladly at your service, Professor."

"Thank you. And now, if you are ready, we will go and do our errands, and meanwhile view the city."

CHAPTER VI.

Three Thousand Years.

"THREE thousand years!" said Professor Prosper absently, as they passed along the street.

"Three thousand years!" echoed Paul; "and yet, by some strange fortune, — whether good or evil I hardly yet know, — I find myself permitted still to live and breathe and to gaze at the pleasant face of the earth. Three thousand years! and yet the sun still shines the same, and the fleecy cloud-ships overhead sail just as calmly, and the wind gives me the same brusque greeting as in the Decembers of old."

"Yes," responded the Professor; "and, as you will learn later, happy childhood plays just the same in mimicry of maturer life; there still reigns the golden age of love-making, accompanied by buoyant hope and castle-building; still there come the soberer joys and responsibilities of middle life; and still each man and woman is followed step by step by the shadow of old age and death. So rolls the world forever through its contrasting seasons. But life's road now is unquestionably much smoother and more comfortable for all of us than it was in your turbulent age of experiment and unrest."

"That is what I am particularly interested to know about. In what respects are you now more at ease? And does this ease extend to all classes? And are all classes happier in consequence?"

"I can answer Yes to your last two questions. Details you must see for yourself. In a general way, however, you will no doubt find the following points suggestive of some of the conditions you may expect to find. Money-getting is no longer the chief goal of effort, and hence many unworthy ambitions have been stifled. Places of power and trust are now filled by strong and trustworthy men; the path to all high places is such that none others can attain them. We no longer have taskmasters, for the simple reason that we no longer have slaves. There is abundance in the way of the world's goods for all, and not so much for any one class as to make them uncomfortable. We have abolished classes. We have less failures and disappointments in our ambitions because the youthful period of experimenting and scheming is past, and we now understand the forces and materials that are at our disposal, and can thus work toward any given end with reasonable assurance of success. History clearly teaches that, in your time, many of your most intelligent and earnest workers failed utterly so far as visible results were concerned. Some of the men of your time whose names are now famous were scarcely known to you, except perhaps as vague theorizers and idealists. From our present point of view we are able to judge the value of their theories, as worked out by later specialists, and justly award them a place among the great ones of the earth who have opened up new avenues of material or intellectual value."

"I can see how that might be so. We did the same by generations that preceded us."

"Yes, but in a less degree, because you lived before the era of truth, justice, and peace, while society was in a ferment, while law was by no means synonymous with justice; while worldly advantage, largely based on a money valuation, was the gauge of success if not of merit; and while the bread-and-butter question overtopped all others."

"Have you no bread-and-butter question now in the world?"

"None of which any private citizen is bound to take any thought. The world produces ample supplies so long as waste, war, idleness, ignorance, and miserliness are not allowed to put their greedy hands in the meal-sack. Under our reign of truth, justice, and peace those buzzards of famine no longer breed. You see, Mr. Prognosis, science, which merely means *knowing*, has now taken the place of experimenting, which means *trying to know*, and consequently implies ignorance. You lived in the Experimental Age, whereby the world was taught many valuable lessons; but it was a world of hardships — how hard you did not then realize, or universal anarchy would have put to the test the great question of all, which you did little to settle. Can you now guess what that question was?"

"Human rights?"

"Exactly. You claimed to be Christians, and your nations claimed to be Christian nations, but — excuse me — your customs and your laws wrought more injustice between man and man than any heathen nations that had preceded you, simply because your power was vastly greater. You ruled by force: to-day the world is ruled by truth; and, under the sway of this benign judge, all things have blossomed and fruited in a manner you never dreamed of. All things human have now lost their sting, only excepting sickness and death; and sickness has been very largely reduced, while death has been deferred unto the day when most men, being feeble and weary, have loosened most of the ties that make life a boon."

For a few minutes the two men walked on without speaking. Paul first broke the silence. "Tell me, sir, do you perceive any evidences that nature itself is growing old? Has the sun perceptibly lost volume and power by radiation?"

"That, Mr. Prognosis, is a question you can better decide, because you have means of comparison. What say you? Do you detect any paling of its beneficent fires?"

"I do not find it apparent to the senses. It seems to me as bright as ever, and its rays seem as warm on my cheek."

"Of course," added the Professor, "we know that, within three thousand years past, there must have been some decrease of light and heat by reason of radiation, some decrease of volume from concentration, some increase of mass from meteoric accretions, and consequently some shortening of all the planetary distances. But these changes are so slight that only our most delicate instruments record them. There has also been a slight lengthening of our days and nights, so that we can now calculate the time when the twenty-ninth day of February will no longer be needed to piece out the uneven years. These few changes have occurred, as your scientists were able to predict, and the same movements will forever continue until the sun finally loses its light altogether and nature dies. There have been measurable changes in the last three thousand years; but, as you have said, none of them are perceptible to the senses."

"I can hardly restrain myself, sir, from asking you many more questions regarding physical science, but this is not the time or place for that. Some other time, if you will allow me, I shall not fail to tax your patience to the utmost."

"You need not fear of wearying me by so doing. Like you, I am an enthusiast on such subjects."

CHAPTER VII.

The Tower of Peace and Good-Will.

"WHAT a magnificent square!" said Paul, as they now entered the same one he remembered crossing in the morning, and he again looked up the eight radiating avenues, between which and fronting upon the square stood various buildings of surprising magnitude and architectural beauty, far surpassing anything he had ever dreamed of. In the centre of the square was a monumental column, and in response to his questioning look, as he viewed its vast proportions and exquisite variety and harmony of decoration, his companion said: "Yes, this is now counted as one of the wonders of the world, and it is unsurpassed in beauty by any similar structure. It is called the Tower of Peace and Goodwill, and was built to commemorate the accomplishment of universal peace among the nations. Its design, as you will perceive upon studying it, is singularly appropriate in every detail to the symbolism which the great artist-architect had in mind. The base is a grand triumphal arch, which, even without the lofty column that surmounts it, would be an imposing object. Grouped around this base are bronze figures of horsemen confronting each other in deadly strife, while between them, and forcibly parting them, stand armed giants. This is intended to symbolize the power of the new civilization to control the spirits of hatred, that would otherwise inspire dissension, strife, warfare."

"I understand."

"On the lower portion of the outer wall, above the plinth, you will observe a series of bronze tablets in bas-relief. These include historical representations of all modes of warfare practiced by the ancients, and clearly show its savage character and terrible destructiveness. Above those is a contrasting series of tablets illustrating the conquests and glories of peace; and over the grand arch is the rising sun, typifying the dawn of peace. Rejoicing in its rays, on either side, are great armies who no longer display implements of bloodshed, but banners bearing emblems and mottoes of good-will. And see! over all, and in letters that can be read by all — by even you, for they are the letters in which your Old English was written, is inscribed the glorious phrase: —

'On Earth Peace: Good-will toward Men.'

"In your day you often repeated that same phrase, but it then had no meaning. Your choirs sang it, but the words were drowned by the trample of armies that then made the world an armed camp. Was it not so?"

"I confess it."

"The inscriptions you see on panels let into the upper portion of the wall are words of wisdom spoken by men of all the ages who were in any way instrumental in ushering in the reign of peace, and whose names follow the texts. Among them you will recognize that of Washington, who helped give a death-blow to kingly usurpation, and Lincoln, who aimed a similar blow at one of the primitive forms of human slavery. Those of the great social reformers, that then follow, are of course not known to you. And now, if you please, we will ascend the shaft."

Thus speaking, they passed through the main arch, and entered an inner door leading to a broad, winding passage, having no steps, by which they easily passed to the top of the grand Arch of Triumph and stood among the art-wonders of the level summit.

"Now," said the Professor, "let us take things in order, and we shall soon obtain a general impression of this masterpiece, although a score of visits may be made without exhausting interest in its countless details. Here, at the four corners, you see bronze groups of domestic animals, some standing and some reclining in peaceful attitudes under graceful foliage; and directly over the four arches are colossal statues of four noted men, — I presume you would have called them social reformers, — who would be but names to you if I should mention them now, but you will know and honor them later."

"The labor question — is it yet settled?"

"Oh, centuries ago. There could be no thought of peace until that problem was solved."

"And was it peacefully solved?"

"Yes and no. It was the momentous question in your day. You must remember the continual strife that grew out of it. Like all great issues, it finally forced itself to the front, challenged attention, and compelled action from the best minds, and then gradually wrought out its own salvation as society became organized on a wiser and truer basis. Honesty and justice were the only elements lacking in your day for its peaceful solution. As soon as these forces took the field, the field was won."

"Above us still rises the tower."

"Yes, and all other parts of the structure are but accessories to this. You will see that the shaft of the column is surrounded by a spiral gallery, which winds about it from base to summit. This gallery is supported by a continuous colonnade; and this, together with a beautiful balustrade below, a series of arches springing from the columns, and a belt of exquisite tracery above, forms a shell to the central shaft and gives the outline of the tower as seen from a distance. Within this ascending gallery, on the side next the shaft, is the passageway; and on the outside, next the colonnade, is a grand procession of marble figures, all carrying offerings to lay at the feet of Peace, who sits enthroned on the summit. Here are herdsmen with cattle, shepherds with flocks, ploughmen with teams, wagons loaded with the products of the field, the locomotive driver, fishermen with their nets, and sailors with the tiller in hand. Here are artisans with emblems of their calling, scientists with their inventions, authors with their books, orators, actors, painters, sculptors, architects, musicians, — every phase of effort is represented that in any way contributes to the necessities, comforts, or pleasures of life. Each figure in this vast collection is the work of some noted artist, and it has been an object of the highest ambition on the part of our sculptors to secure a place for their works in this collection. If you like, you can easily glance at all by entering this slowly moving elevator; or are you likely to be fatigued by the trip?"

"Even if I were, I should not know it, for my entire attention is absorbed in wonder and admiration for these marvelous works about me."

Stepping upon the moving platform, they then leisurely surveyed the vast procession that seemed moving with them to the summit, where, at a windy elevation that was at first somewhat trying to his nerves, Paul grasped the railing that surrounded the throne of Peace, and looked down upon the outspread city.

"Well, here we are," said the Professor, again assuming the office of guide. "Here Peace reigns triumphant, upheld, as you see, on a hemisphere representing the earth, with her right hand supporting a staff topped by a crystal globe, the emblem of Truth, and her left hand resting upon a disc-like ring, signifying Unity, around whose edges are inscribed the names of all the nations that subscribed to the Act of Universal Peace. Around her stand figures representing Justice, Order, Industry, and Plenty; and, emerging from the winding gallery and surrounding the throne, are figures of children, bearing their offerings of flowers and fruit, who form the advance guard of the long procession we have followed from below."

"Professor, the display of beautiful objects gracing this monument fills me with wonder that

I will not try to express. Why, they are scattered with a lavishness that one expects to find only in dreamland. I have a half-feeling as if I might now be treading the summit of an air-castle, and as if a sudden stream of moonlight might awaken me to the dim realities of night. But if that be so, then let me dream on forever, for the world in which I have been accustomed to live boasts no such spectacles as this."

CHAPTER VIII.

A Bird's-Eye View of the City.

"MR. PROGNOSIS, before descending to the earth, where you will find we are quite as practical in most matters, if not as prosaic, as the most matter-of-fact mind of the nineteenth century could desire, I hope you will try and take in a general view of the grand panorama of the city and its suburbs that now lies spread before you. Your eyes will soon become accustomed to the distances."

"But I feel too giddy to look down."

"Let us then look afar at first. There to the east glitters the bay; and here you can follow the windings of the rivers that pour into it, each dotted with sailless craft and crossed by a network of bridges, especially the great river to the west. The most famous of the bridges, known as 'The Old Bridge,' is very clearly visible directly to the north. It belongs to the same period as this Peace Tower; and, like it, contains a display of statuary that is certain to give you pleasurable surprise. Just across it you see our two far-famed Pyramids — please don't question about them now, for you shall examine them later. To the northwest the most prominent object is Mount Energy, with its accompaniment of the Solar Steam-Works; and to the north you can see the chief scene of my labors, Meridian Observatory. I know that you bristle with questions, but please be a little patient, and you shall have an opportunity to inspect all these wonder works in detail. In the valley below us, which blazes as if by the reflection of a lake in noon sunshine, is our far-famed Sun Palace"—

"Excuse me, but I must interrupt with just one question! These cloud shadows that now and then pass us, are they clouds, or huge birds, or balloons of some kind?"

"They are air-ships. You shall inspect them too, and make an experimental voyage in one, if you like. But let us first complete our bird's-eye view. I think now that you will be able to look below without discomfort, and perhaps you will prefer to study the nearer aspect of the city without comments from me."

Paul gazed down, and gradually absorbed the more prominent features of the animated picture at his feet. He saw that the eight avenues radiating from the Peace Square were all extremely wide; and he now noticed that, extending along the centre of each, were open archways revealing a subway, in which he could see lines of moving railway cars. At the crossings, the underground streets were covered by the bridge-like structure which evidently composed the surface avenue through its entire length. Each avenue was two-storied.

"What," asked Paul, "is the purpose of the tall masts that I see scattered so thickly through the city? It cannot be that you permit telegraph and other wires to be strung overhead?"

"Certainly not! The subway gives ample and safe accommodation for all wires and pipes. These masts are simply supports for electric suns by which we convert darkness into day, so that midnight and noon are scarcely to be distinguished in Tone. I believe, in your time, that you were just beginning to discover the usefulness of electricity as an illuminator and motive force."

"Yes, but we found it expensive to produce, impossible to store, and, at times, as unmanageable as a young lion."

"We have now domesticated it. It took many centuries to gain a complete knowledge of its laws, but we now look upon these as simple enough, and we handle it with perfect safety. As to expense, we catch it direct from the sun's rays and from the winds and waves. You will easily comprehend the details when you visit Mount Energy, that monster pile to the north-west with a cap of white, like a snow-covered hill."

"Your buildings — how few, yet how vast they are!"

"Yes; each covers an entire square or block."

"And, viewed from this point, each seems to taper like a pyramid."

"That is the form of construction we have adopted as most convenient."

"But it would seem to be wasteful of space."

"Not when you consider that the centre areas are now entirely covered, excepting the necessary air and light shafts. We simply transfer the space you practically wasted as areas, to the façades to our buildings, thereby affording a much larger surface for the play of air and direct sunlight, although the structures themselves are two, three, and four times as high as you thought it safe to pile them. At the same time, the streets are likewise left open to sunshine and air. You will readily understand that, with vertical buildings of such height as these, our streets would otherwise be converted into sunless alleyways. Convenience and safety of entrance are also secured by this method of construction; and, by allowing a little strip of garden along the successive terraces, we convert each building in summer time into a green and blossoming hill. But this is one of the subjects that you will better understand when you come to examine the two great prototypes of this class of buildings, which I pointed out to you as the 'Pyramids.' They were the happy thought of a master-architect who lived many centuries ago, and who designed them with special reference to the needs of mechanics and others having small incomes. Land in the cities had become so valuable that small houses were no longer practicable, even for the comparatively wealthy; and tenement houses became dangerously tall, and unhealthily sunless and ill-ventilated. The change in construction he advocated was so radical that it met with much ridicule, until submitted to practical test on a grand scale in the 'Pyramids;' but the result of that test was strikingly successful in every respect, and proved conclusively that the designer's claim of maximum comfort and health combined with minimum expense for rent and maintenance was as firmly founded as his broad-based structures. Although each one, in its accommodations, represented a good-sized city, both were speedily filled with occupants, and leases have been greatly valued ever since."

"The expense of building must have been vast."

"Yes, the first expense was; but when you remember that they have now stood for many centuries, and are still in perfectly good condition to serve for as many centuries more, you will understand that this investment by the municipality has proved highly advantageous. We learned by your experience that it does n't pay to build, merely to tear down and build again. The spirit of iconoclasm has been well-nigh rooted out. We build to stand — our legal, as well as our stone-and-mortar structures."

"In spite of this desirable solidity of which you speak, I find a suggestion of singular lightness and cheerfulness in your architecture."

"Yes; and you will find that this is largely produced by the extensive use of glass and of gilded and silvered ornaments. We seek the free distribution of sunlight in every possible manner, and whatever can admit or reflect sunshine is gladly introduced in our buildings. The vines and shrubbery and bay-windows on the terraces also help to break the long cornice lines, and give lightness in effect as well as variety."

"I shall now," said Paul, "be particularly interested in examining your underground world and the construction of those two-story streets; for I was formerly employed by a railway company, and the question of safe passage through thickly populated districts was always a perplexing one."

"Let us then return to the lower world. You see, here we have another moving platform that will speedily transfer us to the street without any exertion on our part. See, the long procession of statues seems to clamber behind us as we make our circling descent; and here we are again, safely deposited in the public square."

CHAPTER IX.

The Underground Railway.

"As you see," continued Professor Prosper, "we now stand upon the upper street, or what we call the 'highway,' which is reserved for pedestrians and pleasure vehicles."

"But I see no horses."

"Oh no, we do not allow the use of horses in our cities. With the continued increase of traffic, it was found that they were a leading source of dust, filth, and unpleasant odors, and they also impeded pedestrian travel unnecessarily. At the same time our needs gave rise to a great variety of wheeled vehicles propelled by electricity or compressed air. You have evidently not noticed that, beyond the next row of elms, is a roadway filled with electric vehicles, continually passing. These make no dust, no sound, are easily guided, and, under favorable conditions, their speed far exceeds that of the fleetest horse. In all our cities, horses have been relegated to the training-school and the arena."

"But of course they are still used in the country."

"For pleasure purposes, yes; but not for mere motive power, for they would be too expensive. Electricity and compressed air do all our drudgery."

"You continue to amaze me."

"I understand that, yet you must prepare to be amazed in many other particulars far more important than this. But, as I began to say, this 'highway' is, in fact, a scaffolding, built sometimes of stone, but more often, during late years, of a peculiar preparation of aluminium, which is now the commonest of all metals, and particularly adapted for purposes of construction, owing to its lightness, strength, and freedom from injury by oxidation. It is also beautiful; do you not think so?"

"The iron that we used must certainly give it the palm on that score."

"We of course use aluminium for all our common household utensils."

"But how do you obtain it?"

"From clay, by the simplest possible mode of reduction. It is one of the mysteries why you failed to discover it."

"It was not because we did n't strain every faculty."

"No; you strained too much. You looked too far. You held the secret in the hand, and forgot to open the hand."

"Very likely," sighed Paul. "The microscope has no doubt given the world more useful hints than the telescope."

"Well, on this 'highway,' as you will notice, are the main entrances to dwellings, hotels, and commercial warehouses, while below are other entrances where all merchandise and bulky articles are received direct from the City Service freight-cars. In the middle of the subway are the transit lines for passengers, separated by broad passages from the freight tracks, and with power elevators that give easy access to the 'highway.' But let us take a trial trip, and you will then see for yourself."

Paul took one parting glance about him before they descended, fascinated by the bright faces of the great throngs of people who passed him.

"You apparently have no beggars in your streets," he said, half questioningly.

"I should hope not. Oh no, beggary is one of the many things of the remote past. It was merely a result of certain unhealthy conditions, including waste, extravagance, avariciousness, crime, and disease, which flourished in your time, and fruited and dropped their natural seed."

"But you cannot have abolished crime by legal enactments."

"No; but we have so reduced, where we have not entirely removed, the chief inducements to crime, including poverty, excess of wealth, injustice, and ambition for undeserved power, inevitably leading to tyranny, that it is now infrequent. While I was recently engaged in consulting newspaper files dating from the nineteenth century, I was painfully struck by the fact that nearly all the news most prominently heralded related to crimes, accidents, and wars or rumors of war. Although the world is now much more densely populated, and the means of communication nearly instantaneous, our daily newspapers seldom make mention of crimes or accidents — simply because they seldom occur; and of course we no longer have our nerves excited, pleasurably or otherwise, by news of war or rebellion, as those are conditions quite impossible under the present régime. In brief, Mr. Prognosis, the news in your day was mainly detective news, while ours nearly all relates to social life, science, art and amusements."

While thus speaking, they had descended the elevator to a broad stone platform skirting the main track. There were four pairs of rails in the central portion of the subway; and on the track next the platform where Paul was standing, he noticed a car at rest, into which persons were entering by side doors and taking seats.

Just at this moment a long train, drawn by some invisible force, flew rapidly by him, on one of the inner tracks, and to its side was attached a small car like that which stood before him, which was speeding forward on the same near track. He watched attentively, expecting to see the two small cars collide. But, just in the nick of time, the small moving car was cast off and came to a standstill, while the other small car was caught up by the train, which never slackened its tremendous speed, and whirled out of sight.

"Beautiful!" cried Paul. "I don't at all understand how it is done so easily, but I see that it is done, and I see that you have settled the question of rapid transit without reference to the number of intermediate stations."

"Exactly so! The small car, as you have observed, acts as a tender, allowing passengers to join the main train and then take their seats in calmness and comfort while it is still running at full speed."

"It is of course dropped in the same manner."

"Yes, it works both ways. Each tender is carried to the next station on the line, and then successively all along the circuit."

"But there must be cross-lines — how are collisions prevented?"

"Easily enough! All the lines in the city are run under one general management, and all precisely on time. In fact, the several trains act like several parts of one vast machine, and the movements of all are as accurately timed as the beats of a clock, which is perfectly practicable under this system."

"But how is it that the people can safely change places while the cars are in such rapid motion, and especially the aged and infirm?"

"There is little motion, as you will soon see, for the road-beds as well as the cars are perfectly constructed. There is no difficulty about that. But see for yourself. Here is a tender awaiting us. And here comes the train — and here we are aboard the train — and the tender dropped, and another at our side! Did you ever see anything easier than that?"

"Never! And now — if you please, Professor, I would like to know something about this new motive force of which you have spoken. I presume it is used on these trains, is it not?"

"Yes. Well, it is based on a very simple but peculiar application of compressed air. I should need diagrams to fully explain it. But I can now say that this compressed air is conveyed to all parts of the city by pipes, the source of supply being a short distance out of town. To-morrow, if you like, with Marco as a guide, you can visit the central works; and, if I am not mistaken, you will see something worth your while."

"I have no doubt of it. The only fear I have is, that you may show me so many wonders that I shall lose my wits. You see, a nineteenth century brain has to expand itself considerably to house the realities of your present."

"True enough. Yet you will find that we do all things in such an orderly manner that we also do them easily as well as rapidly; and you will soon learn to do the same. Life is much easier now than with you. You, as I understand it, were always in a driving hurry, and rather proud of the fact than otherwise. When any one nowadays is seen in a hurry, we know that he is either correcting an error, or that he lacks order and system in his plans. You wasted time, just as you wasted everything else. We value time as our first of all boons — it is our life — and we count every day another opportunity freighted with duties that we take pleasure in performing."

"But does n't this make life a rather dull treadmill?"

"Not at all, because we include all possible pleasures that are not harmful in any way, as part of the duties of life. Dull treadmill, indeed! And that phrase in the mouth of a nineteenth century man! You must excuse me for smiling, please. Why, life nowadays is one round of pleasures."

"But how about your work? Does anybody find work a pleasure?"

"Of course. Why not? The difference between work and play is slighter than you think. Action is the source of all enjoyment. Work is forced action, excessive action, or action to which one's powers are not adapted. Play is willing action in ways that are best adapted to one's powers. We choose our workers and set them to work on this principle. Whatever a man can really do well, he can usually do easily, and he usually likes to do it. If he does n't, then we hold out attractions in the way of higher ambitions, that stimulate him by the drawing process more effectually than any whiplash of want or fear could possibly push him."

"Well, I certainly approve the theory and the principle, but I should n't think it would work in practical life."

"I can only say that, under proper guidance and training through many generations, it has come to work very satisfactorily. If founded on truth, it must work, Mr. Prognosis, just as soon as we give it a full opportunity to work. A correct theory is merely an unrealized truth. Is n't that so?"

"I suppose so; but really, Professor, your remarks suggest to my mind so many problems, and from such a novel point of view, that I don't feel fully competent to pass verdict on all of them. I simply accept your statement that work can be converted into play without the happy victim knowing or caring whether it 's one or the other. The statement interests me, and therefore pleases me."

"And you thereby illustrate the very point of my argument. You thereby convert the hard work of investigation into a recreation. To use an expression from your own day, you therefore 'change your stage-coach into a gentleman's four-in-hand.'"

"I gladly plead guilty."

"And I, as gladly, suspend sentence."

"May it please the judge to listen to another inquiry?"

"Certainly."

"Do you use reciprocating engines for your condensed air?"

"No. The air-wheel is by far preferable. I am aware of the efforts of inventors in your day to produce a useful steam-engine on the rotary plan, and their lack of success; but with compressed air there is much less difficulty. We have no heat to contend with; and soft leather packing, so arranged that it is made tight by pressure, reduces the friction to a minimum. The present engine is exceedingly simple. I will show you plans that I have at home."

"But are these tender-cars started by the same plan?"

"Not exactly. In that case a simple cylinder and piston are placed in an upright position, and at the proper moment the piston is forced up. This rotates the toothed wheel which you see here. Watch the tender we are now approaching, and you will see more than I can explain."

Paul watched as directed. He saw one tender cast off just in time to come to rest at the right point, with its forward end just over a great wheel. Under the tender in waiting a similar propulsion wheel began to revolve, slowly at first, but gradually increasing its revolutions until the departing tender left it at full speed, ranged itself alongside the train, and was promptly hooked on.

"Excuse me, Professor, but I did not see you pay our fares as we entered. Do we do that upon leaving the station?"

"Fares? Oh, there are no fares. All is perfectly free."

"But how are the companies compensated?"

"There are no companies. The Government runs and operates all lines of transportation for either passengers or freight, as well as all other means of communication, by road, wire, or tube, including mail carriage, telegraphs, telephones, and pneumatic-tube service. And all are free — perfectly free. In your time you had started in this direction by making many of your highways and bridges free to the public, and mail-matter nearly so. As the people supply the labor that supports all the public conveniences I have mentioned, they are certainly entitled to their use. Please understand that the people and the Government are one — they are synonymous terms."

CHAPTER X.

The Hospital.

When, after a few minutes of rapid flight in the railway, they alighted at the riverside, the Professor explained that he had stopped at this point in order to give his visitor an opportunity to see one of the several hospitals scattered about the suburbs of the city.

"You seemed interested by references I made to beggary and crime, and it occurred to me that you would like this opportunity to glance at one of our hospitals, which will indicate certain provisions now made for the maintenance of health, and having an important influence on those questions."

"You are very kind. You will find me an interested spectator and listener. But first, please let me ask a few questions. You alluded to disease as one of the exciting causes of poverty, and hence of crime, in my day. You surely cannot have banished disease!"

"Not entirely, yet very largely. Death still awaits us all, and, throughout life, we still suffer those ills to which flesh seems naturally and inevitably heir. But the records show that most of the diseases that brought distress to the ancients were unnecessary; they were mainly such as were directly attributable to poor or inappropriate food, poor drainage, lack of sunshine and fresh air, lack of exercise or too much of it, vice of many kinds, and ignorance of even the simplest laws of physical well-being. By removing those prolific sources of disease, the world first cured the majority of its patients, then prevented further accessions to the ranks, and gradually reduced the liability of recurrence of the same weaknesses in offspring. Indeed, large classes of disorders which you looked upon as incurable are now practically unknown, excepting as sporadic examples that are rather welcomed than otherwise by our physicians."

"What one, for instance?"

"Well, most notably what you used to call 'tubercular consumption.' A case of that kind is now a curiosity; and the patient is promptly removed where there may be no possibility of his distributing the microbes that produce it. I also recall what you knew as 'cholera,' 'small-pox,' 'yellow fever' and 'leprosy.' Let me tell you that we deal with disease as a deadly enemy that deserves no quarter. We first adopt every possible means of prevention. For instance, we respect certain marriage rules that you would no doubt consider arbitrary and harsh, but which have resulted in so improving the world's health that all people now recognize their justness and propriety. No diseased or deformed person who is liable to communicate serious imperfection of any kind to offspring is ever allowed to marry."

"But how can you prevent marriages?"

"By the same means that we effect them — by law; and our laws mean more than mere written statutes. They are founded on justice and right. The public recognizes this fact, and every person feels it for his own interest, as well as for the public good, to see that they are enforced. You were not so blind but that you found it right to prevent a lunatic or a leper from marrying — and you even banished the latter forever as a hopeless outcast. But you nourished in your homes diseases that were even more readily communicable, and quite as dangerous to life and health and moral stamina."

"True — too true!"

"But now let us take a distant view of the hospital, which, as you see, consists of a number of small buildings arranged in a semicircle on the little island before us. There are eighteen buildings in the line, and you will notice that they are divided by walls into three distinct groups. Those to the left are devoted to patients suffering from ailments affecting the mind, including imbeciles and the insane; the centre group to those who are physically ill or injured; while the three to the right are occupied by those who are morally deranged."

"Morally deranged?"

"Yes, I believe you used to apply the term 'prison' to the institution used for the confinement of moral patients."

"They are convicts, then? But why are these associated with your hospitals?"

"Why not? They constitute a part, though happily a small part, of the patients that come under the same management and treatment."

"You astound me!"

"We simply treat them as persons who are morally deformed or ailing."

"But how do you punish them?"

"We know no such thing as punishment in their case. We confine them, partly for their own good, to prevent their doing further injury to themselves, and partly with reference to public safety; but the idea of 'punishment,' in the sense in which it was known to your system of criminal jurisprudence, has no part in ours. Vice and crime are sufficient punishment in themselves."

"Not where conscience is lacking."

"But that is seldom, and especially in the

early history of crime, where our laws mainly apply. In the case of impaired or undeveloped conscience, responsibility would be reduced, and your so-called 'punishment' was liable to be needlessly harsh. It is clear that a person utterly without conscience, or knowledge of right or wrong, would deserve merely the treatment of a beast — confinement."

"Under such conditions, your places of confinement must be of vast number and extent."

"No; I think there are only eight other hospitals in Tone, and they are merely receiving stations. All our permanent patients are in the buildings now before you."

"Why, Boston of my time required buildings of twenty times the number and size for its hospitals, asylums, and houses of correction; and the present city must be many times as populous."

"About twenty times, I believe."

"Professor, I do not yet understand the secret of this wonderful decrease in sickness and crime."

"There are many causes, but none are mysterious or in any way surprising to us now, although some of them may appear so to you. I have already explained to you several of the means by which we have gradually decreased the spread of communicable diseases, until they are now well-nigh stamped out. There was one means that was adopted many centuries ago, which I did not mention, but which has proved of supreme service in the work of purifying the blood of successive generations. It applies to all persons, whether mental, physical, or moral patients, who are ever committed to this institution, and it goes into effect as soon as the Council of Judges has pronounced judgment that the taint — mental, physical, or moral — is incurable and liable to be communicated to offspring. By an instantaneous and painless operation, the patient is rendered forever sterile."

"It seems barbarously cruel."

"Excuse me, but that is because you view the subject from a nineteenth century standpoint, which had no horizon, but was wholly occupied with evils of the hour. Without this wise provision, we should be obliged to keep our patients in confinement throughout their natural lives, for it is contrary to every rule of justice that physical and moral disease afflicting the present generation should be allowed to cast its curse upon a helpless and innocent generation yet unborn. We recognize that we owe something to future generations as well as to those that have preceded us; and we try to do our duty by them in this respect. By this simple precaution, continued through centuries, a thousand taints of mind, body, and morals, that rendered reform in your day difficult to the very verge of impossibility, have steadily been eradicated, until the question of inherited disease, including that of vice, is now one of the minor ones, over which we have almost perfect control."

"But the enactment of such a law must, at first, have aroused bitter opposition on the part of the public. Its very suggestion in my day would have called down universal condemnation."

"My dear Mr. Prognosis, please try and understand that, since the inauguration of the reign of general peace, the people have really been the law-makers as well as the governors. For us to find fault with our laws would be to convict ourselves of error in enacting them. You may be sure that a law of this importance was not adopted until public sentiment had accepted it as right and proper. It first had to meet the test of the White Button standard of truth and justice. That question settled, a public sentiment that has gradually been educated to the acceptance of every dictate of justice simply demanded it. Results have fully proved the wisdom of its adoption."

"And it is still in operation?"

"Yes, though seldom enforced in these days.

Its function was mainly performed in centuries now long passed, when the power of the criminal classes often blocked the wheels of progress."

"You spoke of the great size of Tone. Is it the largest of your cities?"

"By no means. There are scores that are its equal and several that are much larger. The most populous of all in the Americas is located on the isthmus connecting the two continents, which stands at the crossroads where converge all the chief lines of travel, north and south, east and west, by land and by sea. That great cosmopolis of Carrefour has a population of over fifty millions."

"I never heard of it."

"It had no reason to be, when, in your day, South America had hardly given a sign of its magnificent future, and when the entire navies of your globe scarcely equaled those that now daily pass through our inter-continental canals. The city of Carrefour grew naturally from a little port into a mammoth metropolis, by reason of the steady development of all countries south of the equator, which was just beginning in your day and has continued with rapid strides ever since. The formation of new governments founded on the principles of modern civilization, symbolized by this white button I wear, gave opportunities for testing the Costorian theory with a freedom that was impossible under the older governments. The result was a complete vindication of Costor's teachings."

"Costor? Who was Costor? And what was his theory of government?"

"To know that is to know the foundation of modern civilization. To-morrow evening, if time will allow, I will try and tell you about it. This hospital you have just seen is a type of one of the many modern institutions that have been developed in their present form from the clear, straightforward teachings of that master man. You shall know about him later, and then you will understand many things underlying our present ideas and customs that might otherwise appear inexplicable."

CHAPTER XI.

The Pyramids.

LEAVING the hospital, they walked along the paved embankment about half a mile, until, upon rounding a hill, they found themselves at the approach to the "Old Bridge," one of many crossing the mighty salt stream, but the noblest of them. There it loomed before them, and Paul's practiced eye studied the magnificent sweep of its arches. The solid wall above the arches was almost wholly covered by elaborate and beautiful designs, deeply cut in the solid stone; and at the crown of each arch was a projecting keystone, which formed the base of a pilaster-like column, thus dividing the sculptured belt into panels. Surmounting the wall, directly over these pilasters, were huge blocks of stone on which rested bronze figures of all known animals, singly or in groups, the larger at the ends of the structure and the smaller at the centre, in regular gradation. They were all of exquisite workmanship, resembling those on the Peace Monument.

"This," said the Professor, "is one of the chief landmarks of our city, if I may so call it. You would hardly think it a thousand years old, yet such is the fact; the cement that binds the stones is as enduring as the solid granite itself, and the entire structure as indestructible as though carved from the everlasting hills."

"It is grand — grand beyond the power of words!" said Paul, who found himself running short of original modes of expressing his oft-excited admiration.

"Well, let us now follow the upper roadway to the centre arch. Here, at this end, as you will notice, is the 'Arch of the Elephants,' as it is called, which is mated at the other end by the 'Arch of the Mastodons.' Next to these, on either side, are the camels and the behemoths. After leaving the riverbanks come the hippopotami and crocodiles; and, over the centre of the stream, are all kinds of fishes. See! we are now among the fishes. And here, from the top of this central arch, we have our best view of the Pyramids, to which I called your attention from the Peace Monument. Please understand that we have not wasted our time and substance in reproducing those old Egyptian tombs, which are as famous in our day as in yours. Ours are quite as large, but they are for the living. You shall see for yourself."

As they mounted the avenue that led from the "Old Bridge," Paul continued to gaze with increasing wonder on the two massive piles cutting the horizon before him, that had every appearance of two pointed mountains firmly planted on the plateau. They were located about half a mile from the river, one on either side of the avenue, and surrounded by groves of trees. They stood in sombre majesty, their form suggesting strength and permanence in the highest degree. As the wondering spectator approached nearer, he could see that their sides were covered as with a fresco of many tints, broken by spots of color and reflected light; and their vast proportions became more and more overwhelming.

"Can it be possible," asked Paul, "that those are the windows of human dwellings which I see in sparkling lines along those stairlike terraces?"

"Windows? yes; and dwellings? yes — more than four thousand dwellings in each pyramid, and very good ones too, supplied with every convenience as well as every household necessity of this most comfortable age. The South Pyramid alone has a present population of about twenty-two thousand persons."

"They strike me as more like ant-hills magnified into mountains than human habitations."

"Well," said the Professor smiling, "that is just what they are sometimes called. But the people who live in them are mostly artisans, who are both industrious and proud of their industry, and therefore not averse to being likened to that intelligent little six-legged worker. But you will see — you will see! We will inspect this southern ant-hill."

Paul spoke scarcely a word during the remainder of the walk, but kept his eyes fixed on the pyramid they were now rapidly approaching, which seemed to expand in height and bulk with every step he took.

"On each of the four sides," explained the Professor, "there are several converging lines of inclined railways, all entrance being by the exterior; and here we now are at Station No. 29. Step into this car and we will go immediately to the summit. I often come here to enjoy the charming view from the upper terraces, and also to breathe the invigorating air, for the breezes love to visit here even when they desert us in the lower city."

"But I should think it would be extremely hot on a breathless summer afternoon."

"Oh no! for it is then a bower of vines and shade trees. Do you not see that every entrance has its little strip of soil, planted with trees and shrubs? In summer these gardens are more beautiful than I can describe."

"And in winter, is it not frightfully bleak and windy?"

"No more so than in any place where air and sunshine have free entrance. The dwellings are so constructed that they can be made perfectly snug and comfortable in the coldest weather, with abundance of hot air that can be turned on at any moment; while the railways afford the easiest possible communication with the rest of the world."

Seating themselves in the car that awaited them, they started on their upward climb, proceeding rather slowly, while the conductor continued crying out "Fourth!" "Fifth!" and so on up to the forty-fourth terrace, when they were as near the top as the Professor cared to go.

"Ah!" said Paul, as he sniffed the pure and invigorating air, "this is indeed better than the rookeries we called 'tenements,' built in vertical blocks in narrow, sunless streets, where the working-people in our cities were huddled in their so-called homes."

As they walked along, the Professor explained that each terrace was fifteen feet in height and depth, and that each dwelling had a frontage upon it of twenty feet. The flooring of each was four feet above the terrace, so that the door was reached by a few steps; and under the main windows of each were low broad windows serving to light and ventilate the lower or basement rooms. He further stated that, in most cases, a single dwelling consisted of four principal rooms: two in front, besides the hallway, and two at the rear; while still others, without light from the front, were carried further into the interior and formed excellent sleeping apartments, as they were fairly well lighted and perfectly ventilated by central shafts, down which the sun's rays were directed by an ingenious system of reflectors.

"But how is it possible to utilize the central portion of this mountain of stone and iron and glass?"

"At its base it is honeycombed by chambers used as municipal storehouses for surplus food. The lower two tiers consist of a vast number of heavily-arched vaults devoted to cold storage; and on the outer margin of the second tier, between the vaults and the dwelling apartments, is an encircling arched corridor, the floor of which can be flooded and frozen over at any time, even in midsummer, and thus be converted into a skating gallery."

"How is the process of freezing accomplished?"

"By merely releasing compressed air under high pressure from pipes communicating with

Mount Energy. This gallery passes entirely around the structure. The remainder of the interior is devoted to innumerable markets, shops, audience chambers, dining-rooms, etc., lighted artificially and ventilated through many flues opening out on the terraces or through vertical air-shafts. Ventilation is further effected by draughts of cold or hot dry air, supplied by elaborate systems of pipes, which also serve to cool or heat the several departments. All the rooms are lighted by electricity, so that they can be made to glow with midday glory whenever desired. In brief, Mr. Prognosis, everything that heart can wish is obtainable by the dwellers of this Pyramid without ever visiting the outside world. It is simply a fully organized city, piled on end instead of being stretched lengthwise."

"But how about fire? A general conflagration would be a serious matter in such a building."

"Accidental fire is something we no longer dread. With you, I am aware that it was a continual menace, and it not only meant millions of waste every year, but also cost the lives of many persons. Now we use only fireproof materials for building; and, if the contents of any suite of rooms become ignited, fireproof doors are barred upon them, and a volume of steam introduced that quickly subdues the most threatening blaze. But we depend less on the fireproof qualities of materials than on preventives of fire and constant care and watchfulness. No expense was spared in the construction of this building, and the investment was a profitable one, for it is just as serviceable to-day as when the masons rang their trowels on its walls a thousand years ago. In like manner, no expense is now spared in adopting every possible preventive of fire; and this has also proved profitable, for no serious conflagration has ever occurred, and no life has ever been sacrificed. Immunity from accident in the past is not allowed to cause any relaxation in the present service of the fire-patrol; but a single alarm would immediately summon a corps of trained men, furnished with every modern means of fighting the destructive element. The records clearly show that our largest dwelling houses are by far the safest in this respect."

"These exterior terraces certainly afford a convenient means of exit in case of danger. There is no longer any possibility of people being roasted alive while clinging to lofty window-sills within sight of all the world, but utterly beyond the reach of human aid."

"That is true, and that is one of the arguments used by the architect who designed the Pyramids. As populations were massed more and more in the great cities and the vertical buildings rose loftier and loftier, the danger from this source steadily increased, for smoke proved a more deadly enemy than fire. Both smoke and fire can now be speedily escaped by occupants, and help can be promptly afforded from without. But the record speaks for itself: a thousand years — and not a dweller in the Pyramids has ever lost his life from fire."

As they slowly descended, Paul glanced into numberless dwellings, schoolrooms, stores, markets, and places of amusement; and he readily admitted that he had never before seen anything so neat, cheerful, and comfortable. He especially noted the peaceful and happy look of all the people whom he passed. They had no resemblance to the careworn and discouraged faces that he had learned to think inseparable from those who worked with their hands in the humbler callings of life, or depended upon those who so worked. Their cheeks glowed with health and their eyes with happiness.

Paul spoke to a little girl who stood at one of the doorways. She responded politely, but evidently did not understand him. As he rejoined the Professor, the latter said: "She is telling her mother that you are a 'sailor man.'"

A little later, a young man greeted the Professor, and they gladly accepted an invitation to enter his home. The Professor explained to Paul that this was an employee at the observatory, who had a minimum income, so that his quarters would well represent what could be done with small means in the way of housekeeping.

"Thomas, do you think your wife would object to our looking into all your rooms?"

"She shall speak for herself, sir, if you please." And he introduced a healthy young woman, neatly dressed, of whom he was evidently not a little proud, and she seemed well worthy of his regard.

From the combined sitting-room and parlor they passed to the dining-room opposite, both of these rooms looking out upon the trellised terrace; and then to the bedrooms, in one of which lay a sleeping child, and below to the kitchen, laundry, etc. There was not only perfect neatness everywhere, but evidences of taste abounded in the way of pictures, books, wall decorations, and musical instruments, that the visitor had little expected.

"Excuse me," said Paul, "but I do not see how you manage with your washing, in the absence of an area. Our back yards were mainly devoted to the duty of clothes-drying."

The wife opened a large closet, and explained that this was her drying-room, where she had but to hang the wet clothes and admit a powerful current of hot air. The ventilation of all the rooms was evidently perfect, and they were all lighted and cheerful. Paul was free to confess that his own house was not one whit more comfortable as a home.

After leaving the apartment, he said: "Professor, one of the points I still fail to understand is this. You seem to have developed a new race of dwellers as well as a new species of dwellings. I fear, if the tenement class of my day were given the freedom of this place, they would soon reduce it to their own level of disorder, filth, and degradation. Of what account would be tiled floors, and porcelain walls, and all accommodations offered by running water, ventilators, hot-air currents, and electric lights, in the hands of ignorant and shiftless persons having no appreciation of their value, and no knowledge how to intelligently care for them?"

"Precisely. But the preliminary work of educating the working classes in the art of home-making had been in process many centuries before these Pyramids were raised. The women are mainly responsible as the home-makers. One reason why your mechanics had such poor homes is perfectly clear; the women of their class, whom they naturally took as wives, received little home training and no public instruction in the serious duties of life which they ignorantly undertook. They did not know what housekeeping meant. They did not know what home really meant. They consequently lacked a requisite to home-making that even wealth and trained servants could not fully supply. Ignorance such as this, of the first principles of life, is now impossible. The compulsory education of these days means something, and it means quite as much to women as to men. It means the emancipation and the happiness that go hand in hand with knowledge and ability. You rightly surmise that the slatterns of your tenement-houses would soon make a slatternly tenement-house of this palace. But let me tell you that a corps of women such as Thomas's young wife, who tells me that she is a graduate of the Home-makers' Institute, would find or make a way to convert even a tenement apartment-house into an abode of beauty and comfort, whose attractions would make a home-lover out of any husband worthy of the name."

"Then you are disposed to look upon your Pyramids as a result rather than a cause?"

"Partly, but not altogether. Such things are always reciprocal to a greater or less extent. A neat and well-appointed house of course helps to arouse the pride and ambition of the young housekeeper; but it is a diamond in the rough, and opaque until she has polished it and taught it to catch the sunshine. These Pyramids and other great dwelling-houses of similar design simply represent one of the many means which have been adopted to help educate our working people to found — each his own castle, each his own shrine, each his own something worthy to work for!"

"Are workmen encouraged to marry and to make homes for themselves?"

"Of course! in every way that seems practicable. We are now a nation of homes. There can be no stable general government unless it rests upon an aggregation of home governments; and it is recognized that whatever makes home-life better and happier contributes directly to the stability of the national life."

"The fact that your population is more homogeneous than in my day helps to make this possible."

"Of course, time is a physician that can help cure many evils, but every individual is to some extent responsible for the tendency of his time. There must be constant education of mind and manners, or time will only make matters worse."

They walked for some moments in silence. "One more glance," added the Professor, "and then we are done for to-day. Here is the grand central hall, which overtops the honeycombed series of storehouses forming the nucleus of this vast pile. This hall, as you see, divided by avenues and streets, is the business centre of this little world. The numerous domes of glass that light it from above are the lower extremities of shafts that pierce the building vertically and act like great arteries through which sunshine and air can circulate."

From a lofty gallery Paul looked down upon the brilliant scene of activity beneath him, and then aloft to the golden ceiling, now sparkling with myriad suns of electricity. The space, the color, the glow, the warm pleasant odor, the throb of distant music, the nameless emotion of a dream that is not known to be a dream, dazed his senses. "Show me no more wonders!" he plead, "for I cannot longer compass them. Please lead the way, that we may move and keep moving until heaven once more encircles us with its restful curve of blue!"

The Professor understood. They passed to the open air, saw the winter sun just kissing its hand from the western hills, took the cars again, and in another half hour were seated once more in the subdued light of the Professor's study.

CHAPTER XII.

A Dinner at the Restaurant.

AFTER bathing, Paul seated himself on the sofa in the study, with his dog Smudge at his side, and before he knew it, fell sound asleep. When he awoke and looked dreamily about him, he found the Professor still busy at his table. Smudge aroused simultaneously, and thrust a paw into his hand.

"Well, Mr. Prognosis, that hour's nap will do you a world of good. That you might not be interrupted, my family are already taking dinner, and it has been arranged that you and I shall now go and have ours at one of the summer-garden restaurants, conducted under municipal supervision, at the Palace of the Sun, that forms an interesting feature of winter life in Tone, in which I feel sure you will be interested. The fact is, Mr. Prognosis, we give a great deal of attention nowadays to the question of health; and, both as cause and effect, we have become a nation of gormands, — gormands in a good sense, — people who make a science of eating, who know the best, and are consequently satisfied with no other. I want the pleasure of introducing you to one of the most famous of these restaurants. It is only a short walk from here."

The walk, which proved only too short, was soon taken; and they then approached a public square which Paul had not before seen, surrounding what seemed an immense conservatory of glass, its lines of light diminishing in distances that clearly showed this to be by far the greatest building he had ever gazed upon.

"This," said the Professor, "is the Palace of the Sun; but please ask no questions about it, for you shall have an opportunity to inspect it later. I have purposely approached the rear entrance of the restaurant, so that the Palace itself may retain its novel attractions until some occasion when you have ample time to do it justice."

They now passed through a triple gateway into a garden, and entered a handsome building resembling a club-house, where they left their outer clothing in the cloak-room, and then ascended the grand staircase to a hall of great dimensions, and surpassing in beauty of detail anything of the kind that Paul had ever seen or dreamt. A suffused and mellow light from some unseen source made artificial day; and bowers of roses, and orange-trees, and trellised grapes, and plashing fountains, made a tropical garden of the room itself, which seemed reflected in the scene without the windows; while through the warm and perfumed atmosphere laughed a merry breeze of orchestral music. All the windows were open, and birds fluttered in and out. The new-comers soon made themselves comfortable in a secluded nook, where a waiter immediately attended, as if flashed from the rugs beneath their feet.

"I have to confess," said the Professor, "that I never once thought of inviting you to lunch to-day, being engrossed by the interest you showed in all things. That was unhealthy, and consequently very wrong, and I beg your pardon."

But Paul made confession to the fact that he had been so tired before the nap that he was then in no condition to eat.

"I hope that you are quite rested now."

"Perfectly, and ready to see anything and everything in the way of new wonders that you may be pleased to summon with your witch's wand."

"I am glad of that, for, after dinner, I have a literary or scientific treat in store for you. Well, now, what would you particularly like to have? Whatsoever the world produces is now to be had for the asking."

"Anything you will kindly set before me will be acceptable — always excepting cabbage and cauliflower."

The Professor laughed, and remarked that he was rather fond of cauliflower, and had seriously contemplated ordering some; but, out of consideration for his guest, he would of course omit it.

"On no account! Please yourself, and I promise to be pleased. Some of your dishes will no doubt be strange to me, but I am sure they will be good; and, with the exception of the two vegetables named, I can eat anything I ever saw served."

The Professor readily assumed the command thus conferred upon him, and soon had the opening course of a savory repast upon the table. Just where it came from was not apparent to Paul, but there it stood smoking before him: first, a golden-colored soup, with an odd name but a delicate flavor; then, some wonder of a fish, quite free from bones, and with a highly appetizing sauce; and next, a small roast fowl, with numerous side dishes of vegetable preparations, most of which were new to him. After the dessert followed a variety of fruits, wholly unfamiliar but peculiarly delicious; and finally, a welcome old friend in the form of a cup of fragrant coffee.

As they sipped this, the Professor asked: "Tell me, Mr. Prognosis, now that you have had an opportunity to recover from your first feeling of wonder, how did our Pyramids strike you?"

"Well, sir, I can only repeat that they are certainly abodes of the blest as compared with the city tenements of my time, which I suppose were their prototypes. You could not imagine, sir, if you were to try, what those tenements really were — shadowed in narrow courts and alleyways, dark, mildewed, squalid, filthy! And, without seeing them, you could not imagine the wretched condition of the creatures who lived, or rather who drooped and died, in them. You could not imagine the horror of the rumshops and other dens of vice that always encircled them, — vile haunts of crime which, like fungous growths, fattened on what they destroyed, and exhaled their miasma to increase if possible the loathsome odors of the street. You could not imagine the degradation of the children born and bred amid such surroundings, — unhealthy, ignorant, void of all good or desire for good; spawned like reptiles, and then thrust forth to beg, starve, pilfer, murder, and further spread the contagion of disease and sin. Oh! sir, it is too pitiful to even think of. Let us not speak of it further."

"But were there no true men, no strong men, no willing men and women to undertake the task of reform, however hard it might be? Was nothing done to rouse public sentiment to an appreciation of the wretched condition of fellow human beings? I should think that the pleasure of life, even for the fortunate, would have been destroyed by the contemplation of such misery, or by the mere knowledge of it even if they turned their eyes away."

"Oh! we had prophets among us, and reformers, and noble men and women who were willing to lay down martyr lives to better the condition of their degraded brothers and sisters. But it was a well-nigh hopeless task. Many of their most heroic efforts seemed only to result in intensifying the evils they sought to remedy. They seemed perfectly powerless, and the candle of Christianity that had kept the world in hope for many centuries seemed about to die out. You see, the evils of the day had their roots too deep down in the customs of the past; they were the outgrowths of numberless generations of moral and social servitude, unwholesome traditions, evil thoughts and habits, and gross instincts, that allied their victims to a condition worse than that of brute beasts. They had no hopes, no good ambitions that could be aroused, no consciences that could be appealed to."

"Excuse me, but do not be too sure of that. They were certainly sunken in the lowest depths of misery, but consciences, — most of them still had consciences, and they still had possibilities of ambitions mightier than the mightiest of temptations. Vice no doubt was bred in their very blood; but so also, I must think, was a lingering love of virtue; and, with God's help, it has come to pass that strong men and women, working in his name through generation after generation and century after century, and gradually reinforced by stalwart recruits from the ranks they sought to help, have finally raised the standard of morals, both private and public, to a height you dared not hope. What you have seen to-day is not the result of any one act of any one person or of any million of persons, — though Costor gave direction to concerted action, — but of the combined efforts of all individuals who have thus far lent their influence, by even the simplest word or act, to the cause of truth and justice. That 's the only way public sentiment is created, and Public Sentiment rules this world as God rules heaven! To-day, Public Sentiment says all men have equal rights, if not equal capacities, — and it means and enforces what it says. To-day, Public Sentiment pronounces vice degrading, and ignorance the mother of vice, and says that neither shall be tolerated. To-day, Public Sentiment pronounces labor ennobling, and it ennobles the laborer. That 's all there is about it."

The Professor was evidently getting excited, and Paul was not unwilling to follow him into the brisk outdoor air. He was also glad to know that they had in prospect a walk of a mile before reaching the next scene of surprise.

For a time neither spoke; and Paul had a full opportunity to examine the faces that passed him. He looked in vain for any that suggested vice, hunger, poverty, or even care. The streets were crowded, but no one was in a hurry, though all seemed bound on some pleasurable quest.

After a time, he ventured to inquire whether it was not found difficult to supply the various needs of the present increased population of the world.

The Professor at first answered a little sharply: "No, sir! We save what you wasted! We work, while you played at work! We give Nature and her vast forces an opportunity to work for us! And we know how to wisely use what we have!"

Later on, he explained that the art of preserving all kinds of perishable food had been brought to great perfection, and that vast reserves of food were continually stored in all corners of the world, as well as in such reservoirs as the Pyramids in Tone and other chief centres, in order to guard against short crops resulting from drouth or other unavoidable cause. "With the population the world now has, this is a prime necessity. We waste nothing, but preserve and store all that we have no present need for; and the oceans and continents are fairly alive with fleet messengers that herald the first sign of lack, and haste to distribute wholesome food wherever it is most needed."

The coffee was evidently beginning to exert its benignant influence on the Professor's nerves, by allaying his irritation at the inexcusable ignorance of the nineteenth century people. "I will say this," he remarked confidingly: "the progress you scored during the latter half of your century of strife, in mechanical science and also in the enfranchisement of your working classes, was never equaled in any like period of the world's history."

CHAPTER XIII.

The Meeting of the School of Sciences.

By the time they arrived at the lecture hall, both men were quite refreshed. It was located in a stately granite building whose dome glittered far above them, which the Professor explained was exclusively devoted to the uses of the Learned Fellows of the High School of Sciences. During the few minutes that preceded the opening of the meeting, Professor Prosper passed around the hall, greeting his friends and greeted by them on all sides. He was evidently as popular as he was well known. He kept Paul close at his side, and presented him to many of his friends with the words: "This is a valued acquaintance of mine, Mr. Paul Prognosis, who has a remarkable history, and whose knowledge of Old English so far exceeds my own that I feel highly honored in being allowed to name myself as his pupil."

"Is it possible?" — "Most remarkable!" — "We shall certainly hope to welcome him as a fellow member!" — remarked the several friends. "I trust that I may soon be able to announce a paper by you, Mr. Prognosis," said the president. He then mounted the rostrum, brought his gavel down with a bang, called the meeting to order, and read a few letters and formal notices.

As he did so, Paul had an opportunity to examine him. He was certainly a noble specimen of intellectual man. The great electric sun that illuminated the auditorium seemed to invest his shining bald head with distinguishing radiance. "Strange!" said Paul to himself as he gave a stealthy glance about the room, "I believe every man present excepting myself is bald — hopelessly bald!"

After the preliminary business usual in such assemblies, the president stated that those present would have the pleasure of listening to one whom it was unnecessary to introduce, as he was known to all — their honored fellow member, Mr. —, Mr. — alas! he had forgotten the name. He searched among the papers on his desk, readjusted his glasses, and very calmly continued, "our honored fellow member, Mr. Winestine — Mr. Mark Winestine."

During this episode, the venerable president continued making a series of little bows in the direction of the speaker prospective, while the reflected light from his shining scalp continued

to describe a variety of curves which reminded Paul of the light-ribbons he used to make when a boy, by twirling a flaming brand. He fell to speculating on the nature of these curves of light, whether they were concentric, parabolic, or cycloidal. While thus absurdly employed, Mr. Winestine began speaking, as follows: —

"It is a remarkable fact that, since natural history became a science, more than fifty well-known species of mammalia, and more than double that number of oviparous animals, have become extinct; while many others, not yet wholly extinct, are practically so, inasmuch as they are no longer found in a natural state. Such extinction of great classes of animal life has been mainly accomplished by direct and systematic warfare in the interests of humanity.

"One cannot but rejoice that the great carnivorous beasts of the feline, canine, and ursine families no longer exist. We must, however, except the great white bear and the foxes of the frozen North, which still hold undisputed possession of their strongholds.

"Of the giants of the Asian and African forests, the elephant alone remains, and he only as a domestic animal. The hippopotamus, rhinoceros, and that terrible reptile, the crocodile, and his kindred, are all swept forever from the face of the earth; while the fierce lion and tiger have long ceased to devastate and make afraid. The world is also well rid of the entire serpent family, a long wished-for riddance that has but recently been effected. But it is now accomplished; and as in the case of certain diseases once common, there is no danger of a repetition of the pest that for so many centuries ravaged all the edens of this world.

"Besides the above-named classes of animals, whose forced retirement from the living fauna causes no sentiments of regret, there are some others, including the fur-bearers and those whose flesh has been prized for food, which have been hunted to extinction, including that wonderfully intelligent rodent, the beaver, and also the otter, the fur seal, the noble bison, the great elk of the North, and the guanaco of the South. These, unfortunately, are now only known by their fossil remains and by the excellent works of ancient naturalists dating up to the twenty-fifth century.

"At the same time there are many other classes of animals whose food qualities have particularly recommended them to our care, which have not only been preserved, but, owing to the destruction of their natural enemies, have rapidly increased, — in some cases so rapidly as to become seriously troublesome to our farmers by reason of their numbers. Of the birds described by the ancients, very few have succumbed to the changing influences of time. Some few species have ceased to exist, while many others have become vastly more numerous, and particularly the insectivorous varieties, which have been so protected by man, by reason of their usefulness, that swarming hordes of insect life which used to destroy the vegetation of entire countries are now reduced to insignificant numbers.

"I deeply regret that time allows me to but barely mention the subject that most interests me in this connection — the one to which I have devoted my energies for many years past. You all know to what I refer. My forthcoming treatise will afford an opportunity to fully canvass the topic. You will therein see that I have attempted — with what success, it is for you to determine — to rid the world of one of the last vestiges of animal life that all concede to be not only useless but highly prejudicial to human interests — I refer to domestic rats and mice. A combined and continued effort is needed to destroy forever these active and prolific little rodents. Local efforts have been temporarily successful, but fresh incursions from neighboring localities have soon filled their enemies with confusion. It is only through the combined efforts now about to be instituted throughout the world that we may hope to soon class these troublesome vermin with the already long list of extinct species."

Mr. Winestine here bowed to the president, who, being engaged in taking a sip of water, neglected to respond to the salutation.

Mr. Johnsmith next read a paper on "Artificial Modification of Climate," in the course of which he remarked: —

"Fifty years ago to-day I enjoyed the proud distinction of having my scheme for changing the ocean currents approved by the Grand Council. I had thought out the plan while still a boy, had often written on the subject, and often urged it upon the attention of this very body of scientific men — or, more correctly, upon those who then composed its membership. But all was of no avail, until I conceived the idea of practically demonstrating to the world the correctness of my views by constructing an accurate model of the Atlantic Ocean, with its coast-lines and its varying depths accurately reproduced in correct scale. The currents were set in motion by mechanical means, and the proper degree of heat was imparted to the tropical regions by submerged warm-water pipes, while the polar regions were subjected to a refrigerating process. This apparatus was so adjusted that the actual temperature of all parts of the ocean, and also of its many currents, was correctly reproduced.

"I must confess that it looked somewhat like the scheme of a madman to thus presume to control the mighty currents of the ocean; but the topography of the ocean bed and its influence on currents was already so well understood that I was able to draw conclusions much less wild than they were at first regarded.

"The idea had taken strong hold of me that artificial barriers might be so placed as to direct the arctic current into mid-ocean, and, at the same time, to divide the Gulf stream into two currents that might bathe and materially raise the temperature of the northern coasts of America and Europe.

"You know the result. What was theory is now reality. By placing comparatively small artificial reefs at certain points that I indicated, the habitable portions of two continents have been very considerably increased, and now afford room for the spread of our rapidly increasing population. The success of the undertaking teaches anew the power of coöperation,—shows anew that whatever work is undertaken by the Grand Council of Nations, whatever its proportions, must and ever will succeed."

Professor Speculo was next introduced, and opened his remarks in a manner that showed him to be quite familiar with the platform.

"You have often listened to me while recounting the dry details of astronomical discovery, and I trust that I have already prepared your minds for an adequate understanding of the stupendous spectacle that is to be presented to our eyes in a few short hours from now. In my address this evening, I propose to hold up to your mental vision a picture, as seen in the focus of the great reflector, of the grandeur of the Sirian system.

"The magnificence of that far-off luminary, which is the centre of a vast system of luminous and non-luminous bodies, is so great that the human mind fails to grasp the idea that a statement of its known volume would convey. Imagine, if you can, a sphere glowing with light and heat so intense that our sun, bright as it seems, is pale and ineffectual in comparison. Imagine, if you can, that this fiercely glowing body has a diameter of upwards of twenty-five millions of miles. Then picture to yourself a score of planetary suns revolving about it, which, in stellar phrase, are in its immediate vicinity, but, in fact, some of them are about two hundred solimeters from the main body."

"Professor, please," whispered Paul, "what is a solimeter?"

"The earth's mean distance from the sun."

"So I supposed. A famous measuring-rod, truly!"

Mr. Speculo continued : —

"Some of these luminous planets are of half the diameter of the sun, and give a brilliant light, while others show only a faint red light. Others still, though they must be of enormous magnitude, are seen only by reflected light. When you know that we have been able to detect the non-luminous bodies of the Sirian system, you will appreciate to some extent the wonderful achievements of modern optical science, which have enabled us to extend our vision across the incalculable gulf that separates us. If you can grasp the meaning of three hundred thousand solimeters, you will know what that gulf is; and then, returning to Mars, we cannot but feel that it is a near neighbor."

Paul succeeded in keeping his attention fixed for a few moments longer, with the hope that some further reference to neighbor Mars might occur; but finding that the speaker was spreading his wings among systems more and more remote, — so remote, indeed, that even Sirius began also to seem a neighbor by contrast, — he leaned his head on his hand as comfortably as circumstances would permit, and prepared — what! what was the meaning of this ? — he hardly recognized it as belonging to him — his head was completely bald like the rest of those present! He had become a Learned Fellow indeed! But how had this happened, and when had it happened? "Smudge will scarcely recognize me," he murmured, as drowsiness again overpowered him, and he again supported that now unfamiliar smooth poll on his hand and dropped off into a quiet little cat-nap.

From this refreshing sleep he was aroused by a lively, red-faced speaker, who, much to his astonishment, announced as his subject: "The Analysis of Odors, and Analysis by Odors." What the speaker's name was he did not hear, and he never afterward learned, but his remarks included the following surprising statements: —

"Yes, gentlemen, it is very fortunate that a subject so fascinating as that of odors should have been left by the ancients wholly untouched, and therefore fresh for us to investigate with an interest quite unique. The questioning minds of the past that ransacked the universe for new subjects for study were apparently baffled by the subtle character of odors. Those prying ancients in a manner defrauded scientists of this age of much glory and self-satisfaction, by forestalling us in nearly all directions in our search after original truth. This subject, however, was a sealed book to them; and, for that matter, it might have remained so to us and to all time, had it not been ordained that the Tu Ling family were to live and afford us the means of studying this obscure but highly interesting subject.

"This remarkable case of abnormal development in the human species has no parallel in any record of the past that has come down to us. The extraordinary sense of smell possessed by the members of this singular Tu Ling family so far surpassed its ordinary development in man that it may almost be regarded as a sixth sense. The scenting power of the hound, which unerringly tracks his master's horse over snow and ice, even though many other persons have subsequently followed the same path, has ever excited wonder and admiration. Yet these Tu Lings were in no degree inferior to their canine rivals in the power to discriminate all scents. They could do all that the best scenting dogs can do, and they could do much more, for, being intelligent human beings, they were able to describe, name, and classify all possible odors.

"Under the direction of Dr. Probe and myself, a systematic analysis of these ethereal emanations was begun some ten years ago, and continued, with occasional periods of rest, for about four years.

"The members of this Tu Ling family were two brothers and a sister. All were in delicate health, and not strong enough for continuous effort, so that our work was necessarily intermittent; but the true character of odors was soon foreshadowed, and the great practical value of the inquiry realized. During the frequent pauses in the work of examination, many delicate instruments were perfected, mainly the result of the patient labors of my learned friend, Dr. Probe; and toward the last the progress of our work was more rapid. The Tu Ling family are now all dead, but a complete account of their contributions to science is now on record. They lived long enough to fully verify the results of our experiments, and to rejoice with us when Dr. Probe finally succeeded in making odors visible."

The speaker then described in detail some of the instruments referred to, though the vocabulary employed was such as to make these quite unintelligible to the astonished visitor; and he further stated that these instruments now offered an all-valuable means of detecting the most ethereal, but none the less potent, emanations constituting the medium in which mankind lives and breathes and has its being.

Enthusiastic applause greeted the close of this learned paper.

The chairman announced that the following papers might be expected at the next session: "Rate of Absorption of the World's Waters by Crystallization," by Professor Ring; "Retardation, as shown by Observations on the Standard Pendulum," by Professor Calculus; "Prime Importance of a Correct Understanding of Old English of the Nineteenth Century Period," by Professor Prosper; and "Observations in the Coal Mines at the North Pole and along the Lines of Covered Railways approaching thereto," by Dr. Peter O'Dactyl. He also remarked that Dr. O'Dactyl would present specimens from those celebrated mines, including some remarkable fossils that were quite new to science, one of these being especially interesting, namely: a *minordynodigiteriumrodentum*.

The meeting was then dismissed, and Paul and his companion returned home through the now quiet streets, though still lighted as at midday.

"Well, Mr. Prognosis, I hope you enjoyed many of the statements you have heard, which afford hints as to some of the subjects that are now attracting public attention."

"I did, and I shall exhaust your good nature at a later time by making inquiries about them. One thing I am particularly curious to know. What is the standard pendulum that was alluded to?"

"Oh, that is an instrument located in the basement of the building we have just left, which beats thirty strokes per minute, and enables us to accurately compare the second of to-day with that of any past period of which we have records — and such records are numerous and exceedingly valuable."

"I do not think that I understand its importance."

"Do not try to, to-night," said the Professor kindly. "I will arrange that you shall examine for yourself the mysteries of the great pendulum."

CHAPTER XIV.

A Glimpse of Country Life.

"AND now, Mr. Prognosis, whenever you feel drowsy from your unusual day's work of sight-seeing, you will find your chamber in readiness for you. Remember that you require a good night's rest to strengthen you for another and even harder day's travel to-morrow under the guidance of Marco, who is nearly as untiring a traveler as your dog Smudge. By the way, where is Smudge? He must be lonely, and I don't see why he should n't be allowed to enjoy our society at least till bedtime. Perhaps, too, it will help to make you feel at home in our house if he takes kindly to a bearskin shake-down which shall be placed in your chamber."

The Professor passed into an adjoining room, and, a moment later, the noble animal came bounding into the library, where, after manifesting his affection for his master in canine fashion, he spread himself comfortably at Paul's feet, and appeared an interested listener to the conversation that followed.

"I feel quite refreshed, Professor, and not inclined to sleep at present. If you are not tired, I should be best pleased to hear you talk."

"On what subject, for instance?"

"On any subject pertaining to improvements in man's position in the world, that have resulted from your later and more highly developed forms of civilization."

"I shall be delighted to thus oblige you, for, in fact, I am always fond of lecturing, so long as I can be sure of an interested audience. But please suggest some special topic to begin with, as the field is large."

"Several subjects immediately occur to me," said Paul reflectively, "as leading ones in my day, such as ownership of property, real and personal, which of course includes farm-lands as well as city buildings. I should be extremely interested to know something of the methods of modern agriculture, for, without some radical changes in this department of human industry, resources must be severely taxed to meet the wants of the population that now, as I understand, covers nearly the entire continent."

"Very well; let us then begin with the last of your inquiries — that about agriculture, which also involves the question of land ownership. In the first place, you must keep clearly in mind the fact you have already stated, that a population, vast beyond the imagination of the nineteenth century, now occupies not only the American continent, but nearly every other habitable portion of the globe; and also that such habitable portion has been greatly increased during the later centuries, as was suggested in the remarks of one of the speakers to-night. Riverbanks that the beaver once overflowed by his engineering feats are now populous with towns; every town of old has become a city; every city a metropolis; every metropolis a cosmopolis, — of which Tone is a fair example, — with its every human dwelling and workshop a little city in itself, towering to the sky."

"And the fields, the pastures, the grain prairies, the woodlands — are they still here?"

"Yes; though they would probably be scarcely recognizable to you at first glance. To support a population, whereof every thousand of old represents a present million, and where every unit of this million now lives in comparative comfort and plenty — this means myriad changes in methods of production and distribution. There are now few if any waste places; Nature never wastes, and man has learned to take Nature at her best and conform his ways to hers. Horticulture has supplanted agriculture, and every acre is studied and stimulated to do what it can best do, just as every man is expected to exert his best faculties in his most suitable field of action."

"And how do you prevent waste?"

"In many ways. Whatever is produced is preserved, for waste is recognized as a form of wickedness that must mean want to some one, even if the waster himself is exempted from suffering the inevitable penalty. For instance, every berry, every fruit, however perishable, is promptly submitted to the improved processes that chemistry has taught, and so prepared that it shall be ready for future need. To a considerable extent, the waste of past ages constitutes the riches of the present era, and helps to fill to overflowing the vast storehouses of food products that now gird the globe and prevent all possibility of hunger."

"And how about transportation?"

"That problem has been satisfactorily solved. No one centre is allowed to become overstocked with the world's goods at the expense of less favored outskirting provinces. Where the need is, there fly the needfuls. Railways, and lines of road-vehicles propelled by power, net the land; while the seas are highways over which processions of buoyant ships, built of aluminium instead of iron and propelled by electric motors, bear their brimming food baskets. Thereby, the Grand Council of Nations is able to deal with the globe as the market gardener of old did with his garden plat: whatever corner is best suited to a certain product, that corner is devoted to that product and to that alone. Most of the fruits we ate at dinner were grown in Africa. That country is now the world's hothouse, and the scent and flavor of its products make glad every table in the world, while the grainfields of the North return their appropriate quota. The luxurious wastefulness of constraining Nature to half-do things, out of latitude and out of season, is no longer practicable."

"And the farmers—do they not still own their farms, and have the right to do as they will with their own?"

"Within certain limits—yes; but they no longer have the right to buy or sell the lands they occupy, for the reason—which some of your far-sighted thinkers perceived, and which experience has proved to be founded on principles of justice—that the general public has a direct interest, and consequently a prior right, in the improvement and productiveness of all lands, and is consequently responsible for results. The breadth of land under cultivation must be proportionate to the needs of the public, with an ample margin of excess to meet contingencies. It was discovered that a question of such vital importance to the public at large could not be trusted with safety to the will of irresponsible individuals; but that the improvement of lands, to insure the best results, must of necessity be under the management of authorities appointed as the public's representatives to secure its highest good."

"You speak of the improvement of lands. In what does that consist?"

"Primarily in the building and vitalizing of the soil."

"What do you mean by its building?"

"We have been long accustomed to supply soil to barren places."

"How do you obtain the necessary material? It would seem to me that you must merely rob one district to enrich another."

"Not at all. We actually manufacture soil. We follow the lead of Nature, and simply supplement and hasten her processes. All soils, you must know, are produced by the disintegration of the rocks from weathering and the addition of accumulations of vegetable mould. The rocks furnish the chief elements: silica, alumina, carbonate of lime, magnesia, etc. But, in the case of natural soils, only a small proportion of these have the proper admixture of the elements needed to produce the best crops."

"I am still at a loss to understand where you obtain materials for new combinations of earths."

"I will give you an example. Let us take

the case of a rocky hill, covered with boulders and a thin soil, adjoining which is a large tract of heavy clay-land, wholly unproductive. The clay is glacial drift or boulder clay, and very deep. Well, we go to work with our great pulverizers and grind up all the loose rocks on the hill; and the boulder clay in vast quantities is reduced to powder by the same agency. A portion of the rock dust is then transferred to the clay-lands, and the clay dust to the hill. The hill is thereby freed from loose stones, and covered to its summit by a deep, productive soil, laid on in terraces, while the clay-lands are made light and warm by the admixture of rock dust. Then, by the annual addition of leaf mould from the forests, and such artificial fertilizers as are known to be most suitable to the crops desired, we gradually convert such waste places, that in your day seemed hopelessly barren, into lands equal in productiveness to the richest river valleys."

"The process is evidently expensive."

"Certainly, and it would hardly be undertaken by individuals, who, looking upon life as short, are apt to work for immediate results, without much reference to the interests of future generations. But public expense in this direction, which was really demanded by public needs, has made returns by the thousandfold.

The increase in government revenues thus secured has alone been sufficient to change penury to prosperity."

"The practice is excellent," said Paul, "and it must, of course, have vastly increased the bounty of Mother Earth; but even then, I should hardly expect that your farm products could keep pace with the demands of your growing population."

"Up to this time," answered the Professor thoughtfully, "the means of food supply have proved ample. The world is wide, and some large districts still remain unimproved, so that similar development in the future is still possible. Moreover, our forest-lands are also held in reserve for future necessity, and in them we have vast districts yet left to draw upon. From what I have already explained, you will readily understand the necessity of government authority in controlling all lands and requiring of farmers that certain breadths be planted, and with certain plants best suited to the particular soil and also most needed to meet the annual requirements in the several lines."

"Such authority must sometimes be oppressive to the farmers."

"Not at all. It simply consists in indicating to the farmer what his farm is best calculated to produce, and what products are to be most in demand. By thus preventing over-production in any one line, it helps to keep prices stable, and prevents speculation in food products, which, in your day, was a tyrannous vice. The uncertainties that attended the lot of the farmer as you knew him made him a very different sort of person from the farmer of to-day. Agriculturists — or horticulturists, more properly — are now a very thrifty class, and they constitute a large proportion of our population. Farming is now a favorite industry, as affording healthful occupation, variety of interests, and generous rewards; and most of our young men are perfectly contented, if they are so fortunate as to secure good leases."

"I presume you know that it was quite otherwise in my time. Then, very few boys had any fondness for the hoe, and one and all gave their best thought and energy to seeking how it might be escaped, and a city clerkship secured in its place."

The Professor laughed. "And was n't that quite natural? The conditions that then surrounded farming were all against the farmer. Farming had not been reduced to a science, and it involved so much menial labor and so little development of the higher faculties that the young men saw little in it to stimulate their best ambitions. Moreover, the results of their labors were so handicapped by inadequate means of transportation and artificial fluctuations in values that their efforts were always more or less speculative. From lack of knowledge, the work was irksome; while the profits, when there were any, had a fashion of mainly accruing to the benefit of transportation companies, monopolists in the form of middle-men, and speculators. Was it not so?"

"It 's only too clear that your historians have hunted some of our evil tendencies to their holes."

"Moreover, you seem to have taken no steps to make country life attractive. The cities absorbed everything that was educational or amusing. Now, the social attractions of the farming districts far surpass those of the cities in many ways; while the cities are so numerous and so accessible that all the advantages they possess are easily obtained by those living in the country. Every country village has its pleasure-house as well as its public library; and telephones and pneumatic tubes make these tributary to the city centres."

"You have pictured, Professor, what appears to me quite an ideal state of suburban society; and I begin to understand how successfully you have dealt with the question of land monopoly and landlordism, that once gave opportunities for so much tyranny in some parts of the world. I should now be glad to know how other kinds of property are held, and whether you have any legal provisions preventing the accumulation of vast wealth by individuals or companies, which might be detrimental to the public welfare by permitting selfish control of production and prices."

"We have no evils of that kind to contend against. If any such danger arose, there is law enough and righteous public opinion enough to root it out at short notice. The public has learned to have small patience with individual usurpation of any of its privileges and birthrights. The tyrant of individualism has forever been put down. His hoarded and sluggish millions are now the lively small coins of the populace, begetting a hundredfold in the hands of an intelligent and industrious people. Custom is still a leading force that governs men, but custom founded on probity is now the rule of life; and business ethics are so firmly grounded among us that any infraction of our well-established customs would subject the offender to a prompt and effectual reprimand from his fellows. This is generally sufficient to bring avarice to its senses; but in places where moral evolution is less complete than with us here, — and there are such places, — laws of limitation and restraint are brought into action.

Such laws include provisions for a special tax on individual possessions judged unduly great, which are designed ultimately to re-absorb into the public purse any incomes that are excessive beyond all reason."

"In spite of all the precautions you take, do you never have anything like famine or great scarcity?"

"Famine—never; and scarcity is rare. The general average of production throughout the world varies but little; and any surplus is so easily stored and so perfectly preserved that there is really no part of the world that need go hungry. There have been occasions when destructive fires or floods, and especially those interfering with means of communication, have resulted in want in certain districts before the outside world could lend assistance; yet such disasters are extremely rare and only temporary."

"But your crops must sometimes fail?"

"Yes, sometimes in certain sections, but never in all. So far as drouths are concerned, human agencies are competent to prevent much damage so long as rivers continue to flow; but the destructive effects of early frosts or of excessive rainfall are still beyond our control, and these occasionally cause temporary disturbance in supplies. But the usual surplus is supposed to be ample to meet contingencies of this kind for at least a year in advance; and attention is immediately directed to adopting special measures for supplying the deficit."

"Of course, Professor, many other questions are suggested to me by what you have already explained. May I ask a few?"

"As many as you please."

"Do the farmers own their homes and other buildings, and have any legal tenure on the lands they occupy?"

"The lands are simply leased by the Government to the occupants, who hold them as long as they please by paying a certain stipulated rental. They erect their own homes and farm-buildings."

"Some of these newly-improved lands of which you have spoken must be wonderfully productive. How does the Government secure an appropriate return?"

"If the improvements are made by the Government, the return is derived from increased rental. If made by the occupant, the reward belongs of course to him. Occupants of inferior land sometimes appeal to the Government for aid in making improvements, on the condition of paying a stipulated increase of rental. The ordinary rules of business prudence determine what shall be done in such cases."

"And the farmer himself — tell me, Professor, what has become of him, in this process of agricultural evolution?"

"He has simply taken his proper place in Nature's beneficent plan. He is no longer a beast of burden. He works still — works more industriously than ever before; but he works hopefully, as he was meant to work — with his brain as well as his back, as planner and director rather than as brute force. He works intelligently, with agents that he understands, and in the direction of assured results, so that every stroke counts. He has trained the forces of Nature to do his brute work. He has even taught them to relieve his brute companions of a large part of what was formerly their accustomed labor. Oxen no longer painfully drag the plough through stony ground; horses no longer pant and quiver under thrice normal loads. Steam and electricity and motive forces whereof your century had no knowledge now form the muscles of the farmer's arms, and catch their power from the sun and the winds and the tides. The farmer has ceased battling with Nature, and taken her into willing copartnership."

"I suppose there are enough white-weeds and beetles to keep him from becoming lazy."

"Well, pretty much all the weed pests and insect pests have either been yoked into service, or left no opportunity for propagation. Even the so-called accidents of Nature are now seldom complained of, but from them her laws have been codified. Knowledge has become power in its broadest sense."

"And pleasure — has that any part in the scheme of the forty-ninth century, so far as the farmer is concerned?"

"Ay! to an extent that the nineteenth century knew not of. Mr. Prognosis, we have learned that willing work, in fields fitted to the capacity of the worker, is of itself one of the highest forms of pleasure; and freedom from all fear of future want, for himself and members of his family, — which is now placed within the reach of every man desiring to become a citizen — contributes to assure that contentment and peace of mind that alone can give to leisure any possibility of pleasurable recreation. In brief, Mr. Prognosis, and as a sort of parting salutation, I am glad to tell you that the experimental age in farming is past; the age of realization has come; the earth blossoms like a rose, and man laughs in the rose-field that Nature and he have together created. Good-night! and pleasant dreams!"

"The same to you, Professor. Good-night! Well," muttered Paul, as he prepared for retiring, "I suppose I might sleep comfortably in this strange costume, but it would probably be more restful not to. Marco got me into it readily enough, but I really need him to help me out. Smudge, I don't suppose you can explain the mystery, can you? This must be the line of separation. But I find no buttons. Ah! these buckles and snaps no doubt perform the same function. Presto! and in an instant I am ready for bed."

A thought suddenly struck him, and he peered cautiously into the looking-glass to observe the effect of his new headgear — or lack of it. He looked more than once — first solemnly, but finally with laughter so immoderate that he feared he might disturb the sleeping family. "Well," he said, "my admission as a Learned Fellow is practically assured. The learned president cannot beat that!"

PART III.

THE CRYSTAL BUTTON.

CHAPTER XV.

The Library.

PAUL awoke at daybreak thoroughly refreshed, and soon proceeded to the Professor's library, where, being of a decidedly bookish turn of mind, he longed to acquaint himself with the rows of volumes that literally walled the room. But to his regret and vexation, he found himself a stranger to the pages of printed stenography that constituted the bulk of the collection. However, a little roll of tinfoil, that he discovered to be the morning newspaper, lay upon the table; and by placing this in the phonograph, with which he was already acquainted, he was enabled to listen to its news, as if spoken by a person face to face with him.

Then again he began to examine the treasures on the shelves, and was happy to find that many compartments contained rolls similar to the newspaper, which needed only the phonograph to give them voice. Among these he came across one entitled: "History of the Rise and Fall of the Republic of Washington." "Rise and *Fall!*" he repeated, emphasizing the last word. "That is news indeed — the saddest news that I could hear. But ought I to be surprised? Was it not written on the wall, even in my time? Let us see how it begins." And here are the observations with which the chronicle opened: —

"In the history of the rise and fall of nations, there are, in many instances, periods of such brilliancy and beauty that they shine out from the records of time like beacon lights along the shore. Such a period is the one wherein the Republic of Washington was established. It marked an important era in the progress of enfranchisement. It was the work of a noble band of reformers, whose standard was self-government. Before proceeding to describe it, the careful student of history should recall one universal fact that is a necessary preliminary to correctly understanding its lesson, which is briefly this. During and preceding all periods of unusual national prosperity and mental activity, that always denote the working out of some great public question, when representative men rise to proud eminence, we may always expect to find a high standard of public virtue. Whether the form of government be simple or complex, whether a dynasty or a democracy, whether the ruling powers be many or few, we ever find that public spirit is ennobled by a lofty ideal, and that the representatives of that ideal are men notable for a high degree of unselfishness, manly integrity, and exalted ambition.

"On the other hand, the existence of a people characterized by a low ideal and by leaders who are notorious for double-dealing, faithlessness, and treachery, clearly marks a period of decay, which is invariably followed by moral torpor, then feverish unrest, revolution, chaos, and finally by reorganization on a foundation of greater simplicity and stability. The biographies of individuals who have been leaders are chiefly instructive because they present a key to the character of the public and condition of public morals of which they are the outgrowth. No ruler is a tyrant till he is backed by a public spirit of tyranny; no leader can be lawless unless he is the exponent of a lawless public spirit; no leader can be the characterization of dishonesty and fraud unless he is inspired and supported by a public spirit that is likewise contaminated. As wise and powerful governments have been created, so also have they gone to their downfall — by reason of the combined and long-continued influences of every act of every individual composing the population. Upon every such unit, every such individual person, rests in due proportion the responsibility of rise and fall, progress or degeneracy, on the part of a people."

"Ah!" sighed Paul, "I have no heart to read more. If this rule be founded on the eternal verities, and I believe it is, what else could be the meaning of the flaming horizon down which the setting sun of the nineteenth century sank, than just what the title of this fatal history indicates? I do not need to hear the details. I will not hear them! We kept hoping for a prophet to arise. Perhaps he spoke, but we hearkened not. We were disposed to lay the blame on our leaders; but while each man attended selfishly to his own petty cares and desires, content to be served, and had no time and no desire to serve others, what could we expect of those whom we exalted to our high places, but that they also should be creatures of selfishness, fashioned after the shape of those by whom they were fathered. Alas! and alas! for the aspirations of those who hoped against hope in those evil days!"

The next phonograph he took up proved to be a compendium of common law, which was not attractive to him. "But what is this drawer devoted to? — the largest in the room. Physics.

Ah! now I am more at home. Here is the pith of the accumulated research and wisdom of thirty centuries. Oh, for time to study these rare records! I will just see what this tape has to say. It seems rather abstruse — this opening observation: —

" 'The ether of space is primordial matter in equilibrium. Its tendency to expansion is equal to the cohesion of its atoms. It is residual matter from which systems have been formed. Being continuous throughout space, and having no centres of concentration excepting at the widely separated nebulous clouds, it is practically free from the effects of gravitation. So small is the mass of matter that constitutes systems, as compared with the space whence it has been gathered, that if the sun and all its planets were to expand and again fill the space they once occupied, the space reaching to the mid-regions between us and the other systems, the result would be as if a mustard seed should swell until its atoms occupied a space forty miles in diameter. By this figure we can realize the tenuity of primordial matter, and understand the reasons of the wide separation of the stellar centres.'

"Well, well!" said Paul, "this is a rather vague beginning, but I am evidently going to find a feast before me. Ah! here is a tape devoted to electricity. I wonder if they have solved the secrets of that subtle wonder. Oh, yes! but pretty much all the words in which the story is told are new to me. I see I shall have to go to school again, and begin in the primary class, before I can understand much about the modern development of the sciences. I suppose I ought to be somewhat discouraged, but I do not feel so. 'More!' and ever 'More!' is the scientist's cry. This next alcove is evidently devoted to astronomy. What splendid atlases! And some of these, I see, have titles and inscriptions which I am able to read. I suppose they are counted among the ancient works. Here 's 'The Planetary Systems of the Three Principal Stars in the Belt of Orion,' and 'The Age of the Sun and Promise of its Future,' and 'Mean Temperature of the Tropical Regions of Mars, and Average Humidity of its Atmosphere.' Treasures upon treasures! What a house of knowledge I am now privileged to visit, where the seers of the past are prepared, at bidding, to step forth and solve all mysteries of the physical universe! Time! time! give me but time and continued use of my mental faculties, and here will I satisfy some of my hunger for solid facts."

At this point the Professor entered, with a cheerful "Good-morning, friend Prognosis. I see you are also an early bird. I heard you moving about, and guessed what you were doing. But I fear you find some difficulty in getting at the meaning of our most recently printed books. Let me help you. Don't speak of it as trouble — it will give me pleasure. To begin with, the title of the book you hold in your hand is 'Natural History and Destiny of Man,' — here 's what you called evolution, carried several strides further than you ever imagined; the next is 'The True Social State as it now exists, compared with that of Former Times,' — which may sound mysterious, but it 's sufficiently suggestive; this is 'Best Method of Checking Population within Reasonable Limits.' That sounds startling to you, no doubt, but it 's a proposition we have been forced to meet. In your time, war, pestilence, famine, and unchecked diseases of many kinds, were agencies that amply performed the task; but, such are the sanitary provisions of the present time, that the world would soon be overstocked were it not for wisely adjusted limitations. Life may now be regarded as a privilege.

"Here in this next alcove are sets of encyclopedias, in which the sum total of knowledge in certain important branches of study is presented in brief. Here we find 'Flora and Fauna, Past and Present;' and here, a huge set of volumes with the single title 'Modes,' — not fashions, please understand, but the best possible modes and processes applicable to all mechanical arts, as epitomized from the annual reports of the Central Bureau of Demonstration. This series includes the matter from the final reports of that learned body, which is a kind of court of last resort; and, as the publication of each book is delayed for many years after they have completed their investigations, so as to eliminate errors and reconsider allied questions that the public may propose, the review of each subject, as here presented, may be considered exhaustive and final. Specialists of the highest talent throughout the world have been engaged, for centuries past, in carrying forward the comparative and demonstrative tests of which these books are the outcome; and they therefore show, so far as it is possible for the human intellect to understand, the best possible methods of securing all materials and forces that nature affords, and applying them to the needs of mankind."

"As I understand you," said Paul, "this, then, is the expressed substance of all possible invention, filtered, refined, and concentrated, and finally bottled in this compact form for ready reference."

"Exactly."

"But how many occupations are thereby dispensed with! Where are the inventors now?—

that great army of dreamers and experimenters, poor as church mice, yet buoyed by hope though a hundred times disappointed in accomplishment — working tirelessly day and night, starving themselves and their families, yet always filled with glad visions of future wealth and leisure; and then, at last, when their labors were crowned with success and they joyfully gave the world a new rung in its ladder of upward progress" —

"What then?"

"Then — having the mortification of seeing some man of business, the handler, reap their reward, — and, too often, even the honor, — while the patient worker, out of pocket and out at the elbows, went ruefully in search of something new. And what have become of the patent officials, patent solicitors, patent lawyers, patent swindlers? Well, well! some of those could be dispensed with and yet give the public no inconvenience."

"The patent system was long ago outgrown. Its usefulness vanished as soon as the age of science supplanted the age of guesswork and experiment. The age of mechanical discovery is now practically past."

"Then you must miss one of the joys of life. Professor, I have myself been an inventor and a patentee, and I know what it means. It is a rare pleasure to accomplish what no one else was ever before able to accomplish — to see a dream gradually develop into a solid reality, to see the world first sniff at it and then snatch at it, and to know that the creation of your mind has become every man's servant and benefactor. Even though the shrewd man of business might reap all pecuniary benefit, he could no more deprive the inventor of this proud satisfaction, than the book publisher or picture dealer to-day can defraud the poet or artist of his joy of paternity."

"But we have no cause for inventors now."

"So I understand. But again I ask: What has become of those peculiar powers of the human mind that were formerly directed to the duty of conquering the world of matter? Without war, the art of war must be lost and the sword must rust in its scabbard."

"True; but it is better so."

"Is it better that any faculty of the mind should be lost or dwarfed?"

"No; but it may be directed to wiser and more beneficent uses. Nature dispenses with useless members, and preserves and magnifies others. The eyes of caverned fishes disappear, while those of the hawk are sharpened by necessity. Use broadens a single toe and claw until they become the iron-like hoof of the horse, while disuse shrinks and shrivels the companion members until no external trace remains. You must understand that, under the favorable conditions which now surround the human race, all powers for evil are crippled, while those for good are given every possible opportunity for development. The 'survival of the fittest,' which was a new by-word in your day, is now a gospel. The sword of war may rust, and well it may; but the bloodless mace of peace has a mission much more fitting and nobler far. The energies that your inventors too often wasted in profitless hide-and-seek with the powers of nature are now directed toward perfecting instruments of every kind for enriching human lives. Our workers no longer feel their way and stumble blindly among unknown materials and forces, inflicting public injury in ignorant attempts to chain giant forces, as your electricians too often did; but we now walk forward by straight and familiar paths to desired ends. Please try to understand, Mr. Prognosis, that the age you called 'Mechanical' we now refer to as 'Experimental.' Your most knowing scientist would find himself ill at ease in to-day's primary class in mechanics."

Paul said nothing more on this subject. What could he say?

CHAPTER XVI.

The Downfall of Old Forms.

"By the way," said the Professor, "this crystal ornament on the lapel of my coat must have often excited your curiosity, though you have modestly refrained from questioning me in regard to it even when I have alluded to it. You will find this symbol, as well as the apple blossom, repeated in one or another form in nearly all our modern art works, and you might think it some talisman, some remnant from the age of superstition, if I gave you no explanation of its meaning. Like the apple blossom, — which, in its season, is used as a like emblem, — it recalls an event in the world's history which was in the nature of a crusade, and which led ultimately to the possibility of establishing a Council of Nations and inaugurating the period of universal peace. It symbolizes an object that appealed to the sympathies of all men and women, without reference to the particular religious beliefs held by them, or lacked by them, and thus afforded common ground for the adoption of an ideal and inspiration that should be universal. Until you understand the token of this white button, you cannot understand the secret springs that animate modern civilization."

"You of course greatly interest me, sir, although I have no idea to what you refer."

"The whole subject is explained quite fully in this book, and it would well repay your careful reading; but it is unfortunately printed in our modern characters, which are, of course, like black-letter to you. However, during the hour before breakfast I can give you a general conception of the main facts, if you like."

"There is nothing I should like better."

"Excepting to find your home."

"I am even willing that my home should be lost for a little while longer, if I can thereby gain knowledge of a secret apparently so precious."

"There is no secret about it. It is simple history. Well, the book is entitled 'The Crystal Button.' That sounds somewhat sensational, does n't it?—as if an estray, in the form of an amorous poem, might have elbowed its way into my rather serious collection. But you will find nothing more serious in this room. The opening chapters describe in detail the general downfall of the European monarchies, which tumbled at last like a row of blocks."

"All this is new to me."

"Yes, I know; but it happened not long after your time. And you must have seen abundant handwriting on the wall. You must have known the natural and inevitable results of such an artificial state of society, such foolish sectional pride, and such a preposterous attitude of governmental forces, as then existed in Europe. Why, there before your eyes, with its plaints ever in your ears, groveled a noble continent, packed with intelligent and industrious people, who, for reasons we are unable to understand, permitted their hardly-earned substance to be mainly devoted to the worse than useless purpose of supporting great armies of idlers, whom you dignified by the name of soldiers, whose only object was to perpetually menace and challenge neighboring nations. These armies, please remember, were composed of their ablest-bodied and most capable workingmen, and, not only was no use made of them, but they were supported in idleness by those who really worked, and supplied with the costliest of all luxuries — military armaments. Why, Europe might much better have transported, for the time being, its young and middle-aged men thus enrolled, and thereby saved the cost of their maintenance. The women and children would have fared better in their absence, and could then have lived in peace.

"Such waste of men and means could not, of course, go on forever. When one nation lengthened or strengthened its walls, all the others were compelled to do the same; and, the broader its opportunities, the more onerous became its responsibilities. In those days, the very pride and strength of a nation meant its weakness. The growing disease pointed its own cure. Pride's pocket-book was at last emptied. Military glory was attacked in the rear, and compelled to droop its banners. It then lost its hold on the public sentiment. Then, suddenly, public opinion took in hand its gorgeous regalia, gave it a single hearty shake, — and there came an end of it all. What had appeared to rule the destinies of Europe was discovered to be merely the straw-stuffed jacket of a field scarecrow, hoisted on a stick. The stick removed, its backbone was gone; and it came to ground in a disordered heap. Glittering armies melted like frost pictures on a pane, and puppet princes became hunted outcasts; while democracy calmly proceeded to sweep from the boards every rag that royalty left behind, and set up in their place the simple modern system of government by the people.

"We say that the mills of the gods grind slowly; but it now seems strange that men did not sooner lend a hand to make them grind somewhat faster. Certainly, society now has more intelligent knowledge of its powers, a deeper sense of its responsibilities, and far higher faith in its destiny. We now read, as a piece of grim humor, the statements of your historians that Europe, when first liberated, laid the fault of all its woes on the shoulders of its princes. That is a kind of philosophy we do not countenance. Your princes were but flesh-and-blood men till public opinion raised them to thrones and bolstered them there. As soon as public opinion removed its artificial props, down came the princes — somewhat less than men. This is a chapter in your painful history which is hardly comprehensible to us."

"When do you say all this happened?"

"I do not now recall the precise date, but it was not long after the two Americas had proclaimed democracy."

"And England — did even England have to succumb?"

"The English monarchy did. The only wonder is that her wise men did not act sooner."

"And Russia?"

"She was the last and most stubborn. But no power on earth can withstand the assaults of public opinion when thoroughly aroused to action. Well, in the midst of the chaos, and confusion, and biting poverty that followed the monarchical downfall in Europe, and by reason of the resulting shock that electrified the world's conscience, there arose a new reformer, a new prophet, with the simplest of all doctrines on his lips, the most cheerful of gospels, and a manly earnestness of manner that made him brother to all men."

"You say, Professor, that he came by reason of the shock. Does the modern mind look upon prophets as the outcome of emergencies?"

"Just that. To have a prophet, there must be prophecy in the air — that is, a general desire and expectancy on the part of the public; and then some great public need must arise to summon him to the front. A prophet is merely the mouthpiece of the public's highest and best hope, when, for some reason, that hope must be voiced. You may think it strange that any man of the twentieth century should have been able to catch inspiration sufficient to place him high among the world's prophets. If so, that is simply because you failed to understand your times. They were times of ferment. Education was sufficiently general so that the masses began to understand their power, but they were not yet skilled in exercising it wisely. Although capable of all things, they effected comparatively little excepting to discourage old forms. But that was no doubt a needful preliminary. For the time being they lacked what all men then lacked to a fatal degree — moral stamina. In your great labor revolts, the reason for their frequent failure was not lack of strength — there was superabundance of that. It was because your workingmen, as you seem to have called your masses, — now, all of us are proud to be known as workingmen, — were inspired by no better principles than those against which they revolted. They demanded independence, but, when they had it in their hands, it too often became lust for gain — honest gain if practicable, but gain anyhow! Their leaders wrung privileges from those above them, only to deny the same privileges to those below them. The vice of the age was in every man's veins — idolatry of money. Till that idol was dashed from its pedestal, there could be no hope of the reorganization of society on any basis of permanent improvement.

"Such were the conditions of universal chaos that opened the way for the prophet of the twentieth century. Who should raise the new banner under which the world could reform its broken ranks? In his make-up, it was evident that at least three conditions would be demanded. He must possess such knowledge of the lessons taught by past as well as current experience, that his point of view should cut a semicircle behind him as broad as the world's history. He must then be drawn by the guiding star of a single idea, and that idea must be a moral lesson of some kind, which should so possess his own soul as to make him wholly unselfish in all his motives, and give him the fearless and untiring devotion of a heaven-inspired enthusiasm. He must also be one of the people, familiar with all their hopes and sorrows, and yet lacking the vices and prejudices common to his fellow-men. But how was this condition possible? It seemed impossible. Yet, as events finally turned, the challenge for such a leader was answered by a man in whom great sorrow and mental shock had so purged all selfish concerns of life that he was practically freed from all the limitations of his day. In brief, all three conditions were fulfilled in the person of John Costor, whose life and work I will now try to briefly describe."

CHAPTER XVII.

Appearance of John Costor, The Apostle of Truth.

PARTLY reading, partly conversing, the Professor gave the following summary of the subject.

Unlike all previous prophets, nothing is unknown or in any way mysterious about the biography of John Costor. Little of interest occurred during his early life, but that little he freely told, and such were the news facilities of the twentieth century that all he told was faithfully recorded. We have no legendary lore about him.

He was of Scandinavian parentage, and had the strength and devotion characteristic of that hardy people, but he was born and bred on the Great Lakes of North America, and his early life was divided between the cities and the loneliness of the lakeside hills. His frequent references to Niagara Falls, then at its acme of majesty, now past, give evidence that he caught some of his inspiration from early familiarity with that mouthpiece of nature.

He passed his early manhood in outdoor labor and wholesome obscurity; but he was a careful observer and intelligent reader, and was justly considered a leading authority on questions pertaining to political and natural history. His mind had been bent in these directions by the early teachings of his father, who was a school-teacher, and the son proved his ablest scholar. He finally married, moved into the new country of the northwest, and made a thrifty home for his wife and children. Although commonly counted a silent man, he is represented as having been peculiarly boyish and merry when in the society of his family, in whose welfare then centred his every life-interest.

One night, while he was absent from home, his wife and children and several near relatives were murdered by Indians, who were then in revolt against the Government of Washington and consequently against all its white people, on the ground that solemn pledges had been broken and treaties trampled upon whenever the wishes of the whites came in conflict with those of their humble wards.

It was on a June morning when he returned on horseback, singing a ballad and filled with glad anticipations. In the place of house and home and family, he found a heap of ashes and the charred remains of his loved ones. The shock was too much for even his powerful organization. When his neighbors found him, he sat beside the grave of his wife, that he had heaped with apple blossoms, holding a crystal ornament he had taken from her neck, and saying: "Even as you have always been the soul of truth, so this bit of clear crystal is an image of your spirit." For many weeks he was like one distraught, wandering about the ashes of his former home as in a dream, muttering: "Truth, truth! All that was mine is sacrificed to the ogre of political deceit!"

To the astonishment of all who knew him, he joined the very band of Indians who had committed the crime, and became a trusted companion of the chieftain. It was thought by some that his mind was gone, and that he was consequently not responsible for this erratic course, while others shook their heads and prophesied that his present aim was to discover and pursue with fearful vengeance the authors of his woe. In after years, when an opponent publicly assailed him with this charge, he silenced it with the simple declaration: "In Truth's name, it was as you say. I then lived in darkness such as I trust you may never know, but it was darkness that preceded a brighter daydawn with a broader horizon. I have put night behind me. In Truth's name, my friend, let us now join hands to lead the world into sunshine." And he who was an opponent became a life long co-worker with Costor in his great labor of love.

It was afterward learned that the chieftain whom the stricken man joined was indebted to the elder Costor for some great boon in early life and also for a winter's home and schooling. When he learned that his braves were the murderers of his friend's family, he bared his breast and said: "Let the blow fall here. But spare my people. Their homes, like yours, are gone. The whites were to blame, but you were not to blame." Then Costor joined hands with the chief, and with him went into exile among the hills.

So it was that, for five years, nothing was heard of John Costor; and such was the rapid succession of exciting events then attracting public attention that his life-tragedy was well-nigh forgotten. But a wonderful work of preparation was going on in that remote Indian camp. The lonely white man became like one who has ascended a mountain-top to commune directly with the sun and stars. In the simplicity of the lives of his new friends, wherein the struggle for food was the foremost object of all action, he read anew the story of humanity. Stripped of all robes with which civilization of the nineteenth century covered its moral deformities, he found in his mates men whose only cry was "Food!" This was also the beast's cry. But these were not beasts. In some of their impulses they seemed more admirable in his eyes than the more polished offsprings of the cities. In many instances they showed themselves more truthful. This native chief of the tribe, royal in face and bearing, resolute, untiring in labor, and frank to a degree that perhaps had no equal among the state rulers of his day — what was his true position in the scale of human development? Might he not hold a higher rank than some of his more fortunate white brothers, whose civilization was a word of contempt in his ears? In this retired world of introspection, attracted and finally won by the simplicity of his new friends, and with conscience pricked to do some good deed to them and to the world, in reparation for the act of revenge he had purposed, John Costor finally caught the seed of an inspiration which, in the mighty march of events, was destined to fill the world with blossom and fruit. "By Heaven!" he one day exclaimed, as he gazed on the crystal button he always wore, "in all that I find fair, it is truth that makes it so. And all that is wicked and miserable and unhappy shows untruth in some form scowling beneath its mask, however painted and gilded. All that was dear to me in this life was sacrificed to the ogre of untruth and its broken pledges. I now stand alone in the world, with eyes opened and with hands free. The world, smitten by the results of its errors, awaits a new spring of action. It is clear to me that here we have it. I now devote myself to the sacred cause of Truth. By her ministrations, and by hers alone, can the world hope to find clues leading to prosperity and happiness!"

When Costor emerged from his obscurity, he was well prepared for the solemn duty to which he had dedicated himself. His mind was thoroughly imbued with a deep sense of the wide-spread evils resulting from falsehood, deceit, and all forms of injustice. He rightfully believed that, if every man could be induced by any means to lead a life of absolute truthfulness and simple honesty, all forms of injustice and wrong would in time be swept away. The many tangles of belief and theory that held men in bondage or antagonism, he sought not to unravel. "Time will cure these errors," he said, "if truth continues to be the constant watchword."

Thus, a stranger and unannounced, Costor appeared one day in the suburb of one of the great cities, and began to speak. It was at a time near the anniversary of his great sorrow. The apple-tree that shaded him as he spoke was a snowdrift of white and pink bloom. He held a spray of it in one hand, and in the other, the crystal button which formed the text of his discourse. He told his story with simplicity but strength. There was nothing at all remarkable about the beginning he made. It was a small beginning, and its growth was slow.

After a while, when he became a little more sure of himself, he entered the city, and began a series of rather homely but very direct and forcible addresses. Here his audience speedily increased. His subject was always the same — Truth. The silent man was gradually finding a tongue, and it was soon admitted that such a tongue never before spake the English language. In debate, he was like a trumpet voice from the sky, whose every word thrilled his hearers to their very souls. His audience began to include all classes, rich and poor, and educated as well as illiterate. "Truth, truth, truth!" was ever the topic of his discourse, but he was never-failing in his resources for freshly presenting it. He discreetly avoided all mention of religion or politics or philosophy, but kept the same clear note forever resounding. He never generalized, but addressed himself to every hearer as an individual, saying: "I speak the gospel of Truth, which means peace on earth and good-will toward men. Let every man be true to himself and to his fellow-men, and Eden will again blossom on the earth. I have no word to tell you of the life hereafter, for I do not know, — but this I do know, that untruth is the serpent whose poison now taints every fountain of private and public life. Scotch that snake in the grass, and law will then mean justice, power will mean ability, work will mean abundance, and duty well done will crown all with happiness." Such was the general current of his thoughts.

Here, again, he is quoted as saying: "Let us now reason together aloud, just as each one has no doubt reasoned by himself, in agony of soul, when there was none to give comfort. I believe that I can give you comfort, — no, not give it to you, but give you the secret by which you can gain the boon, if you will only do your part.

"Each man of us is capable of living a larger and better and happier life than he has thus far known. I believe this, — I know this. Why, then, do we continue to suffer? It is not merely because we have to work. Work does not mean unhappiness. Work of the right kind, and in right quantity, and with the right recompense, is what you and I and all of us want and demand, in order to take a first step toward happiness. If any man now within reach of my voice is afraid of work, let him understand that I have nothing to offer in answer to his cravings.

I speak as one worker to another. If you are that other, hearken! and I will try to make my voice the voice of your conscience, even as it is of my own.

"Each one of us is capable of a higher destiny. Each one of us really loves truth, virtue, and the performance of kindly offices. All men love these qualities in others, and are even ready to worship them as godlike attributes. Why, then, is man denied the full enjoyment of these and other ennobling virtues, which are necessary to his happiness on this earth?

"Is it not because he feels he must protect himself by a defensive armor of caution, tempered with suspicion, and reinforced by a helmet of secrecy and a shield of deceit? He fears evil ways in others, and proves by frequent experience that his fears are well founded. He would be glad to have faith in his fellow-men, but even his childhood was made unhappy by wounds from the arrows of deceit. Do you remember the first time you ever detected any one in an untruth? It may have been a brother, a trusted friend, — it may even have been a parent. Can you now recall the shudder that then ran through your whole being? In that very hour you were cast out of Eden. You then looked into the serpent's eyes, and it was Eden no longer. Do you shudder now when the serpent's hiss of untruth sounds at your side? Do you recognize it as a hiss? Do you not sometimes admire it in others and even cultivate it in yourself, as one of the weapons, one of the diplomacies, of current life, necessary if one would keep his place in the moving phalanx? Is it not a fact, to-day, that man's ordinary intercourse with his neighbor and even with his closest friend, however pleasantly conducted, is marked by considerations that ought only to find expression between open enemies?

"Where lies the blame? Of course it is easy to say that such unworthy phases of human character are inherited from the barbarism of past ages; that they have been kept alive and nourished by the degenerating influences of warfare and the animosities growing out of fanatical differences of creed. When our consciences are pricked, we are all too ready to anoint the wound with excuses of this sort. We also say — you and I — that such are the settled customs of the world, and we must conform ourselves to them, or be pushed to the wall. I ask you, in all honesty: would it not be better, then, to be pushed to the wall? And are we not already against the wall? And are we not constantly pushing and drawing others to it, — which is much worse? And are there just now in the world, where all is chaos, any customs so settled and of the nature of cornerstones that it would not be well to search for the flaw of deceit upon them, and if it appears, to topple them over, come what may? By the eternal verities, my brothers, I tell you there is nothing stable in this universe but Truth! I tell you that one thing is now lacking, and only one thing, and that thing is Truth! The time has come for that new and higher and nobler civilization which is man's heritage on earth as soon as he is willing to grasp it; and here is the only key to heaven-like civilization. I believe it is the civilization of Truth that the world now awaits; and, until that is attained, welcome chaos!

"The godlike power of creating this new civilization of Truth — which is to quell our righteous anger, feed us and our families, give us peace, and fill our hearts with contentment and happiness — is within the keeping of every man before me. Let us look no longer behind us, but stop right here and understand that the world's to-morrow is the fruit of to-day, and that 'the world' is only a way of aggregating a great number of you's and I's. Your to-morrow and my to-morrow is the fruit of our to-day. There is nothing on earth to prevent our turning this city into ashes before another nightfall, if we — the people — will to do it! But will ashes and stones feed the hunger and longing that is now in our souls? There is nothing on earth or in heaven to prevent our making this city a brighter and better and more heaven-like place before nightfall, if we — the people: you and I — will to do it! What do you say? Shall it be ashes? You cry No! Then let us try the other way. Never fear the result. Truth must prevail in the end. What we now want to do is to help it prevail at once.

"Do you ask me how? Are you really filled with a burning desire to know how? And are you willing, eager, to do your part? To each of you, as an individual, I now appeal, and ask you to make this promise, not to me, but to yourself: 'I will try, from this moment henceforth, to be true and honest in my every act, word, and thought; and this crystal button I will wear while the spirit of truth abides with me.'

"That is the 'Truth Promise' — the beginning and the end of the gospel I bring you. Do you know of any just reason why you should not make this promise to yourself? Is it not worthy of any man? And even if it should not always prove easy to keep it, is it not worthy of the best efforts of your lives? If you think so, put the button in your coat, and say the words aloud as I repeat them: '*I will try, from this moment henceforth, to be true and honest in my every act, word, and thought; and this crystal button*

I will wear while the spirit of truth abides with me.'

"But see, my friends, that the button is promptly removed whenever you are untrue to it. It means something, — it means everything! See that you are not false to that meaning!

"This beginning is easy, friends, but the hard part is yet to come. Let us now organize societies throughout the land, for mutual help and encouragement. We must not only thus pledge ourselves in the most solemn manner to abstain from all falsehood and deceit, but we must help others to do the same. That will suffice. All other virtues will thrive, if the soil is kept free from the weeds of untruth and hypocrisy."

CHAPTER XVIII.

The Order of the Crystal Button.

"SUCH, in substance," said the Professor, "were the simple teachings of this latest of the prophets, John Costor. There was nothing particularly new about them, excepting the burning enthusiasm with which they were communicated. I am sorry I cannot give you a better idea of the peculiar force of his oratory. I have read you only a few disconnected extracts from various addresses, and I cannot but feel how inadequate these are to give you a just conception of the man and of his work.

"He simply spoke from a full soul, and labored with an untiring devotion only possible in a truly great reformer. Few listened to him without feeling that he was inspired. His skill in tracing the chief evils that beset mankind to sources that his hearers could not dispute was marvelous in its logic and its power to convince even the most cavilous; but his success as a public speaker was due to his profound convictions and unceasing work in support of them, rather than to mere novelty of utterance. 'Preaching,' he once said, 'moves men as the wind sways the branches of forest trees, and its influence is generally as transitory. The most impassioned appeals are soon forgotten. What then? We must organize, bind ourselves individually by the stoutest pledges to life action governed solely by principles of truth and justice, and then work from within outwardly.' On this basis, he proceeded to form, in each city he visited, a local society of his followers, who at the start isolated themselves to some extent from the rest of the world. These societies took strong root and flourished mightily. Their form of organization was extremely simple, and of a character that could challenge no man's prejudices. 'I bring you no new doctrine,' he often repeated. 'Think what you will, believe what you must, but do only that which you know to be right, and all will be well!' Of course, no man could take exceptions to such a doctrine as this.

"I should add that he always objected to being referred to as a 'labor reformer,' although he ranks foremost in the long and honorable list. His claim was that of a moral teacher, appealing to society generally and not to any particular class, and he purposely took no cognizance of any special subjects of grievance, such as the labor question then involved, it being hopelessly complicated in his day. He confined his attention to the sole purpose of establishing a pure mode of living and truthful dealing between man and man, and expressed his entire confidence that this of itself would suffice ultimately to settle the labor question and all others that were vexed, whatever their immediate cause. In this expectation he was not disappointed. The observance of strict truth, honesty, and fidelity removed all sources of complaint in the field of labor, as a fresh wind from the sea banishes mist.

"Well, Mr. Prognosis, as I have described Costor's early course of action, this may seem to you — it must seem to you — a humble and unpromising start for a reorganization of society that was destined to revolutionize the world; but such was the result. The ripe seed of moral development was in his hand, and it was winged like that of the mountain ash. In the general whirlwind of political and social disturbance that was then overturning creeds, governments, civilizations, this watchword of 'Truth' was caught up as the one idea that all men, of whatever nation, or language, or religion, could understand and take seriously to heart. It was an idea that was far from being inert. As events proved, it was a heaven-sent seed dropped on fallow soil in that period of universal anarchy.

"Costor was peculiarly energetic and skillful

as an organizer, and, as soon as he had assured the success of the movement in all the principal centres of thought in America, he proceeded to Europe, gathered preachers of every tongue and representing every phase of popular belief, and scattered them as missionaries throughout the globe. Never before was a revival so speedy, so thorough, or so lasting. As I have said, it was promoted through the instrumentality of societies, that is, by organization, which underlies every form of development in the modern world. These societies, local and small at first, rapidly increased in number and membership, giving a nucleus around which clustered men and women of all shades of all religious beliefs, or lack of all, and shedding beneficent moral and social influences in every direction. The permanence with which these maintained their organization was quite remarkable, but it was evidently the result of the extreme simplicity and nobility of their object. A single, solemn recitation of the 'Truth Promise' and wearing of the crystal button made any person a member of the local society; and it was finally arranged that a member of one was a member of all. Almost without exception, such societies prospered and finally came into possession of abundant means, yet it is not recorded that any theft or defalcation ever occurred within the ranks."

"And did the societies build great churches?"

"It would hardly be correct to apply to them that name, in the sense in which you were accustomed to use it. I should tell you that Costor wisely took every possible means to impress the public with the fact that his order was not a religious organization."

"Was he, then, prejudiced against religion?"

"Not at all. But he explained that the prejudices existing between religious organizations were so frequent and so strong that it seemed wise to avoid all complication with religious questions. 'It is better to have it clearly understood at the start,' he once stated, 'that the aim of this Order of the Crystal Button is to promote the well-being of its members only so far as this life is concerned. It does not conflict with any religious organization, but it is hoped that all members of all churches will feel drawn to enroll themselves with us. If they do not, the fault will lie with our own members, in not making the purpose of our order understood. Its sole object is to encourage the development of truer, nobler, and happier life.'"

"What, then, was the character of the buildings erected in the place of churches?"

"They are more properly club-houses, which are kept open both night and day, and devoted to all purposes that mean education or social amusement. The auditorium or lecture-hall is merely an incident. Millions of money have been devoted to such club-houses, and also to schools, hospitals, and all other agencies that promise to ease or better the condition of mankind.

"The moral effects of a strict adherence to the new rule of life were such that intercourse between members became very attractive, and an era of good fellowship began to dawn which added much to the enjoyments of life. In the course of time, it therefore came about that many sought admission by reason merely of the social attractiveness of the organization; while to be received into full membership was regarded as one of the highest social honors. When this stage was reached, the final success of Costor's effort was no longer problematical."

"But tell me, Professor, — am I to understand that the work of rehumanizing mankind kept pace with this work of reorganizing society? In the efforts made in my time to better the condition of mankind, it was man himself who proved the stumbling-block. Too often he did not wish to be helped, — he would n't be helped!"

"Very true. Costor met the same difficulty, and it was by no means overcome in his day. But he was not discouraged by that. He used to say: 'If we are sure we are on the right path, we fulfill our duty by keeping to it and drawing others to it. The longer and the rougher the path, the greater need of making the best possible speed, and the greater the glory in finally attaining the goal. Let us each do his best to-day, and have faith in to-morrow.' As a matter of fact, the world mounted slowly to the plane it now occupies. Generations passed, centuries passed, while the work slowly progressed. But the progress was steady. As you have suggested, humanity often proved itself weak and wayward. But Costor had expected that. It is recorded that he once expressed himself as follows: —

"'Humanity — it is its own worse enemy! In the process of improving plants and the lower animals, we have unresisting materials to work upon, and results can be calculated with some confidence. The production of well-formed heads and delicate features in men descended from ancestors of the lowest moral condition is of necessity a work of many generations. It is true that an individual with the head and neck of a savage may, by education, acquire the manners and address of a person of real culture and refinement. Even then, tread on his toes, and, before he can restrain himself, up leaps the savage, with the tiger look in his eyes! In re-humanizing degraded humanity, the head must be enlarged at certain points, the neck reduced, the nose straightened, the cheekbones and jaws remodeled. To do all this must require centuries, even if a single subject, perfectly passive, could be freely experimented on throughout that period. What, then, is to be done with subjects short-lived and selfishly inclined, biased by superstition, perverted, brutalized, even to the point that truth is no longer recognized as good.'

"Costor, you see, well understood all that. Yet he was never discouraged, but he pressed on bravely with his work, always progressing, even when the movement was not apparent. The roots of truth, once implanted, showed a tenacity that even untruth never had; and, under the fostering care of the 'Crystal Buttons,' as members of the new guild were called, the weeds of society were gradually crowded out. Costor lived to see the work of reformation well begun; and his numerous disciples afterward developed many wise means of perfecting its organization and spreading its growth. From small beginnings it steadily grew into a healthy tree, whose branches promised to bear fruit that should nourish the world."

CHAPTER XIX.

The New Civilization.

"THE centuries rolled on," continued the Professor, "and the activities of the Crystal Button societies continued to enter into the warp and woof of political as well as social life, and give a brighter aspect to all. The well-disposed portions of society throughout the world finally accepted the new rule and lived up to its teachings with more or less fidelity.

"And now, Mr. Prognosis, we come down to the time when the crowning glory of the new order of things is at hand, — the accomplishment of permanent and universal peace among men. Naturally enough, the initial movement in this direction came from the Costorians, whose clear-sighted leader had long before predicted this as an outcome of the principles he taught, when they should be sufficiently developed. Indeed, he had constantly urged his followers, and especially his teachers, to work steadily toward this end.

"When, in the judgment of the leaders of

the order, a suitable opportunity offered, they issued a call for a council of all nations to be held in the interests of peace. Such had become the influence of the allied societies, and such was their world-wide distribution, that this call met with a prompt and favorable response from every nation addressed, most of which were democracies, and having Costorians of high-standing in nearly all positions of trust. The council assembled at the great city of Carrefour, located on the isthmus midway between the two Americas, whither the fleets and railways found easy access from all parts of the globe. Perfect harmony attended the sessions of this remarkable congress; and, before the sittings were ended, a plan was adopted and signed by every representative present, which promised, and in fact accomplished, the total extinction of warfare between nations. This enactment was afterward approved by every government, and even some of the savage tribes gave their hands to the solemn compact. An international police was maintained for some years to check any lawless tribes that might fail to keep their pledges, but the event proved that even these were unnecessary, as the disturbances of the peace that occurred subsequent to the action of the congress were few, and easily quelled by local authorities. A Court of Arbitration for each of the grand divisions of the world was shortly afterward established, for the purpose of deciding any disputed questions presented at their annual sittings; while those of international character were referred by such courts to the Grand Council of All Nations, whose decisions were final. Ample opportunity for discussion was thus allowed, but none for controversy.

"Peace at last! The new era had dawned! Those who have experienced the cheer that follows reconciliation after long estrangement from former friends, when mutual trust and cordiality once more take the place of cold reserve and jealous watchfulness, will understand the outburst of unspeakable joy that resounded throughout the world as the glad tidings were flashed over the wires that the great act, so long hoped for, had finally been consummated. Through the successive ages of stone, iron, bronze, and silver, civilization had finally passed to the attainment of its crystal age of Truth.

"Thus it was that the Crystal Button conquered the world. Thus it was that, from the ashes of thrones and false altars which had been cast down, arose a single pillar of crystal, to which all nations looked up with fresh hope. The hope was not disappointed. It rejuvenated the human race."

"This, then," said Paul, "is the keystone of your present blessed civilization."

"Keystone, arch, foundations, — all! The time for the moral reformation had come, and 'Truth' was its watchword. Art had given the world all the instruction it had in its keeping: truth in the representation of outward nature, which means beauty. Science had taught its lesson: truth in the understanding of nature's methods. But moral truth was still lacking.

"You see, Mr. Prognosis, we are now accustomed to divide history into three distinct stages of development. The earlier civilizations we call 'the first' and 'the second,' and our own 'the modern.' The first and second were sectional and partial, and they were not sufficiently grounded on fixed principles to maintain a continuous existence; while ours is complete and universal, — or rather, I should say, it is destined to be. It has placed the human race on the direct road to its highest development, and is based rather on moral than intellectual qualities.

"The achievements of former ages may be briefly classed as follows: the first civilization developed art, architecture, and literature; the second, music, mechanism, and science; and the modern, peace, social order, and permanent government. As you study further, you will not fail to see that we are rich in inheritance from the great minds of the past, to which we have added the remarkable moral progress that has resulted from the reformation first started by John Costor. It was moral tone that you chiefly lacked in the nineteenth and twentieth centuries. It was the general want of truth, not only in act, but in thought and sentiment, that lay at the bottom of your every form of individual and social and political vice. At least, so it seems to us now, as we calmly review the past."

"I cannot say nay."

"But now, Mr. Prognosis, let us to breakfast, after which Marco will be your companion for the day; and then this evening we can renew our conversation."

"May I suggest the subject of that next conversation?"

"Certainly."

"Your form of government is what would most interest me."

"That, then, shall be our evening's text."

PART IV.

A DAY'S RAMBLE WITH MARCO MORTIMER.

CHAPTER XX.

The Standard Pendulum.

THE Professor led the way through a corridor to the breakfast-room, flooded with sunshine, where he introduced his guest to the already assembled family, saying: "This is my new and remarkable friend, Mr. Prognosis, whom you already know something about. We must try and make him feel as much at home as circumstances will permit. I take pleasure in introducing Mr. Prognosis — my wife, Madam Prosper; my daughter, Helen; and her school friend, Miss Eldom. And here comes the prospective new member of our family, Marco, whom you have already met, who is to do the honors to-day."

Paul felt that he took his seat a little awkwardly, but this feeling soon vanished in the presence of an ease and sociability that won his heart. Madam Prosper was one of those motherly old ladies who immediately give a halo of home to any room in which their armchairs are located; and the young ladies chatted with him with a gentle yet perfectly sustained manner, that relieved him of all feeling of conversational responsibility.

No allusion whatever was made to Paul's singular past, but the subjects talked of were confined to the scenes of his yesterday's walk with the Professor, and to a variety of topics of current interest, including duties that the young ladies had planned for the day.

"I fear," said Paul, "that I am seriously interfering with these plans by capturing Mr. Mortimer so unceremoniously."

"Not at all," answered Miss Helen. "Marco has so many engagements that we no longer count upon him as our conductor by day; but we hope to have him with us in the evening, and to have you, too, Mr. Prognosis."

At the close of the meal, Paul felt as much at ease with each member of the delightful household as if he had been acquainted with them for years.

After brief parting salutations, and many injunctions to be sure and return promptly in time for six-o'clock dinner, he and Marco proceeded to the thronged streets, on their way to view the standard pendulum of which the Professor had spoken on the previous evening.

On entering the Hall of Sciences, Marco presented a letter from the Professor, which gave them immediate entrance to what was known as the "Pendulum Chamber," located in the basement of the building. Paul noticed that the walls of the chamber were composed of solid stone blocks of enormous thickness, and the room was quite dark until the attendant illuminated it by a glare of electric light, when, suddenly, the elaborate appliances of the great instrument stood revealed before him.

Without speaking for several moments, the two men watched the measured vibrations of the great pendulum as it swung between its heavy piers of polished stone, slowly telling its beads to the time of double seconds. There was a strange kind of solemnity in the silence and regularity of its movements. It was as if the finger of Time itself were counting the heartbeats of one whose hours were few and the minute of departure inexorably fixed. The only sound was a slight but distinct click at the completion of each stroke.

"We are indebted," said Marco, in a half-whisper, "to the scientists of old France for the theory on which several of our modern appliances are based. Their invention of the metric system of weights and measures is the foundation on which the value of this fine instrument depends. We still possess the originals of their standards of measurement, including those composed of the various metals and metallic alloys, as well as of glass. Those painstaking Frenchmen gave us not only their accurate standards, but also the exact length of the pendulum that in their time beat seconds. Thanks to them, therefore, we are to-day able to make comparisons that are of great interest.

"Let me first show you the construction of the pendulum, and we will afterward go into the computing-room, where the professor in charge will tell us some of the lessons it has already taught.

"You will observe that these piers, and the base on which they stand, are all cut from a single block of stone and in a single mass, while the foundation below is also solid rock. You see, here, that the tops of the piers, which are close together, have, for bearings for the cross-head of the pendulum, two large flat jewels. These bearings are diamonds. Resting on these are the knife-edges of the cross-head, which are also made of thin slices of the same gem.

"On the top of the cross-head is this elaborate micrometer regulator, which lengthens or shortens the pendulum. This appliance indicates accurately the one-ten-thousandth fraction of a millimetre of movement.

"Now look beneath. Here the lower end of the pendulum-bar swings very close to this stud of platinum, which is deeply imbedded in the stone. At the present time, the distance between the pendulum-bar and the stud is a fraction less than a millimetre. Here is an electric lamp, so arranged that, as the pendulum swings past the stud, an instantaneous flash is made to pass between the two points, and thence through a lenticular glass, which greatly enlarges the beam of light in one direction, so that a very slight variation of length can be detected in the enlarged band of light, which can then be accurately measured.

"The great clock that is operated by this pendulum runs so nearly to the true time that the variation in the course of an entire year is only a small fraction of a beat. Human skill can go no further in this direction."

"But the influence of varying temperature?" said Paul questioningly.

"Of course, a perfectly even temperature must be maintained. To secure this, the room is inclosed by the three massive walls through which we entered by closely fitting doors; and the normal temperature is 70° Fahrenheit, so that the presence of observers does not tend to change it. The heating apparatus is outside, and the entire mass of stone is kept at a perfectly uniform temperature throughout. You will readily understand, Mr. Prognosis, that it required many days for these massive walls to become once warmed through, and you will also understand with what tenacity they hold the heat, once absorbed.

"The distance from the stud of platinum to the diamond bearings is absolutely unchanging, delicate measurements having frequently been made without detecting the slightest variation. Thus the length of the pendulum beating double-seconds is always known by simple inspection with the beam of light."

"You seem to be quite familiar with this wonderful piece of mechanism," said Paul.

"Yes, I have often visited here with Professor Prosper."

"May I ask in what special work you are engaged?"

"I have not yet finished my studies in the Government schools, but I hope to become a civil engineer, if I succeed in passing the examinations."

"If you fail, what then?"

"The Board of Examiners finally determines to what field of labor each Government pupil is best adapted."

"And is there no appeal from their decision?"

"There is no need of that, for they are far better able to judge of the comparative capabilities of men than the men themselves are. Their duty is to see that every pupil who places himself at their disposal is put in the right place."

"And you will be satisfied with their judgment?"

"It would be foolish for me to feel otherwise. They will know, not only what my capacities are, but what field is open for me. When my working age arrives, they will see that I am put to work without the loss of a day."

"I shall be interested to know more about this."

"I will tell you with pleasure. But now, if you will please to follow me, we will make a short call on the professor who observes and records the movements of the pendulum."

"I think it was mentioned, at the meeting I attended last evening, that he would soon read a paper on the subject before the Society."

"Very likely. He is no doubt deep in his figures by this hour."

They emerged from a dark passage by which they had entered, and ascended to the computing-room on the ground floor. Here Paul was introduced to the elderly gentleman in charge, who received him with a somewhat absorbed manner, but presently explained the contents of the room and the nature of his duties. Unfortunately, his language was so technical that Paul could comprehend very little, yet he gathered enough to understand that the retardation of the earth's axial motion was a familiar subject. He also learned that the present length of the pendulum was appreciably longer than it was at the time when the French standards were made, and that computations, recently completed, confirmed in a remarkable manner the deductions of an astronomer who had arrived at substantially the same results by an entirely different method. The professor showed his visitor numerous thick volumes filled with solid mechanical work, the results of several years of labor; but Paul was none the wiser for anything he could learn from them. Feeling himself decidedly out of his element in the presence of his kind host, he took the first opportunity to tender his thanks and withdraw.

"I 'm afraid," said Marco smilingly, as they regained the street, "that you have been more impressed than edified."

"I confess it; but the fault is mine. There must be give and take to make conversation worthy of the name, and I was unable to give. But the pendulum, — I shall always be thankful to you for showing me that."

CHAPTER XXI.

The Air-Ship.

"If you will allow me, Mr. Prognosis, I will now offer for your approval the day's programme that Professor Prosper suggested to me. It includes visits to the Central Observatory, Transcontinental Railway, and Mount Energy. Do you find this programme attractive?"

"Decidedly so."

"I will suggest that we take them in the order named; and, as the Observatory is several miles out of town, this will give you an opportunity to test one of our air-ships, or aerial cars."

"An air-ship? Well! wherever Miss Helen is willing to trust you, I'm sure I can safely follow."

"The station is within this inclosure, and I see by the bulletin that the Observatory car is just ready to start. Here we are between its vast wings! And now we are rising! Does it make you feel at all uncomfortable?"

"No more so than if I were aboard a passenger elevator in a building."

"There, now we have the proper elevation, and are taking our course. What do you say to this as a comfortable mode of travel?"

"It seems like a dream. In my dreams I seem to have been in this car before, and to have flown in it to the ends of the earth. Pray tell me how long such machines have been in successful use?"

"Oh, for centuries; but the task of so perfecting them that they should not be attended by danger was long and often discouraging."

"I know something about the difficulties of the problem. We tried many methods in my day, but they were dismal failures. We at last came to look upon aeronauts as dreamers, and upon flying-machines as simply toys. At the same time, one had only to watch the flight of a seagull to feel that here was a mode of motion that put all others to shame."

"It was the theory thereby suggested that helped retard the development of a practicable machine. It must have been soon after your day when there appeared an inventor who very confidently went to work on that basis. Said he: 'If a seagull, of such and such weight, and such and such length of wing and tail, and such motive power, can sail in the teeth of a northeaster, I see no reason why I cannot construct a mechanical bird that will at least be able to swim the aerial sea and direct its course in lines nearly parallel with the course of the wind. I propose to do just that; and if I succeed, then I think I can do more.' Model after model, of the most ingenious description, proceeded from his fertile brain and hand. The theory seemed all right. Did not the gulls visibly demonstrate that? But here was an instance where practice permanently declined to obey the rein of theory. The wood-and-iron bird refused to cousin with the flesh-and-blood seagull. While there appeared every possible reason why it ought to work, it simply would n't, and there was an end of it!"

"The defect, I imagine, was a simple one,—lack of a nervous system."

"Very possibly. Well, then followed a plain mechanic, without any theory at all, beyond this: 'To get horse-power, I don't need to build the model of a horse; and to get wing-power, I have no use for a feathered bird. I just want an every-day sort of machine. To make it swim in the air is easy enough. How to steer it is the puzzle, and I propose to solve that.' With little talk, but years of hard work, he finally completed a rather clumsy and complicated model that attracted little attention beyond jibes, — when, lo and behold! it worked! That model, gradually simplified and perfected in its details, was the prototype of the beautiful little machine we now occupy."

"May I ask you to please explain its principles and its parts?"

"The main portion, as you see, consists of a horizontal canvas web, stretched tightly over a light circular framework; and through the centre of this passes a bamboo mast, extending both above and below the web. This affords ample means for securing numerous wire stays from various parts of the framework to both the upper and lower extremities of the mast. The car we occupy, please observe, is attached to the lower end of the mast, and in this are carried the engines, propelling machinery, and passengers or freight."

"What kind of a propelling device is employed?"

"It consists of a pair of shafts running diagonally up through the canvas and rotating in opposite directions, each shaft being supplied with a propelling fan on either end. The rudder then completes the machine."

"And what motive power is used?"

"A pair of light engines driven by explosives in little cartridges. Nothing could be prettier than the working of these engines, which are hardly larger than toys; and the cartridges themselves are so light that fuel sufficient for an ordinary two or three days' flight can be easily carried. I 'm sorry I cannot invite you to look in upon the engineer, but it is strictly against the rules."

"I can easily understand that he must have his hands full. What rate of speed is attained?"

"It is by no means regular, but is largely dependent on the course and power of the wind. From twenty-five to forty miles an hour is a common rate; but the flight across the continent has been made in less than five days."

"Are such air-ships also used in crossing the ocean?"

"No, that proved too dangerous. Several fatal accidents made a sad end to that experiment."

"Are machines of great size used?"

"All the passenger ships are small, as these are found more manageable; and they are seldom used for freight. The one we now occupy is a fair sample. But here we are at our journey's end, — eight miles in twenty minutes."

"And I do not feel as if I had made a journey at all. Is travel by these air-ships also free?"

"Free? Yes; everything that is recognized

as a convenience for the general public is perfectly free."

"Cheap enough! I have always wished to visit southern California. Now is evidently my opportunity."

CHAPTER XXII.

Meridian Peak Observatory.

"WHAT a beautiful pleasure-ground!" exclaimed Paul, as he left the aerial station.

"This is one of our many public parks, and in the centre of it is the object of our visit, Meridian Peak Observatory. The peak is not a lofty one, but it has a fine atmosphere, and is a favorite summer resort."

With astonished eyes, Paul gazed on the huge structure before him. So far as he could see, the exterior of the Observatory consisted of a single great dome, or hemisphere, to the north side of which was a stone tower. He estimated the tower to be about fifty feet in diameter and at least a hundred feet high. Protruding from the dome, at an angle of forty-five degrees, was an immense shaft, strengthened by innumerable radiating stays; and this shaft rested on the top of the tower. Paul silently regarded this last feature for a moment, and then said to Marco with some excitement, "That shaft must be parallel with the earth's axis."

"You have grasped the idea exactly."

"But how can this great structure have a proper motion around this axis?"

"It is but partial," said Marco, smiling at Paul's quickness of perception, "but sufficient for all practical purposes. Let us go into the office, and there we shall find drawings that will explain the general plan of the works with very little study."

Paul followed Marco into a small side building, where Professor Prosper's name gave them ready admission, and where they stopped to examine the diagrams on the walls.

"Here," said Marco, "is the vertical section. This upper hemisphere, you see, has a corresponding lower half, and both together form a perfect sphere. The lower half is the main structure. It is really a great hemispherical vessel, and floats in a basin just large enough to receive it. This cuplike hull is made very strong, and its deck is the floor of the observatory.

"Here you see the axial shaft, the upper end resting on the pier, while the lower bearing or pivot is down here in the basin, corresponding to the one on top of the pier.

"Here is a drawing which shows, on either side of the hull, as we will call it, a heavy toothed rack, which runs diagonally down the side, and is at right angles with the axis. Each of these racks engages with a pinion which is a part of a train of wheels, moved by an engine. Thus, you see, the hull is capable of being screwed up one side and down the other on this diagonal pivot, thereby tilting it in either direction twenty-two and a half degrees, or forty-five degrees in all. In this way, all the instruments on this floor are made to follow the stars with perfect accuracy for six consecutive hours.

"The engines which keep up the motion have their valves actuated by an independent electrical engine, which, in turn, has a clock regulator. When engaged in planetary or cometary observation, different clocks are connected, which change the rate of motion as desired."

"Every requisite seems complied with," said Paul.

"Yes. And now I wish to show you how firmly all this is put together. You understand, of course, that it is really a vast ball floating in water. Well, the deck or floor is so well braced and so thick that it is practically inflexible. The roof is also strongly made, with heavy iron ribs, and the covering is so arranged with sliding plates that openings can be made at any point or any number of points, as may be required by observers."

Paul expressed himself as greatly interested

by the novelty and completeness of the arrangement. "But," he observed, "it must have been enormously expensive, and I should think that a much simpler method of mounting single instruments would have been preferable. Of course, too, your transit circles cannot be used here."

"That is true," said Marco. "Our transit instruments are in another building on the other side of the great dome; but you will readily understand why such outlay was thought desirable when you see the great reflector. All you have examined thus far are but the mountings of the principal instrument, although they incidentally furnish the best possible accommodations for many others."

They next passed through an entrance on the north side of the stone tower, where an inclined platform led to a door, as if on a ship in the docks. They ascended this platform and passed into the interior. Paul gazed with admiration at the arching canopy above them, which was grand in its proportions and presented a space perfectly clear with the exception of the axial shaft, which passed through the floor at the centre and sloped away to the north side of the roof. It was supported from the floor by iron trusswork. He saw about him several large refractors, turning on pivots and mounted on simple trunnions, together with many other instruments whose uses he did not know; but the great reflector, — where was that?

"These are magnificent instruments," he said to Marco, "but I expected to see something much larger."

Marco smiled, and pointed across the inclosed space to an oval-shaped object covered by a screen. They walked across to its side, and an attendant withdrew the screen, revealing an immense concave mirror, elliptical in form, its shortest diameter being at least twenty feet. It was supported by a metal framework, which reminded Paul of the frame of a monster steam-engine. The mirror sloped backward at an angle of forty-five degrees from the perpendicular, and was so arranged that this inclination could be changed through an arc of forty-five degrees.

"This is remarkable!" exclaimed Paul, "but I do not understand it. It is a much larger speculum than I supposed possible to make; but it has not a spherical curve, and it has no tube or place for an observer that I can perceive."

"True, it has no tube, but the place for the observer is across the hall. Do you see those iron guides running up nearly to the roof? Well, those are the elevator guides by which the other end of the telescope, with the observer's seat, his short tube, and his eye-pieces, are elevated or lowered to correspond with the inclination given to the mirror. These guides are segments of a circle, whose centre is the axis of the mirror. It is now placed for zenith observations, and the chair of the observer is at the bottom. The image, you see, is reflected at an angle of forty-five degrees. Hence its elliptical form and its spheroidal curves. From the eye-piece, the mirror presents a perfectly round disk and produces a perfect image."

While they were looking across toward the observer's end of the telescope, the attendant carefully returned the curtain to its place; and the two visitors walked across to the other extremity.

Paul was deeply impressed by the great strength of every part, and also by the extraordinary provisions for securing absolute accuracy of movement. The short tube was uncovered, and was, in fact, a large telescope. Within the car, or chair, were arranged a great variety of high and low power eye-pieces, spectroscopes, etc. Paul longed for a single peep through this monster artificial eye, which must, he thought, have the vision of a god. He felt himself humbled to the dimensions of a creeping insect, as he considered the smallness of his horizon as compared with that of the tremendous instrument before him; and he left the building with his head still uncovered, as if he were in the Divine Presence.

CHAPTER XXIII.

The Transcontinental Railway.

"FOR variety," said Marco, "we will return to the city by one of these electric road-carriages, which is likely to be quite as swift as the aerial car, and we shall then have an opportunity to inspect the transcontinental railway line. I am sure that will interest you, for it is based on a principle which was only entertained as a vague theory in your century. And, if we lose no time, we shall be able to take a glimpse of the evening train as it shoots by."

"By all means, then, let us hasten."

"The electric carriage must hasten for us. The road to the city from this point is one of the best, and there are no restrictions as to speed, so our driver will be able to show you the possibilities of his machine."

With these words, Marco called a carriage, explained to the driver that he wished to be at a certain point at a certain time; and, without an instant's delay, they coursed down Meridian Peak and into one of the great boulevards leading toward the city, which blazed and glistened in the afternoon sun-glow.

Meanwhile the carriage itself attracted Paul's attention, by reason of its simplicity and beauty, and the surprising ease with which it glided along the level highway. In form, the body was not unlike that of the primitive coupé, giving accommodation to two passengers inside, while the driver occupied an outer and elevated seat at the rear, after the style of the Hansom cab. The source of power was invisible; and, judging by the attitude of the driver, the means of applying it was well-nigh automatic. Marco explained that the electric battery was snugly packed under the seat they occupied, and that the supply of power was equal to about a day's travel with their present load and under the favorable conditions of the road before them.

"And about what speed are we now making?"

"The driver can tell us, as a dial before him keeps that fact constantly recorded, so that he can time himself to make any given distance with the greatest accuracy."

An inquiry addressed to the driver brought the response that, while coasting down the hillside, they had for a short space made a record of twenty-one and one tenth miles per hour, but that this was now reduced to eighteen and four tenths.

Marco further explained that the body and wheels of the vehicle were composed entirely of metal; but such was the accuracy of adjustment that not the slightest sound was heard, excepting the firm, even roll of the wheels as if they clung to a metal track, and the occasional peal of a musical bell as they approached a cross-road or a vehicle going less rapidly than they. The danger of collision was greatly reduced by the fact that all vehicles approaching the city were divided from those outward-bound by a double row of elms inclosing three middle paths for pedestrians, bicycles, and saddle-horses; so that speed was seldom slackened excepting at some of the great crossways.

"So horses are allowed here."

"Yes, we are still outside the city limits."

Between the towering Pyramids they soon swept; down the incline toward the river, alive with gay water-craft; over the Old Bridge, populous with statues; and then, by a swift curve, under the *porte-cochère* of the railway station, where they learned that the evening express was due in two minutes and a quarter. The station-master showed them an indicator in his office, on which the approaching train was shown by an index finger; and, at the same moment, alarm bells began to sound along the roadways. The window of the station was thrown up, and they looked out to see the track.

"But I see no track!" exclaimed the astonished spectator.

"I will explain that later," said Marco. "Here comes the train!"

There was a flash — a glisten — a slight suspension of breath and dizziness as the air seemed caught from the lungs — a little puff of dust — and it was gone!

"Is that a railway train which passed," gasped Paul, "or a whirlwind?"

"That," answered the station-master, smiling at the visitor's surprise, "is our regular evening express, which will land its passengers within sound of the Pacific's waves in twenty-four hours from now."

"And now about the track."

"Before we look at that," said Marco, "I want to propose that we visit the main station and car-shops, where you will have an opportunity to examine the rolling-stock. My object in pausing here was simply to show you a train under full speed."

They therefore reëntered their carriage, took another short course, obtained a permit and a guide, and were conducted into a spacious car-house, where several trains stood side by side.

At first glance, Paul thought each train was continuous from end to end, and it was practically so, although there were provisions for disconnecting its parts and lengthening or shortening it according to the demands of custom. Each train was several hundred feet in length, and the entrance doors were at the sides.

While he stood looking at them, a bell struck, and one of these solid trains moved slowly and smoothly past him, gradually attaining speed, and with such silent celerity that Paul stared after it in dumb amazement as it vanished in the far distance.

"What kind of wheels, what kind of axles, and what kind of roadways have you, to admit of speed like that?" asked Paul; "and what speed is it possible for you to attain?"

"To answer your last question first," said the guide, "our fastest trains travel at the rate of three degrees of longitude [over two hundred miles] per hour. The rails, wheels, journals, and boxes are all either solid, or cased with hardened steel, and are perfectly true."

"I see," said Paul excitedly, — "I see that this is an age of perfection, and that, with the perfect mechanism you have to deal with, you can easily and safely make somewhat over four times the speed we used to boast of. Why not? We did well to accomplish what we did, over the rough jounces of our crooked rails and decaying wooden sleepers. But your track? I have not yet seen any track. I see only these fences, — what is the purpose of these fences?"

"They are the tracks," said the guide, solemnly eying the visitor, as if he did not quite understand the cause of his surprise.

Paul advanced and asked: "On which side of this fence was the train that has just left us?"

"It was on both sides," said Marco, laughing; "in fact, it was astride of this fence. It is simply a single-track railway."

Upon examining the single rail on top of the supposed fence, Paul found that it consisted of a number of steel bars, placed on edge and bolted together by lapping joints so as to make it continuous, and fixed in a grooved capping of cast-iron, all being planed and fitted with the greatest nicety. The lower part of the fence-like support of the rail proper was extremely strong and stiff, having a wide base and being bolted to a solid stone foundation.

Paul walked around the front end of one of the "transports," as he noticed the guide called these trains, and found it to be pointed like the prow of a boat, and the lower part cleft to the height of the rail, which latter was about six feet above the foundation. On the top of the transport was a longitudinal projection, like the inverted keel of a boat, or still more like the dorsal fin of an eel. "This covers the wheels," said Paul to himself, "and the axles are across the top, or probably under the framework of the top." On questioning the guide, he found this to be the case.

"These transports, as you see, are very light structures," said Marco, "great weight having been found inconsistent with great speed."

"I believe you are right," said Paul; "yet in my day we had night cars weighing over thirty tons each, whose carrying capacity was only fifteen passengers, or two tons of dead weight to each passenger carried; while, at the same time, we had cars of only one twentieth that weight which easily carried the same number of passengers and their luggage over the roughest roads. I suppose," he continued, "that a train on a double-track road could hardly be made to attain the high speed that has been named."

"No," answered Marco, "for experience showed that they were liable to jump the tracks, or do something else that was undesirable. You see, this is no experiment. Centuries ago, it was settled that the use of a single track was the only practicable means of combining speed and safety. By this arrangement, the weight is disposed on either side and below the top of the rail, for the transport bestrides its support just as a rider does his horse, thus giving a maximum degree of stability and safety."

"I should think curves, turnouts, and draw-bridges would cause trouble."

"So they would," said Marco, "if we had them; but the rail for a fast line has no curves, and no breaks excepting at terminal stations, where all transfer ways are placed. No switches are ever used on the fast lines."

"A very wise precaution, too," said Paul. "Those old switches we used to tolerate had a multitude of crimes to answer for. But how do you prevent the overhanging sides of this transport from rubbing and grinding against the iron-work below the rail? It must sometimes be 'out of trim,' as we would say of a boat; and this transport is really more like a boat than like any rail-car I have ever before seen."

"Look underneath here," said Marco, "and you will readily understand how that is avoided. Here are horizontal wheels, which rest against the sides of the iron support. When speed is attained, these wheels separate a little, by an arrangement worked by the swift passage of air through the clefts dividing the two parts of the transport. Thus they come into action only when the motion is slow, as in starting or slowing up. Moreover, as you doubtless know, great velocity insures stability. A body moving with swiftness shows no tendency to oscillation. And here again, on the roof, is another device intended to preserve the proper poise. It works automatically. You see this longitudinal rib on top, which covers the wheels. It looks smooth and continuous, but it is, in fact, cut out in various places between the wheels, and these cut-out sections are mounted on upright shafts and turned to the right or left as the car tilts, however little that may be; and the swift current of air, striking these rudders, helps further to keep the transport vertical and steady. If you were to ride in one, I think you would be surprised to find how perfectly this quality of steadiness has been attained."

"No doubt, no doubt! Indeed, I am now ready to believe that the generations of master-minds that have dealt with these questions since my day have removed all difficulties which puzzled railway managers in my time. Yet these points cannot but present themselves to my mind, and suggest questions. For instance, supposing the engineer should forget to apply the brakes at the proper time, I should think, in case of a smash-up, that a transport and its passengers would be demolished beyond recognition."

"Unquestionably," answered Marco; "but we do not throw as much responsibility on human agency as you were accustomed to do. We supplement man's powers by every possible mechanical contrivance. These brakes all act automatically. Whenever the transport approaches a point on the road where a regular stop is to be made, the brakes are thrown into action by an attachment to the track, or, rather, to the frame that supports it. A long, swelled projection on the frame actuates an arm on the transport, and thereby throws on the brakes and shuts off the steam at the same instant. This, of course, applies only to regular stopping-places. In case of emergency, the engineer uses his judgment, but we leave as little to his judgment as possible."

"I suppose it is all right," said Paul, "but we used to have an idiom to the effect that 'accidents will happen in the best regulated families,' the truth of which we frequently exemplified; and I should think such speed would be fruitful of disaster. Imagine another train coming in contact with it from behind, as was not uncommon in the early days of railroading; why, not a person in either transport could escape instant annihilation."

"That can never happen," said Marco, "for the positions of all transports are known at all times all along the line; and in case one made a stop from any unexpected cause, every other would be immediately notified by telegraph, and none would be allowed to leave a station unless the track were open to the next principal station."

"That is a good arrangement. Yet I should still expect trouble of some kind would result from such speed. I should expect, for instance, that the wheels would sometimes fly in pieces, and come crashing through the middle wall into the passengers' quarters."

"All I can say is that it does not happen. Of course, every possible precaution is adopted. The wheels are of the best quality of steel forgings, and no more liable to break than a circular saw, which can safely be run at double the speed."

"I should suppose, also," continued Paul, "that engines heavy enough to drive these carriages could hardly be worked fast enough to turn the wheels at the required speed without great loss."

"A very good point," replied Marco, "but I will answer it by showing you the engine itself."

Walking down to the middle of the transport by which they were standing, they entered the engineer's compartment, and Paul soon perceived how this difficulty was overcome. High overhead were the axles of the great driving-wheels. These axles were provided, not with cranks, but with gears. The gears were rather small-toothed, very small and bright, broad-faced, and arranged in pairs, two wheels being placed side by side, the teeth not corresponding in position. The crank-shaft, which passed through from side to side in the space between the tread of the driving-wheels, carried two pairs of crown wheels and engaged the four pairs of pinion wheels on the axles above. The speeding-up was about three to one. The steam cylinders were horizontal, and placed as near the middle of the shaft as possible. All the arrangements were very beautiful, and they commended themselves to Paul's practiced eye as perfection realized.

"Well," said Marco, as his companion completed his survey, "what do you think of it?"

"I think," said Paul, "as a jockey might, after inspecting a famous horse, — 'it looks as if it had ninety in it.' But do you find no difficulty in starting these engines?"

"We probably should," answered the young engineer, "but we avoid that liability by employing an auxiliary starter, worked by compressed air, which gives it a good send-off. The engine is perfectly capable of making a start from a standing position, but it would be a little slow."

"I understand. Now, one thing more, if you please, and if time will allow. I should like very much to see something of your system of electric signals. I shall probably not be able to comprehend them, but even a glance at them would interest me, because I have given considerable attention to that subject."

They walked toward the manager's office, and as they did so, Paul watched the great transfer platform slowly moving the transports into position for starting. He also saw another of these movable sections of the road in a monster turntable, waiting to receive one of the transports, which, like a land steamer, was gradually swinging about, as if at her dock.

Upon entering the office, the young man directed Paul's attention to a long case, which had a double slide in front, and a metallic back on which were engraved the names of cities.

"There," said Marco, "this represents the length of road from here to Megothem, two hundred miles or an hour's distance from here. These are the names of the stations along the road, and these little moving objects represent the precise positions of all the transports now *en route*, either going or coming. Whenever a stop is made by any one of them, a gong is sounded, and this signal is repeated when it starts again. The manager, by a glance, can thus keep the run of things as speedily and accurately as he can tell the time of day by looking at the clock."

"We used a similar device in connection with

our passenger elevators in buildings," said Paul, "so I can readily understand how the principle might be extended and applied in this case. It is excellent. Has the manager also some means of communicating with the trains while in transit?"

"Oh, certainly. Each transport is in telegraphic connection with every station on the line, so that messages can be passed to and fro whenever desirable."

"Good, very good! And the result is" —

"No accidents," broke in Marco, "and no opportunity for accidents."

CHAPTER XXIV.

Mount Energy.

"Now, then," said Marco, "prepare to be again surprised, and supremely so, by a sight of what we call 'Mount Energy.'"

A further short course in the electric carriage brought them to the outskirts of the city, where they alighted at the foot of a rocky hill; and on its brow Paul beheld a lofty rampart or tower of stone, circular in form and more than two thousand feet in diameter, surmounted by what appeared to be a naval display of tall-masted vessels, sailing in stately procession around the margin of its summit. "Well, well!" exclaimed Paul, "I don't understand at all what this means."

"This," said Marco, "is one of many similar towers from which we mainly derive our mechanical power, and this is the largest. Here is where we produce the compressed air that moves our cars and drives our machinery; here are located the electric generators that give us light; and here we separate hydrogen from water, that it may be used for warming our houses in winter and cooking our food. These processes are chiefly performed by power caught directly from the winds. Mind you, we no longer look upon the winds of heaven as uncontrollable and pitiless forces that are to be feared and shunned. We invite their coöperation; and, with a little ingenuity in handling them, they have become very docile and helpful friends."

"I see, — you have tamed our eagles into domestic fowls. But do you not find them rather inconstant? I should suppose that their wings would often be becalmed, and that your machinery would soon stop."

"That is where the ingenuity comes in," said Marco. "Like most other difficulties, this one is not insurmountable, as you will soon see. But before I try to explain, let us walk up the incline leading to the working level, and there you will be able to see and understand for yourself most of the appliances that are employed."

The terraced road before them, after reaching the summit of the hill, entered a long arched roadway or sloping bridge that led to the top of the wall, where an arched opening gave entrance to the interior. They slowly climbed this steep incline, stopping frequently to take breath, and also to enjoy the charming panoramic view of the contrasted scenes of city and country life by which they were surrounded. Out of the sunshine they then passed through the topmost arch and last tunnel, that led through a solid wall thirty or forty feet in thickness, into the midst of the animated scene of the interior. Paul was fully prepared to be surprised, but the reality far surpassed his expectations.

The entire roof of the vast tower was slowly revolving above their heads like a horizontal wheel. At intervals between the circumference and centre were lines of iron framework, forming circles within each other, and these frames supported a great number of wheels on which the roof rested and revolved. Attached to the iron frames and operated by the wheels were innumerable condensing engines, and other strange-looking contrivances that Marco explained were electric generators and hydrogen liberators. Upon inquiry, they learned that, as the breeze blowing was moderate, only one fourth the entire number of machines were at present connected; but that, with a high wind, all could easily be pushed to their full capacity, and the amount of work they accomplished, as exhibited by tables of figures, was beyond the power of Paul's mind to grasp at once.

"Before we go up on deck," said Marco, "I

may as well explain the principal features of this wind apparatus. You noticed the solidity of the wall through which we entered. Well, on top of this wall is a circular canal, extending around the whole structure. Floating in this canal is an annular vessel, nearly filling it, which carries the principal weight of the deck that covers the entire area, and also the weight of the masts, sails, and rigging. The wheels on which the deck rests help incidentally to support it, but are mainly employed in accumulating and transmitting the power."

While Marco thus spoke, the visitors reached the great central shaft, around which curved a stairway, and this they followed until they stepped through an opening at the top and stood in the midst of the revolving platform, surrounded by sunshine and the flash of white sails. In the centre arose an iron tower or mainstay, that seemed to pierce the clouds; while around the rim of the deck, at regular intervals of one hundred feet, stood the masts, uniform in height, and much higher than the mainmasts of the largest ships. Sixty of these masts completed the circle. They were held firmly in position by stays radiating from the iron tower, and also by stays extending from one to another and to projecting spars resembling bowsprits. Each mast was provided with a double series of booms, swinging both inwardly and outwardly, the lower ones being very long, while those at the top were shortened like the yards of a square-rigged ship. On these swinging booms were arranged the sails, which opened and closed like the wings of a butterfly, trimming themselves automatically to catch the faintest breeze. Paul could easily see that the strength of the masts, sails, and rigging was calculated to withstand the most furious gale, and that no reefing was ever necessary. The great circular ship was always in working order, day or night, blow high or blow low, without the need of ever calling poor Jack to tumble up and spread or shorten sail.

Paul gazed without speaking upon the great white wings as they swept noiselessly, but irresistibly, around the grand circle. He felt small and weak as he contemplated the proportions of this marvelous work of human hands, and estimated the enormous horse-power it must represent. "There is really a sort of majesty about it," he finally ejaculated.

"I think so, too," said Marco, "and I often pay a visit here to get nerved up, as it were."

"I begin," added Paul, "to see the significance of all this. In the rapid succession of unaccustomed sensations I have experienced during the past two days, I have had little time for thought; but I can vaguely feel rather than understand what this means. The world's coal-fields are no doubt exhausted, and you have no fuel for either steam-power or heating purposes. Consequently, you are obliged to resort to this mode of obtaining power through the medium of compressed air, and to this mode of securing heat through hydrogen and light through electricity. All are produced here, and the power that produces them is that of the winds."

"You are a keen observer, sir," said Marco, "but not altogether correct in your premises. As a matter of fact, our coal supply is not yet exhausted, but vast quantities have been wasted, and we never allow ourselves to use coal for producing power so long as we can conveniently substitute wind or falling water, and our steam is mainly produced by the heat of the sun's rays."

"Steam by the sun's rays?" said Paul inquiringly. "Ah, that was Ericsson's prophecy. But have you really learned how to secure useful work from the sun?"

"Yes, indeed," rejoined Marco. "In the long, hot days of summer, when the winds are light, it is a powerful auxiliary, on which we have learned to depend. We no longer complain of hot weather: we know it means cheap power, that will be carefully stored and prove invaluable in a thousand ways. The sun apparatus is at work to-day, and, if you are ready, we will immediately visit it. It covers the south wall of this structure, and we can descend by this elevator directly to the works."

"One more question, first," said Paul. "I see you have two strings to your bow for the production of energy; but supposing wind and sun both fail to lend their shoulders to your work, as they must at times, what then happens?"

"The same as usual," answered Marco. "Everything proceeds; nothing stands still. We merely make a draft on the surplus energy we always keep on storage, which is intended to be sufficient for at least a full month's supply without assistance from any other source. The supply has never yet been exhausted."

"How can you store sufficient compressed air to meet such a requirement, and where do you store it?"

"Storage is not difficult. For instance, the wall that supports these upper works is a vast water cistern, which is sunk far below the surface of the ground; and resting upon the water is the air-receiver, which is of the full size of the interior space. This is open at the bottom, and rises as the air is forced into it. It has a vertical range of one hundred feet, and is loaded to maintain a pressure of three atmospheres. It is not an open inverted cistern, but is formed like a honeycomb of upright hexagonal cells, and these cells communicate with each other by openings near the top, so that the pressure is equal and constant."

As Marco spoke, he drew Paul toward the elevator; the door opened, and they took their seats in the car, which rapidly descended.

"I see," said Paul; but he said the words a little dubiously.

CHAPTER XXV.

The Solar Steam-Works.

At the bottom of the elevator shaft, Paul and Marco entered the engine-room of the Solar Steam-Works: this extension to the main structure was crescent-shaped, and extended from the southeast to the southwest, covering about a third of the main wall. The floor was occupied by a long line of powerful steam-engines, following the curve of the wall, all vigorously, but noiselessly, at work.

"The heating apparatus," said Marco, "which is the chief attraction for us, is on the floor above; and if we ascend by the eastern entrance, we shall see it to the best advantage, as the sun is now on the west side."

Passing up a spiral stairway, they entered directly into the steam-generating room, and Paul experienced still another novel sensation. Some moments passed before he was able to collect his faculties and intelligently observe what was going on about him. He then saw that, on the side opposite the main wall, was a cavernous horizontal recess, walled with white fire-brick, and within this recess a perfect network of pipes. This pipe cavern extended all around the outer inclosure, while the wall above the brickwork, and also the roof of the great crescent extension, were composed entirely of glass, the height being the same as that of the main structure, namely, two hundred feet, with width about the same. Paul next noticed that the main wall was entirely covered by mirrors, all so adjusted in frames that they were made to catch and reflect the sun's rays directly into the cavern below and upon the pipes, which he now understood were intended to answer the place of boilers; the movements were automatic, turning with the sun, and all that were now exposed cast their quota of rays full into the boiler recess. The effect of the flood of light which, at first glance, seemed to radiate from the boilers to the mirrors, was dazzling beyond description, and it was difficult for Paul to conceive that the blazing interior of the boiler receptacles was not really a bed of live coals. Marco explained how the morning sun illuminated one half of the mirrors, how the noon sun illuminated both halves, and how the present afternoon sun again expended itself on one half.

"It is much easier than you might at first suppose," said Marco, "to thus generate steam from the sun's rays, the heat being directly applied to a much larger heating surface than could be reached by fire."

"Yes; but the degree of heat thus accumulated is what I most marvel at."

"That is merely a matter of mathematics. We have only to catch and convert into power the solar heat falling upon an area ten feet square, — that is, one hundred square feet, — and we secure energy equal to the force of five or six horses. The power placed within our reach by the sun's rays and the winds is, you see, exhaustless, and equal to every need of man in the way of motive and mechanical force. But I should add that both these sources of power, limitless as they are, would be of little practical use to us without the medium of compressed air through which we make the application. In your day, you had little conception of what a wonderful agent of usefulness you held dormant in compressed air. It is always ready for work, and it waits our pleasure though unused for years. When needed, we have only to turn a valve, and this willing servant instantly answers our summons. With equal facility it turns the delicate little rotaries for the lightest task, or the immense engines employed in our factories and forging works. It is ready for the jeweler's blowpipe, or for the blast furnace.

It cools and purifies the chamber of the invalid, or blows the organ, or dries vaults and cellars. In innumerable ways, it is now an indispensable helper."

"I can understand that," said Paul; "and I can also understand one important advantage it possesses as compared with steam. With steam-power the fire needs constant attention as well as the boiler. Moreover, to be effectual, — to say nothing about being economical, — it must be operated constantly during working hours. It must oftentimes, therefore, be in active service for long periods, and at considerable expense for fuel and care, when there is no work for it to do. I can understand that, with compressed air, supplied by a system of pipes, there is no call for constant attention, but it is always on duty when needed, and can be shut off the moment it has filled that need."

"Moreover," continued Marco, "a further saving is made in our large workshops by having each machine, to which power is applied, driven by its own independent air-wheel. In fact, nearly every machine nowadays is made with its power-wheel as an integral part of the mechanism, thus saving both first cost and wear and tear of shafting, pulleys, and belting, and also the waste of power required in constantly driving them."

"That's an improvement, certainly," responded Paul. "So you connect each machine directly with the supply pipe, do you?"

"Exactly."

"An improvement, unquestionably! I know that by my own experience."

Leaving the boiler-room, and descending by stairs to the engine-room below, they again passed the long row of engines and so out of the building, whereupon they reëntered the electric carriage, and were whisked down the hillside avenue.

CHAPTER XXVI.

The Palace of the Sun.

"ARE we now bound for home?" asked Paul.

"Yes; but I will suggest that we make one more call on the way. In the Solar Steam-Works you have seen one of the modes in which we use the direct rays of the sun as a helpmate in our work. I would now like to show you how we also use them as a pleasure-giving and health-giving agent. If you are not too tired, I want to introduce you to what we call our 'Palace of the Sun.'"

"The very name is enough to banish weariness, if I felt it; but I am not at all tired."

"From the crest of this hill, you will be able to get a good idea of its external appearance."

A few moments later, the young man directed the driver to make a turn to the left, where, after a short ascent that led to a paved terrace in front of a temple-like structure, a glorious view of the Sun Palace suddenly burst upon them. There was no need to ask, "Is this it?" In the little valley beneath them lay a billowy sea of glass, glittering in the late sun-glow as though a thousand suns were imprisoned within its crystal roofs. A park, of dimensions that seemed to Paul more than equal to the familiar Boston Common of his own day, was closed in by glass, as if it were a vast conservatory. A central dome of glass towered hundreds of feet above the streets below, and five circles of lesser domes and arches surrounded this, gradually decreasing in size until they stooped to the outside walls of glass. Glass, — everything visible from this height was of glass, and everything was aglow with sunshine.

"It is certainly marvelously beautiful," said Paul; "but to what use is it put? I seem to see streets and buildings within it, as if it were a miniature city. It now occurs to me that it must have been in this fairy world that I had the pleasure of dining with the Professor last evening. But the structure, — does it inclose an international exhibition of some kind, planned on a scale that makes it a world in itself?"

"No and yes. It is not at all one of the exhibitions of mechanical devices, such as became common in the latter half of the nineteenth century and grew to gigantic proportions in the century following. Then, when the science of mechanics was in comparative infancy, and the code of knowledge possessed by one generation became the primer of the next, such comparative reviews of recent discovery were invaluable; but now we have little or nothing new to learn along those much-traveled lines. Yet it is, indeed, a world in itself, — a tropical world, where summer always reigns, and where nothing is ever allowed to enter that does not bring blossoms, or perfume, or music, or smiles, or happiness in some form; nothing, I should say, other than humanity. Many of those who live here are invalids, or would be invalids if required to face the rigors of our climate during the seasons of change. Here it is always June, and here every precaution is taken to assemble all possible conditions that are favorable to health and vitality. Instead of sending our invalids to far-off health resorts, we have brought to their doors the best of all sanitariums, where friends and medical experts can be within easy reach, and where they are surrounded by all that art can furnish to amuse and stimulate them. But you shall see, — you shall see!"

Upon leaving the carriage, they entered, by a series of swinging doors, upon a central avenue lined with flower-beds and tropical trees, among which flitted and caroled numerous birds. A delicate fragrance of orange blossoms was in the air, and distant music lent an added feeling of restfulness.

"You may find it a trifle warm," said Marco, "just after leaving the outer air, but you will soon become accustomed to this temperature, which is never varied throughout the year, but is maintained at a standard that is considered most conducive to the health of animals and plants. Those who, like myself, find the sharp nip of the winter wind a pleasure sometimes call this little realm 'Effeminacia,' and it is a fact that those who constantly dwell here have less vigor than we outsiders; but they unquestionably have remarkably good health, and live to an astonishingly ripe old age. One of our humorists once remarked that 'invalidism in Effeminacia is immortalism.' It is a famous winter resort for all classes, and its many hotels are filled to overflowing during that season. It is also the chief centre of gayety in this region; and its constant attractions in the way of music, theatricals, art exhibitions, and merrymakings of all kinds make it a rendezvous throughout the year."

"It certainly appears a paradise, appealing to every sense."

"And also to every creature comfort. That is its object. So far as health and pleasure are concerned, human skill has conceived nothing more perfect than this little Eden. Of course, we have many public works that exhibit far more genius, but this is a happy combination of strikingly beautiful elements. To the achievements of skill there seems to be no limit; and so long as man possesses the power of thought, he will constantly be engaged in adding something to the sum of human knowledge and to visible manifestations of that knowledge."

"Very true. The old adage that 'the present builds upon the past' still holds, no doubt, and the accumulative process that has been active ever since pre-glacial man fashioned his first rude weapons of flint is evidently still at work in your more advanced age; but you can hardly imagine how completely a leap of a few thousand years appears to have resulted in the creation of a new earth. How is it with your heaven? Have you also created a new heaven?"

"It was one of John Costor's mottoes that every man should do his utmost to make earth a heaven. He viewed all unhappiness with suspicion; and, in following out that same train of thought, we have found it to be a general truth — with only enough exceptions to prove the rule — that unhappiness is in some way the fruit of either sin or ignorance. According to his teachings, if we could only banish those two conditions from human life, we should live in an earthly paradise that would fit us to feel at home in any future state, however joyful."

"Judging from the cheerful faces of the

pleasure-seekers I here see about us, you would seem already to have realized that dream."

"Not wholly, but enough to encourage us to press forward along the path that Costor pointed out."

The concourse of people to which Paul referred was certainly quite unlike any ever gathered in his day. Up and down the broad avenues they thronged, dressed in the lightest of summer clothing, and gayly talking and laughing. There was no look of care, no feverish haste. It was as if the world were made for them, and their only duty to drink in its delights. Paul watched their happy faces in the doorways and on the spacious balconies projecting from the upper stories of the structures that towered on either hand above the orange-trees and palms. If any of these were invalids, then it seemed well to be an invalid.

Now and then they entered and took a glance at some pleasure-house, where paintings and sculpture looked alive in the warm, perfumed air, and unseen orchestras gave a zest to every sense. The buildings themselves, by which Paul was particularly charmed, showed great variety of material and form. No two façades were alike, but all were graceful, airy, and profusely decorated. Some were built of vari-colored marbles, and others of light-tinted enameled bricks, enameled iron, and terra cotta, while still others were of white glass or porcelain blocks, encased by a framework of bronze.

"And now," said Paul, "that I have recovered from my first impression of dazed surprise, I want to ask how this June-like temperature is thus maintained in midwinter."

"That is the question that suggested our coming here this afternoon. The sun is the only source of heat used. Do you see these long lines of dead-black surfaces that are railed in between the central arbors and the outer passageways? Now look up to the glass roof and see the thousands of mirrors there suspended to the iron framework. Those mirrors are so arranged that reflected rays of the sun are concentrated directly upon these black surfaces, in the same manner that the mirrors played upon the heat generators in the Solar Steam-Works. But here, instead of immediately transmitting the heat into mechanical force, these black accumulators catch it and store it up, and deliver it as it is needed."

"Am I to understand that you can thus retain the heat for any length of time, and in sufficient quantity to maintain the present degree of heat throughout the year?"

"Enough, and to spare. But you shall now see for yourself."

The young man called an official, and explained to him that his companion was a stranger from a strange land, who had never seen a heat accumulator, and asked if he would kindly give a test, showing the power of the heat rays. The official drew from his pocket a slip of black paper and tossed it over the railing upon the surface of the accumulator. It immediately began to smoke, and in a few seconds burst into flame and was reduced to white ashes.

"The sun is getting low," said the official, "and the heat is waning, otherwise the combustion would have been instantaneous. In another half hour we shall cover the accumulators. These are the covers," he continued, pointing to heavy rolls of thick matting that lay on the ground against the railing. "By a touch upon an electric button, these blankets are unrolled and wrapped about the accumulators, thus helping to retain the heat, while beneath the surface are large masses of heat absorbents, in the form of bricks, built up in kiln shape, with air spaces between them. The stored air is thereby kept in circulation, and all heat imparted from without is thus absorbed, as water is sucked in by a sponge; while radiation is prevented by confining walls of several thicknesses of polished metal, which are again covered on the outside by a thick body of cotton fibre. By this means, we can retain the heat for many weeks without sensible loss ; and it is drawn off in pipes, which radiate to all parts of the inclosure and also to the interior of the buildings, for use at whatever points it may be needed."

"It is a great scheme, — a great scheme!" exclaimed Paul. "But now, pray tell me how people manage to exist here in midsummer. On a July day, about three o'clock in the afternoon, I should think they would roast alive."

"Not at all," replied the attendant. "All the glass frames in the roof are pivoted, and can be opened at will by the engineer in charge. We thus admit or exclude the outer air, as may be desired; and whenever the normal temperature is exceeded by even a degree, we open pipes containing compressed air stored at Mount Energy; and this, having parted with its own heat, absorbs so much by expansion that the standard degree is restored in a few moments."

"I suppose your householders also cook by the sun's rays?" said Paul inquiringly.

"No," answered Marco, "not as a rule, but not because they cannot. Some families prefer the process by direct concentration; but hydrogen is our common fuel for cooking, and that too is one of the products of Mount Energy, as you will no doubt remember."

"There is one more question I would like to

ask. In retaining the summer temperature on a cold winter day like this, does not the inclosed air soon become vitiated by the thousands of dwellers here present?"

"Not perceptibly," answered Marco, "although, as I have told you, we outsiders, who are not afraid of the rough caresses of the north wind, think we discover a lack of life-giving quality in this conservatory climate. On the other hand, our specialists in the science of health find the conditions here peculiarly favorable to life. The management employ a large corps of intelligent officers, who give constant attention to the condition of the air both as to temperature and purity; and they have abundant means at command to control it and to prevent its becoming vitiated. Several stations, located widely apart, contain mechanism for detecting and reporting the presence of deleterious gases, by means of columns, dials, and sensitive colors, and the character of the air can thereby be read at a glance, and any defect be promptly remedied."

"Ah! that is as it should be. We used to be surrounded by invisible enemies that meant illness, if not death, and they found access not only to our factories and places of amusement, but also to our homes. Yet we had at command no monitor to warn us of their presence.

Our thermometers and hygrometers recorded little more than our senses told us. The meters we most needed to cry 'Beware!' when the seeds of death hovered about us and our loved ones, — those we lacked."

"We have filled that lack," said Marco quietly. "With the same intelligence that we eat, we also feed our lungs."

The sun had now declined until its heat rays were no longer serviceable; and at the tinkle of a bell, Paul saw the accumulators hide themselves beneath their blankets. Marco consulted his watch, and suggested that they ought now to start for home, as dinner-time was approaching. Walking rapidly down the Avenue of Palms, they left behind them groups of flaxen-haired children playing hide-and-seek among the tree-trunks, took a last glance at the canopy of glass, aglow with sunset tints that seemed to merge with the evening sky, and passed between the buttressed iron towers and flapping doors to the street, where a sudden snow-squall greeted them as they drew the carriage robes about their knees.

"I'm afraid there's something of the tropical plant about me," said Paul, as he sneezed and then coughed.

PART V.

THE CELESTIAL VISITOR.

CHAPTER XXVII.

An Evening at Home.

THE dinner that night, served, as customary, from a pneumatic tube, which proved a prompt and efficient waiter, was a distinguished success; and the animated and cheerful conversation of those present speedily banished the mental weariness which Paul naturally felt after his long tour of investigation.

Of course, the chief subject of conversation was the near approach of the great comet. Before the coming of to-morrow's daylight, a spectacle surpassing all glories of the past would sweep into view. Before the dawn, the prophecy of centuries would become a recorded fact in history. Or if — there was an *if* in the case — if the prophecies of certain pessimists were realized, to-morrow's sun would see the close of the world's book of history. Professor Prosper laughed this fear to scorn. "Why, my dear," he said to his daughter, "this thing has been figured down to such nicety that the course of the comet is known as accurately as that of a horse around a race-track; and there is no more danger of its disturbing our peace than of the horse trampling you in your seat on the grand-stand. Nonsense, my dear!"

Still, there was a sufficient element of the unknown in the matter, and consequently sufficient possibility of the unexpected, to give that trifling sense of alarm that is not inconsistent with pleasurable anticipation, and every eye was bright, every cheek flushed. At twenty-two and three quarters minutes before three o'clock, the celestial visitor would first show its face. One hour and eight minutes later, it would flash by. Time was getting short. No sleep to-night in any part of the world. The close of one era was at hand — but would it mark the beginning of another?

After dinner, the elder daughter exhibited the pride of the family, a baby, that for a short time completely turned the current of conversation and thought from the one great and absorbing topic.

"Did you ever, in your day, Mr. Prognosis," demanded the young mother, "see a finer little fellow than this one?"

"Never, — upon my word, never!"

"Dad, dad, dad," said the baby.

"Why, he is actually speaking!" cried the young mother.

"Mum, mum," continued the baby.

"Don't you hear it? Say mamma, dearest!"

"Mum ma," echoed the crowing child.

The testimony of those present was unanimous that a first step had been taken in the direction of acquiring the universal language.

Paul's attention was next attracted to the fact that no lamps of any kind were visible in any of the rooms, although they were illuminated as if by full daylight; and Marco explained to him that the electric lamps were concealed along the lower edge of the frieze, but that the frieze itself and the ceiling reflected the light throughout the rooms. The finish of the walls of the drawing-room afforded another subject of conversation. It looked like porcelain, and was chastely ornamented in moulded panels, softly tinted with harmonious colors, the whole giving an effect of great permanence as well as beauty. The Professor now came to Marco's assistance, and explained to his visitor that the walls were covered with sheets of opaque glass, set in cement, the edges of the sheets being turned down so as to hold them in place with great firmness. The ornaments on the panels and mouldings were made separately and fused on, and the colors were absolutely fast, having been fixed in the furnace.

"The use of glass, then," said Paul, "is by no means confined to your exteriors."

"Not at all! We employ it wherever practicable, as it insures cleanliness as well as permanence, and is always beautiful. As I have already told you, this is often spoken of as the Diamond Age, and glass is its representative that we use in architecture."

Many exquisite works of art decorated the drawing-room, in which Paul manifested much interest. The paintings especially were marvels of drawing and color; and numerous products in metal, stone, and wood contributed to make the room a veritable art museum.

"You are evidently a lover of the beautiful," said Madam Prosper. "We have a glass screen that we prize highly, which I am sure will interest you. Professor, I think you must have forgotten to show Mr. Prognosis the screen."

"True; but I will immediately retrieve the fault."

The drawing-room was divided into two sections by a wide archway; and from one side, as if it were a sliding door, the old gentleman proceeded to draw a pictured screen, until it filled the entire open space. The pictures were in panels, set in a skeleton frame of metal, and they struck Paul as being beyond comparison the most unique and exquisite he had ever seen. Curtains were so arranged that one picture might be viewed while the others were concealed. Upon close examination, the guest found that these pictures were in some unknown way executed in glass, and that they were transparencies; but they had none of the raw coloring of stained glass.

"What!" he exclaimed, "is it possible that these are photographs of pictures, and that you are now able to photograph color as well as form?"

"That we can do," responded the Professor, "and in my library you will find portfolios of photographs in color which are almost as life-like as the objects themselves. But another process has been used in this instance. The designs shown on these glass panels were painted by Artean, the greatest genius in pictorial art, and especially in color, that the world has thus far known. The originals were cross-ruled, and the entire surface divided into minute hexagons. Small hexagonal plugs of glass, of all possible shades of color and degrees of opacity, were then selected, classified, numbered, and arranged in cases, much the same as a printer's types are kept. A mosaic picture was then formed, giving an effect as nearly as possible like the original painting. This was done on a bed of fire-clay, held firmly in place by an iron casing, protected by clay, placed in a furnace, and fused by a downward blast of hydrogen. By careful fusing, the colors, as you see, have been made to blend so as to perfectly obscure the union of the hexagons and leave this solid sheet of glass. It was then taken from the furnace, and delicately ground and polished."

"The effect is certainly very novel and charming."

"Yes; and you will observe that it can be seen with equal advantage by transmitted or surface light; but the effect is totally changed."

The Professor led his visitor to the other side of the screen, and continued: "There, you will notice that you can see it with the light on either or both sides, and that an infinite variety of effects is thus produced. Madam considers finest the one I obtain by thus covering the terrestrial objects with an opaque screen on the further side, and then withdrawing the light to a low point before the face of the picture, thus gradually lowering the degree of transmitted light. See! we are now introduced to all the varying effects of sunset and twilight, and in a manner wonderfully true to nature. Now, the black outlines of the hills, woods, and edifices stand out in sharp contrast against the background of evening sky, which is as clear and transparent as in nature itself. And now, when the twilight is very dim, I can increase the front light until we have the effect of moonlight. Is it not beautiful? And we can still further vary the result by interposing colored glasses before the light, producing a red or yellow sunset, or the bluish white of moonlight. We sometimes make such experiments to amuse visitors, and I assure you I am thereby able to present quite a varied picture gallery."

"You have already done that," said Paul, "and it is altogether a new experience to one of your audience."

Music was then proposed, and all present proceeded to the music-room, where the elder daughter seated herself before an instrument having keys and pedals, that somewhat resembled an organ. "Is this an organ or a piano?" he asked.

"We call it an eolia. Do you play, Mr. Prognosis? If so, please try, and you will be better able than I am to compare it with the instruments you have named."

With some confusion Paul seated himself on the seat she vacated; and in response to the earnest requests of all, he played a simple adaptation of the national hymn, "America." To his surprise, he found himself quite enchanted by his own music. The result was quite unexpected. Each chord gave forth a rich, mellow note, as of a stroke followed by a prolonged tone, which ceased only when the pressure was removed. When he pressed a key gently, a soft violin tone followed, without any noticeable stroke; and when the pressure was increased, the tone also increased, its volume evidently depending upon the degree of force employed.

"Well, well!" he exclaimed, "you have combined the organ and the piano, and so perfected this union of the two that you have given the instrument expression. It has feeling now."

He repeated the same thought more emphatically after listening to the wonderful music with which the ladies entertained him.

"Can I see the mechanism by which this much-desired result of expression is obtained?" he asked, later in the evening.

The Professor replied by uncovering the strings and exposing the action to view. The strings were arranged in pairs; and, like a piano, it had hammers, while, in addition, each pair of strings had a little tongue pressing up between them, encased with a soft cover. These tongues were made to vibrate rapidly by electrical agency, striking the strings with more or less force as the current was strong or light; and the strength of this current was determined by the pressure on the key.

"I understand the general principle," said Paul, "and I will not trouble you to describe the electrical apparatus; but please show me the slide, as I do not understand how the particular note struck can be acted upon while the others are not, for of course it cannot be that all the strings are raised and lowered at once."

"Certainly not; but you shall see. There, if you will look here, you will find that each pair of strings rest at this point end upon a smooth roller, slightly grooved to keep them in position. This roller is carried backward and forward through a short space by a simple connection with two pedals, one of which raises the pitch and the other lowers it. Only the note struck is affected by the pedal. To accomplish this simply and effectually, much time and ingenuity have been expended upon it, but it is now a very perfect house instrument."

"It is indeed," said Paul. "I do not think I fully understand the mechanism; but the result is certainly satisfactory."

"Now, if you are ready," said the Professor, "we will take a smoke in the library, and discuss the subject we laid on the table last night."

CHAPTER XXVIII.

The Administration of Law.

As the Professor handed his guest a cigar, he suddenly exclaimed: "I have it at last! Mr. Prognosis, ever since I first saw you, in that singular costume in which you abruptly presented yourself day before yesterday, you have vaguely reminded me of some one known before, and familiarly known; but I have been unable to individualize your counterpart. As you rose to take that cigar, the fact suddenly came to me that that counterpart is my old friend, Tom Glide. Dear old Tom! — he was a schoolmate of mine; but I have n't seen him for over forty years. When we parted, I felt that a large piece of my pleasure in life had gone with him; and now — why, I fear I have n't given him a thought for ten years. I really must have a word with him to-night, if he is alive."

"Have a word with him? But how is that possible? Surely, you don't mean to say that you have realized the wildest of dreams that possessed the nineteenth century, and developed mesmeric messengers?"

"Not at all. I shall merely use human agencies of the simplest description. But as the system is no doubt wholly new to you, I will explain it. In these days, although the population vastly exceeds that of your time, every human being is a matter of consequence to the general public as well as to himself, and the public has taken means of identifying its units. Every person, on arriving at manhood or womanhood, is assigned what is known as a 'census signature,'—so called because its adoption grew out of the demands of the enumeration of the people each decade. This 'census signature' is made up of letters and numerals like an algebraic formula, and denotes the city or town of the person's nativity, the name of his family, and the year of his birth. No two signatures are ever precisely alike, so that identity is assured; and all such signatures are carefully registered, and copies are kept at certain stations for ready reference by the public. When a person changes his place of residence, the law requires that he shall register at the proper office his 'census signature' and place of destination. He thus leaves behind him a thread that may be speedily followed, even after the lapse of many years. We will now try the experiment, and see whether we can obtain a response from Tom Glide. His signature, as it appears in this old address-book of mine, is

'A, 66, M, 220, L, 22.' Here, Marco, I wish you would be so kind as to take this over to the nearest census office, and ask them to look up the respondent and put me in communication with him, — to-night, if possible, though the present excitement may make this inexpedient. Or you might first attempt to telegraph direct from here. If he is still alive and the means of communication are all open, we ought to be able to see him in an hour or so."

"See him, Professor?" asked Paul wonderingly.

"Yes; that was not a *lapsus linguæ*. Have a little patience, Mr. Prognosis, and you may perhaps also have the pleasure of seeing Tom Glide."

"Glide was my wife's maiden name," remarked Paul absently. "Well, sir," he added, "if my privilege still holds good, I will begin our evening's talk by asking you how it came about that such a city as this, and such marvelous public works as you and Marco have shown me, were constructed. Possibly, in my day, the world did business on a very limited capital as compared with that you possess; but if cities and public works like these now abound all over the world, capital alone cannot explain their existence. A new kind or quality of public spirit must be behind all. I refer particularly to the Peace Monument and the Old Bridge, which must have cost vast expenditures of money and time. The form of government inaugurated by the Costorian movement you have described would, I should think, involve considerations of economy that would forbid all works where decoration forms a leading feature; and under such a truly democratic condition of affairs as you now appear to have, it can hardly be possible that private means can effect such results."

"You are right," said the Professor, "as far as you go. But we must go back further. First, you must understand that, at the time of the proclamation of universal peace, the various governments of the world possessed an enormous amount of property in the way of war-ships, armaments, forts, arsenals, and the like. These had been sustained and augmented by heavy taxes on the people. Moreover, great numbers of the people were maintained in compulsory idleness in the standing armies. With the inauguration of peace, one of the first questions that arose was, what to do with the war material, that was now useless, and what to do with the soldiers, whose education had hardly fitted them for the pursuits of peace, — indeed, had unfitted them to immediately wear the yoke of individual responsibility. It was finally determined to let the usual revenues accumulate for a time, and to sell all government property that was now useless; and with the vast fund thus supplied, the Government employed the armies about to be disbanded, without wholly relaxing the former military rules, in building a variety of works of public utility and monuments in commemoration of the beneficent peace enactment. But this did not begin to exhaust the fund. Universities of learning were established and richly endowed, extraordinary works of internal improvement were undertaken, art received an unprecedented stimulus, and all industrial pursuits were marked by healthful activity. And still, in spite of steady decrease in taxes, the fund as steadily increased. Then, as Government and people drew closer in their mutual relations, the interests of the two began slowly to be merged. Even in your day, it was one of the signs of the times that small interests were beginning to be absorbed by corporations, and those by giant monopolies. By slow and peaceful steps the same movement progressed, until the Government itself came into possession of such industries as were of peculiarly public interest, including all means of communication and transportation, and life and fire insurance; and the land question was settled in the same manner."

"Certainly, the fund must speedily have been exhausted in that process."

"Only temporarily, for the investment proved remunerative; and later on, the surplus still further increased. The Government simply assumed all responsibility, and guaranteed a certain rate of interest to former proprietors for a certain period. No capital at all was required, excepting sufficient to meet the interest account, and this was covered many times over by the returns."

"Did not this result in great injustice to individuals?"

"Not at all. If it had, the movement would not have succeeded, for the public conscience had been quickened by Costor to regard truth and justice as foundation-stones in erecting the new structure of society. Of course the process was a slow one, and it continued through several generations; but the first step was hardest. The others followed more or less naturally. Under Grant's presidency, it seemed perfectly proper and just that the Government should conduct the postal service. Was it any less proper and just that it should conduct the telegraph, telephone, railway, and express service? And was n't it equally desirable that the Government should sufficiently control the supply and distribution of food products, that no man or clique of men should be able to put the hand on these and say, 'This wheat is mine, and no man shall eat of it until he has paid me my price'? That is not an exaggeration of what used to happen in the nineteenth century, if we correctly understand the records."

"I fear they are only too clear. But how about the land?"

"That was absorbed by the Government in just the same manner, by guaranteeing interest to previous owners and re-letting on equitable terms. At this point, the best skill of the best jurists of the world was required; but long before the scheme of leasing was perfected, it was recognized as far more just than the former method of land-tenure laws, which permitted individuals and corporations to monopolize a large portion of the world's most desirable districts for their own benefit or amusement. As we now look upon it, air, water, sunshine, and land are peculiarly the people's own, and it is with great difficulty that we can understand a state of society in which individuals were permitted to exercise any control over them."

"And you say that all these changes were made peaceably?"

"Yes; they could hardly have been made otherwise. The work was a slow one; it had to be done one step at a time, and public opinion was required to time each step. Whenever public opinion halted in giving its approval to a proposed step, the movement halted Any violence at any stage of the proceedings, or any attempt to make unhealthy haste, would have retarded the movement indefinitely. It grew as a tree, each limb of which naturally stretches out new limbs, and each new limb pushes forth twigs and leaves. The trunk of this tree was established by John Costor, and its root was truth."

"This was certainly," said Paul, "a great stride in the evolution of social science."

"Yes; it is now referred to as the 'Transition Period,' as distinguished from the 'Experimental Period,' to which you belonged."

"And now," said Paul, "if your mind is not too much taken up by the near approach of the great event, let me remind you of your promise to tell me something about your present form of government, and especially of your law system."

"As to the great event," said the Professor, "that will only speed my tongue in the telling. To speak the truth, according to the behest of this crystal button on my lapel, — which, you may have noticed, I removed for a few moments during dinner, — I must confess that, for several days past, I have felt something of that nervousness that probably always precedes the termination of some great work on which one has long been engaged. It was for this reason that I preferred to have Marco accompany you to-day. Madam alone knows my anxiety; and by her advice, I have taken a long nap this afternoon. I therefore feel perfectly rested and in a mood for conversation. You see, my reputation as an accurate mathematician depends largely on the occurrences of this night. I have placed myself on record in the most unequivocal terms as to the course this comet will follow. All other leading astronomers are also on record. To-night the test will be applied. I must also confess to you that there are pessimists, even in this forty-ninth century, who do not take the brightest views of to-morrow, but who, on the contrary, boldly prophesy that there will be no to-morrow. For this reason, I have preferred to have all my family with me here to-night, and have declined to be present with my scientific co-workers at the Meridian Peak Observatory, where, as you saw, the most elaborate preparations have been made for observing and recording every phenomenon of to-night. My telescope on the terrace, which you will see presently, is a comparatively small one; but I prefer to have my family about me in case — in case — But let us now give our whole attention for a few moments to the general structure of our government.

"In the first place, please understand that the government of the continent of North America is merely an integral part of the great structure which composes the world's government, just as one of your States was of the United States of Washington. All are based on precisely the same laws and principles; all are based on truth, which includes honesty, simplicity, and efficiency. In our law-courts, for instance, we no longer have to trust our interests to more or less accidental verdicts of irresponsible juries; we no longer blush at the special pleading of counsel and the desperate efforts of men of eminent ability profaning their position to defeat the ends of justice by their arts of persuasion. We no longer listen to impassioned appeals to the emotions in behalf of known criminals, — even criminals who have admitted their crimes, — or to the badgering and browbeating and character-blackening of innocent witnesses. You will easily understand that much has been accomplished since your day, when I tell you that we now have no lawyers, no pleadings, no juries, no appeals, no exceptions taken, no pardons, and no favors on account of wealth or social position. Justice to-day is indeed blind, as you used to portray her."

"But how, then, are your laws administered? —for you certainly must have laws, and very elaborate ones, that need frequent exposition."

"I will give you an example, to illustrate the mode of procedure in a civil suit. John Doe charges Richard Roe with conspiracy in a certain business transaction, by which, it is alleged, said Doe has been defrauded. He goes to the Board of Examiners, which consists of three, five, or seven men, according to the importance of the case. These examiners summon the parties in dispute, listen to the statements of both, take evidence, and very carefully gather all facts in the case, which are committed to phonograph — to three phonographs — and distributed to three independent boards of judges for decision. The names of the contestants are not known to the judges, and the latter are usually far removed from the locality of the interested parties.

"When the decisions of the three boards are returned to the proper office, the three packets are opened in the presence of the contestants, and two out of three concurring decide the case beyond appeal, unless new facts afterward come to light. The examiners have the power to dismiss trivial complaints as unworthy of notice, and they also perform a valuable service in correcting errors in preliminary papers, and oftentimes as arbitrators in effecting compromises between those who would otherwise invoke the court. Unlike the old-time lawyers, they are in truth legal advisers; and they have no temptation to pervert the law or to delay it for their own emolument. All examiners and judges are educated for the offices they hold, and have been selected from students in the universities by reason of their special fitness, both as to abilities and temperament, to do justice to their lofty calling. The priests of old were not more venerated than these men; and, indeed, their position and its duties are not dissimilar from those of priests, excepting that the code they give instruction from is human.

"You will notice that, by the mode of procedure I have described, no outside influence of any kind can reach the real tribunal, as all contestants are designated by names applied according to a regular formula, which is simply an amplification of the John Doe and Richard Roe that have figured in law for so many centuries. In obscure cases, new evidence may be demanded by the judges, or the parties may have leave to withdraw the suit; but if John Doe has a decision in his favor, then Richard Roe must make restitution in full and pay costs of trial. The costs, however, are very small, as all officers are paid by the Government, and the testimony is caught direct by the phonograph, instead of being laboriously taken down by stenography, and then copied by hand or the printing-press. With a few slight variations, this same system is used for all kinds of cases that are brought before the Department of Justice."

"Small pickings here," said Paul, "for members of the bar. Sergeant Buzzfuzz would hardly find scope for plying his vocation, and his moving appeals would sound sadly out of place."

"The laws themselves," continued the Professor, "are as simple as their administration. No new ones have been enacted for several centuries past, but those pronounced just by the most learned judges were long ago codified, and the code now in use throughout the world may be called the 'Code of Common Sense, founded on Truth.' Moreover, the penalties for criminal acts are sure to fall upon the offender, if convicted. They are sometimes severe, but they are felt to be proper and necessary, and they can never be set aside at the caprice of any one claiming powers superior to those of the judges. They are so clearly determined and executed on a basis of justice that they are even respected by those who suffer them."

"But," exclaimed Paul excitedly, "if you make no new laws, you have no law-makers, and no need of them; and if no law-makers, then no legislative bodies; and if no legislatures, then no elections, no voting, no parties, no politics, no politicians!"

"Your deductions are correct," said the Professor, smiling; "and you may extend your list of defunct officials by adding generals, admirals, custom-house inspectors, kings, emperors, or even presidents; for, in the ancient sense, there are now no well-defined boundaries for official domain other than municipal."

CHAPTER XXIX.

The Government of Settled Forms.

At this point, Madam entered the room, and with her own hands served the gentlemen with coffee. "The whole world is in the open air," she said. "Will you join us soon on the porch?"

"Very soon, dear," answered the Professor, as she retired.

"You do not add," said Paul, "that you no longer have any governments, although I almost expected to hear you append that to your list of outlived institutions. Please tell me, have you a government or not?"

The Professor smiled, and then, after a short pause that lent emphasis to what followed, he added seriously: "Yes, Mr. Prognosis, we indeed have a government — the simplest, the strongest, the most effective, the most enduring government that the world has thus far known, which has been slowly evolved out of the needs of the people. Yet if you should seek for its head, in the person of a single man, you would find none, for there is none. This is a government of established forms. These forms time has fixed inflexibly in the minds and consciences of the people. All the methods of administration have been carefully considered, and gradually shorn of objectionable features; and, so far as human wisdom can provide, they are the best possible forms suitable to existing circumstances. To distinguish it from all predecessors, this is called 'The Government of Settled Forms.'"

"I begin to understand," said Paul: "the fittest survive, in the forms of law and common usage, as well as with plants and animals. But what a vast army of civilians you must have disbanded in the process — greater, perhaps, than in case of the armies and navies. What, in the name of gentility, is left for the poor fellows who have no money, and who really need a comfortable position, with a good fat salary, and little or nothing to do? Something of this kind was a prime necessity in my time. I recall armies of blind tinkers who infested our state capitals and even our national capital — blind as bats to demands of public service, but sharp enough in self-seeking; everlastingly tinkering the laws, repealing the good, enacting the bad; forever puncturing the good old Government kettle for the express purpose of patching it with baser metal. Think, too, of oratory, — how that must have suffered! No more occasion for those splendid pleas of the lawyers who sometimes chained the wrapt attention of the court for weeks at a time, in their attempts to so misrepresent or misinterpret law and justice that neither should by any chance be recognizable by equity. Think, too, of the buncombe speeches delivered in Congress, which so amused the nation by manner that their utter lack of matter was forgiven; and the eloquent stump speeches of the politicians, so filled with sparkling wit and spicy stories that they often succeeded in disguising the painful fact that the utterer of such views deserved horsewhipping rather than applause. It is sad — very sad!" he concluded reflectively, but with an expression of great satisfaction.

The Professor regarded Paul with an amused twinkle in his eyes: "Yes, it is true that many former occupations are gone; but some are still left — enough to occupy all the time and thought of our best thinkers and workers. I assure you there is no lack of work in these days. The only difference now is, that we all lend a hand in doing the necessary work, and we actually accomplish what we undertake, instead of playing with it. The public service still has its coveted positions to offer, but they are no sinecures. They are only reached through the highway of a long course of preparatory experience; and they are only held by those who give ample and constant evidence that they are capable of filling them and are faithful to their responsibilities. Arbitrary appointment or dismissal at the caprice of a person totally unacquainted with the official involved or with the duties of his office, as we read was common in your day, we should consider a gross insult to the common sense of the people, as well as an infringement of the simplest rules of government. Our representatives are what the name implies: they simply represent the best talent that is available for the office, — talent that has been specially chosen, cultivated, and trained for the purpose of adapting it to the duties of that particular office. Public service is now a career of the highest honor, and every public servant glories in the inscription of his badge of office, which bears the words: 'I serve.' Positions of responsibility are no longer subject to the accidents of a capricious popular vote, which, as I study the records, seldom stumbled upon firm ground until it had so woefully wandered into the bog that it must turn back or be engulfed. Please understand that, in this scientific age, we leave just as little as possible to accident, or to the individual judgment of any human being.

We arm him with proper authority, when he has proved himself worthy of it, but we also arm him with ample knowledge of his duties and the prestige of settled and recognized forms, which are in reality merely the crystallized experience of the past. The Government of Settled Forms is very simple, and needs no tinkering. It is universal, having been accepted by all nations. It knows nothing of the uncertainties of law-making, and I am glad to tell you that it knows very little of law-breaking, for law-breaking is no longer amusing or profitable — no longer honorable."

"But neither was it in the nineteenth century."

"Are you sure of that? If so, then your public journals must have sadly misrepresented the condition of things. They ring the changes up and down the full gamut of possible law-breaking, and they seem to prove conclusively that your rich men and your men high in office usually attained their positions through paths more or less crooked, and consequently more or less opposed to law, which means rectitude."

"That is only too true. And yet, Professor, the Government of the United States was the best in the world."

"That also was true, and it was true even in your time. But it had one serious defect.

It was well adapted to a small, homogeneous, educated, and law-abiding community, where the majority could be depended upon to represent intelligence and virtue. Mere majorities, mere numerical strength, — this means nothing, of itself. It may mean the voice of vice, or, what is nearly as bad, indifference or ignorance. Such it finally came to mean, when the prosperity of your country invited to its open doors the adventurers and outcasts of the rest of the world, who, with their countless languages, conflicting customs and religions, and minds wholly untrained to the duties and responsibilities of their new position, produced the most medley and rabble population that any government ever attempted to control. And the reins of government were placed in the hands of these debased majorities. My dear Mr. Prognosis, the experiment was as futile as it was philanthropic, and results so proved it. The time came when the sacred freedom of the ballot had to be protected by more and more stringent laws, until the balance of power could be assured to the saving minority who knew right from wrong and liberty from license. The noble principles of its founders were established on truth, and they have consequently outlived all buffets of fortune, and are engrafted more or less on our present system; but they required the exercise of wisdom in their application. The history of your early government is very instructive, and the world has profited by it in many ways; but it is a remarkable fact that the most highly commended provisions of your first successful experiment in constitutional government should have proved its weak points in practice, permitting those who had been brutalized by want and tyranny in other countries to turn its dignity to derision. As we now look back, it seems probable that only Costor, with his gospel of truth, prevented its disruption and downfall in his day.

"But all difficulties of the past, so far as government is concerned, are now happily ended, and rendered impossible hereafter by the simple operation of the Government of Settled Forms. There can be no general disturbance of the public in these days, for the simple reason that education of an advanced type is now universal, all men and women are usefully employed, and there is no school of poverty or vice for developing a discontented class. Moreover, the population has again become homogeneous, with common customs, needs, language, religion, aims, ambitions. If we were called upon now to trust the decision of momentous questions to the nod of majorities, we could safely do so; but there is no longer any such need. The initial questions have been determined in the stormy past. We are now enjoying the results, and peacefully developing details.

"I have explained the workings of the Department of Justice. The other elements of our government may be classed as the departments of Education, Public Health, Agriculture, Meteorology, and Public Works. These are general in character, and the sub-departments are local in their operation, but under the direction of Division Councils, who in turn are guided by the decisions of the Grand Council of the World.

"The duties of the Department of Education are obvious, and need no explanation. That of Public Health has absolute control of everything pertaining to the sanitary condition of the people, such as the purification of rivers, water supply, disposition of refuse and its useful employment, and the location and character of all places of habitation.

"The Department of Agriculture determines the amount of seed to be sown each year, and the number of animals to be raised, to meet the requirements of the world. This department maintains the food conservatories of which I have already spoken, which are always amply supplied with a surplus, to compensate for short crops. In short, its duty is to see that the world has plenty to eat.

"The Department of Meteorology determines the proportion of forest growth to tillage land, and indicates to the Department of Public Works means of improving the climate, and, to some extent, of equalizing the rainfall. You are probably not aware of the fact, but we are now able, by electrical disturbance on a large scale, to artificially produce a local shower; and there is good reason to suppose that we may some time learn how to control supplies of moisture in the upper strata of the atmosphere with almost the same assurance that we now look to the depths of the earth, through driven tubes, for all supplies of water used for domestic purposes. You will readily understand that, with our present population, our rivers and lakes, even under the most stringent precautions, could not safely be depended upon to fill this need. Even in your day a considerable number of prevailing diseases were unquestionably due to the use of impure water. Your scientists understood this, but your public servants apparently made little use of the knowledge. Men of the very highest attainments are now engaged in this department of the public service; and their work, which is comprehensive, has already produced results of the greatest importance to our physical well-being."

CHAPTER XXX.

Money.

MARCO now entered, and introduced a sudden turn in the current of conversation by announcing that Tom Glide had been heard from, and that he was now living in the metropolis of Volvec, on the Amazon.

"I was obliged to wait," said Marco, "until he finished his dinner; but he is now at leisure, and says he is anticipating great pleasure in renewing acquaintance with an old school-friend. The circuit is open, and you will find all prepared. Mr. Glide presents his compliments, and he is now ready to see you and to be seen."

Paul heard these last words with open-mouthed wonder, but, without speaking, followed the Professor into a small room adjoining the library. The latter advanced to a box, open at one end; and, after so adjusting the electric light as to bear strongly on his own face, he began to talk into the box. Meanwhile, Marco directed Paul to look over the Professor's shoulder; and he then saw, on a glass screen, the image of a man's face, just as it appears in a photographer's camera. It was Mr. Glide, down in South America. Paul distinctly saw Mr. Glide's eager smile of greeting, heard him speak, and then listened as the two friends talked over old times. He also heard Mr. Glide ask the name of the gentleman who was looking over the other's shoulder; at which remark, not knowing what else to do, Paul nodded to the pictured face, and received a similar greeting in return.

"Why! that looks wonderfully like my sister's husband, Paul Prognosis," exclaimed the face in the box.

Both Paul and the Professor gave responsive exclamations of astonishment, and Marco stumbled over Smudge in his eagerness to reach the instrument to hear more. Before there was an opportunity to demand explanation, a confused murmur of voices was heard, and a sharp "Be quiet!" followed by the words, "Please come here a moment, Dr. Clarkson. I want to have the pleasure of making you acquainted with my old friend, Professor Prosper, and also with a friend of his — Excuse me, I do not know his name."

Then came another interruption, followed by an abrupt "Beg pardon, but I find I'll have to cut short this pleasure, in order to join my family and be in time for the comet display. Of course you are also interested in that above all things, just now. Philip, I shall ring you up again in a day or two. Do the same by me, — soon and often. Good-night, old boy!"

"But Tom, — just a moment!" cried the Professor.

"Just a moment, Mr. Glide!" echoed Paul still more excitedly.

But it was too late. The circuit had already been broken, leaving Mr. Glide in South America, and the new mystery unsolved.

"Very strange!" said Paul. "How is that to be explained?"

"I'm quite in the dark," answered the Professor. "I look to you for a solution."

"But I was never less capable of solving anything, excepting, perhaps, this most marvelous of all instruments, that has so weirdly presented to my eyes ghosts of the past in which I once lived. I believe your friend Glide to be my brother-in-law, and I know his friend Dr. Clarkson perfectly well. Why, I spent the evening with the doctor not a week ago."

"Three thousand years and a week, perhaps."

"Perhaps. I confess I am a little dazed, and hardly know what to think."

"We had better, then, adjourn our talk about government until to-morrow evening, — that is, in case we are still spared to be here."

"In case we are not, there is one point I would first like to have explained, Professor. I have now been with you two days, and have neither seen nor heard a word about money. Have you happily learned to dispense with the 'root of all evil'?"

"No. That was dreamt of by the theorists, but never realized. We find it a necessity as a ready means of exchange."

"But why is it that I have no visible evidence of its existence?"

"Simply because, in your excursions with Marco and myself, no demand has happened to arise requiring the use of exchange. When we call a thing public, we mean that it is the property of the Government — that is, of the people; and it is consequently free. The public conveyances we have used are all free. The dinner we took at the restaurant is the only exception I now recall; that will be charged to my account, and settled at the end of the month."

"Settled with what?"

"With money."

"And what kind of money?"

"Paper money, very similar to that you were accustomed to use."

"Government paper?"

"Exactly."

"Based on gold as a standard?"

"No! Just there we have made an important change. Experience showed that no one article, however rare or precious, could be depended upon as an unvarying standard of value. In centuries closely following your own, the scanty fresh supplies of gold were quite out of proportion to the increase of population; and, as a consequence, the purchasing power of the actual metal far exceeded that of preceding generations. Then, again, in the later Volcanic Period, when the whole orb was convulsed and the Continent of Atlantis was restored to us, fresh deposits of the metal were disclosed, so abundant that for a time it lost its distinction as a so-called 'precious metal,' and came into common use even for household purposes. That settled its pretensions, and a new and more stable standard of valuation was necessarily sought. The search was a long one, and accompanied by many disastrous experiments; but the result finally attained has proved entirely satisfactory. One of the first important acts of the Congress of Nations was the adoption of a new and universal unit of valuation, based upon the world's surplus of food products, as accurately reported each decade, proportionate to the world's population at the same date. The result of the computation sometimes shows a slight variation; but this is trifling, as reduction from any cause in one item or in any one section of the globe is nearly always counterbalanced by increase in others. Moreover, the ten years' period for which each standard is fixed is sufficiently long to allow the conditions to become known to the public and to be fully discounted; and there is consequently no possible danger of sudden revulsions in valuation. Do you understand? Government certificates, based on such surplus food products and guaranteed by them, are the current medium of exchange throughout the world; and each such certificate yields quarterly interest to the holder. This is intended to encourage the habit of saving, which is no longer liable to unhealthy development, inasmuch as money has now been shorn of most of the powers and privileges that once made it a despot."

"You no longer, then, have rich men?"

"Oh, yes; but we no longer regard them with envy. On the contrary, they command not only our respect, but our sympathy. They have a right, during lifetime, to all they can lawfully accumulate, though that is little compared with what was possible in former times."

"Why so, when present resources are so much greater?"

"For many reasons, but principally because

the establishment of a medium of exchange having an absolutely fixed purchasing power dealt a deathblow to speculation. Any attempt to artificially raise or lower values would now be vain; and it is only under circumstances where values are variable that any one man, or clique of men, can secure the millions that made wealth in your day a burlesque and a byword. Your attitude toward millionaires seems to us now rather amusing than otherwise. You scolded, but took no measures to prevent. You condemned what your laws and customs clearly permitted, but allowed the laws and customs to remain. You suggested more than you probably had in mind when you used to speak of the 'wheel of fortune.' Every man of you helped to twirl that wheel, and, with every struggle by which you vaguely sought to remedy industrial evils, you only made values all the more fluctuating, and thus gave new impetus to the wheel and new opportunities to your speculators. With the establishment of our Government of Settled Forms came also settled values; and the speculator, and consequently the millionaire, is now merely a picturesque memory of the remote past. By the same means, we also abolished the great army of bankrupts and men and women without means of support, which the 'wheel of fortune' — mainly by accident of sudden variations in value — whirled helplessly, hopelessly, to dependence and wretchedness. Incomes are less unequal now, and all are richer, and better, and more hopeful in consequence."

"You say that your rich men have a right to their wealth during life. What then?"

"The bulk of it returns to the people."

"But how about their relations and friends?"

"They can be provided for during the life of the rich man by the gift of Government annuities, based on a principle derived from your life insurance companies, whose vast interests and responsibilities finally passed, by an inevitable course of events, into the hands of the Government."

"Has your Government, then, become an insurance institution?"

"Yes; and why should n't it? As the people's representative, it is the people's banker and the people's backer. It alone is competent to insure beyond all peradventure; and we take no chances nowadays that are avoidable, especially in matters of such vital importance as this to public as well as private welfare. Government annuities form an essential element of modern life. By a process of development that now seems simple enough, but which was the slow growth of several generations, such annuities revolutionized the system of investment. You will understand that, during the process of absorption by the Government of all monopolies seeking control of staple and needful products, the opportunities for industrial investment gradually decreased, while the means of the general public as steadily increased. Government insurance, in the form of life annuities, gradually took the place of these. By judicious management, under the supervision of several of the world's ablest financiers, these annuities were reduced to a system perfect in every detail. They were made convenient and sure as an investment; and they naturally became popular. Indeed, they became so popular that public demand made them almost indispensable to the position of citizenship. Although there is no law to this effect, it is not customary for any man or woman to become a citizen until thus secured against future dependence. It is also customary, before marriage, for both the man and the prospective wife to be thus provided for; and every child, before it receives the usual birth certificate, is supposed to have at least the minimum annuity that guarantees freedom from physical want. Thus, you see, it is considered incumbent on every person to be protected against future dependence; and the requirement is so clearly for the best interests of individuals, as well as for society in general, that it has willing support from poor as well as rich, and is one of the chief civilizing agents of modern life."

"How does this affect the rich man?"

"As our laws and customs allow him to hoard comparatively little of his wealth, annuities have also become his favorite form of investment, and many an employer has been led to grant annuities to hundreds of his employees."

"In preference to great public benefactions after death?"

"Yes, because real public needs are no longer left to the accident of individual benefactors, but are promptly provided for out of the public funds. Nowadays, the local Government establishes a library or hospital just as it would a bridge — because it is needed; and we are not subjected to the uncertainties of waiting upon the caprice of individuals in the form of post-mortem benefactions."

"What proportion of your people are thus provided for?"

"Nearly all. The annuity system means independence and a certain freedom of action, without which citizenship would be open to many temptations and perversions. It is just at this point that a gulf divides the forty-ninth from the nineteenth century, not only in sentiment but in fact: no citizen in these days is absolutely dependent upon any other person so far as the necessities of life are concerned. The first ambition in life, for woman as well as man, is independent citizenship; and both law and custom encourage this ambition, and afford every practicable means for its accomplishment. What one of your workmen spent for beer and tobacco would now suffice in a few years to assure him a competency. To be poor without good excuse, and consequently to be dependent, is now to be in disrepute."

"Bless me! that sounds unjust."

"But I assure you it is not. Public opinion, educated to its present standard, is never unjust. It does not demand the impossible of its citizens. It simply lends its aid to make things possible that were not so in your day; and then very properly frowns upon those who fail to use the opportunities it affords."

"But I cannot help thinking that you must have lost a certain element of progress in thus making each man independent of all other men."

"Why? We simply make him a free man, as he formerly claimed to be, but was not. We now know what liberty — liberty of action — really means. We discover that it means true manhood and womanhood. It means happiness unclouded by care or fear. It means free and full development of one's best abilities. It means the banishment of an army of evils that previously blocked the progress of civilization: starvation, penury, theft, prostitution, compulsory marriage, child-labor, and a multitude of others that will readily occur to you, which too often had their rise in immediate want, or fear of it in the future, on the part of self or those dependent."

"Your report is so pleasing," said Paul, "that it blinds my judgment; but I still cannot help thinking that such independence must mean annihilation of ambition in a large class. 'In the sweat of thy brow shalt thou eat bread' was in my day a truth that did not need the authority of Holy Writ. We used to be taught and to believe that, except for the struggle for life and the ambitions that maintained that struggle, life would hardly be worth living."

"That was one of those half-truths that are worse than falsehoods, because more difficult to disprove. All I can say is that time and experience have utterly refuted its conclusions. We no longer have cause to struggle for the bare necessities of life; but, for that very reason, our ambitions of youth, our highest and best ambitions, — now no longer liable to be strangled by petty cares of mere animal existence, — are given an opportunity for realization to a degree of which the nineteenth century had no conception. You have already looked about you with searching eyes. What are the tokens you have observed? Have you not seen evidences of exalted ambition everywhere apparent?"

Paul was about to answer with great decision, when Madam entered the room, exclaiming: "Come, come at once! I believe it is already in sight."

The Professor arose precipitately. "Impossible!" He glanced at his watch. "Perfectly impossible, my dear!"

"Come and see for yourself." And she put an arm about him, and drew the trembling man to the terrace, Paul closely following. One glance, and the Professor sank into a chair, saying: "My reputation is undone! I can no longer answer for consequences. That is the position and this is the very instant prophesied by Professor Pessim, and he has already settled up his earthly affairs. Well, let us use our eyes and our understandings to the last." He drew his wife's face to his, while Paul discreetly left the aged couple, and proceeded to the group of young people surrounding the telescope.

CHAPTER XXXI.

The Passage of the Comet.

THE scene that met Paul's gaze, as he leaned on the railing at the edge of the terrace, was of indescribable brilliancy. As Madam had said, the whole world was in the open air. Streets and sidewalks were filled with slowly moving processions of people; dwellings, shops, and places of amusement showed their doors and windows filled with eager throngs; and most striking of all were the house terraces, decorated with colored lanterns, where, amid bowers of rhododendrons and other evergreen plants, were gathered households and their friends, some sipping tea or creams, but nearly all now engaged with their opera-glasses, scanning the luminous stranger that was just coming into view on the eastern horizon.

Utter silence characterized the scene, which might otherwise have been one of ordinary merry-making. No music was heard; and those who spoke, did so in whispers. There was a solemnity abroad that Paul could only liken to that which he once experienced in early manhood, during a visit to a foreign cathedral, when the host was elevated, and a sonorous bell sounded what seemed a call to judgment. He felt, as he did then, like bowing himself to the ground before some unseen but majestic presence. He looked about him to see what others were doing. They appeared almost as quiescent as they were silent. He was oppressed by a sudden sensation as if they were ghosts, or as if he were a ghost in the midst of an assembly of men and women, between whom and himself existed a barrier of cloud through which he could only hopelessly grope, and find naught that was palpable. He pressed his hands to his temples as if in pain, — but he felt no pain. Then he heard, distinctly but distantly, a familiar voice which said: "A few moments, and all will be done. Have no fear!"

Then for the first time there fell upon him a sensation of abject terror. He rose hastily from the lounge where he found he had thrown himself; and a hand grasped his, while the speaker took his place on the lounge and drew him to a seat beside him. Paul looked up in alarm. It was the face of Professor Prosper that met his gaze — or was this Dr. Clarkson? — how like Dr. Clarkson! — and the first words that followed were a repetition of those he had just heard:

"Have no fear!" but somehow they had a different intonation. If it was the Professor who spoke now, it could not have been he who spoke before. Yet it must have been, — it must have been! And the same voice that last spoke now spoke again, saying: "This comet has been seen and studied once before during the historical period. That was in the century following yours, and in the year preceding the first appearance in public of John Costor. Like him, it came unheralded. The multitude, who are always liable to associate contemporaneous events as cause and effect, were wont afterward to look upon it as his herald, and they consequently gave it his name. Perhaps there may have been an element of cause and effect which the multitude never understood. So portentous a spectacle subdued the public mind to a point of unusual humility. Some foretold that it meant the approaching end of the world. The natural result of such a conviction was a deepened sense of the fleeting character of the present life and the all-importance of that which was to come. When this expectation failed of realization, it was then prophesied that the heavenly visitor probably augured the coming of a prophet. The need of a prophet was felt; and in response to that need he came, in the person of John Costor, who was the embodied presence of the world's dream and yearning at that period."

"Please tell me something, Professor, of the appearance of the comet as it then passed the earth."

"There is little to tell. It was one of those things that could not be told. But its appearance as it approached was admirably photographed in countless numbers of views, some of which you can see in my library. Recall the largest and brightest comet that appeared in your time. This one was many thousand times greater than any before recorded. It had been observed for many months in the far distance, gradually approaching our system. Interest in its movements increased day by day, and it finally became the all-absorbing topic. As it drew nearer, it rapidly developed a nucleus of extraordinary magnitude and brilliancy, from which spread away in divergent streams its enormous train, spanning the entire vault of heaven like a bow, and casting a shadow quite equal to that of the full moon. Its path nearly coincided with the plane of the ecliptic, but, unlike the planets, it moved from east to west. This great body, with its deep enveloping mass of hydrogen, as shown by the spectroscope, moved in a flat parabola almost directly toward the sun, foretokening a short perihelion distance, if not actual collision with the source of light. Some apprehension was then felt by astronomers that, on its return, it might pass in dangerous proximity to our orb; but as the actual distance at perihelion could not be known until after the passage, the width of parabola would be less as the comet passed nearer to the sun, or greater as it made a longer turn. Thus, although nearly in the plane of our orbit, it might not come nearer to us on its return than on its approach to the hot bath in the sun's atmosphere."

"And what in fact happened?"

"As it became lost in the rays of the sun, all eyes were watching for its reappearance on the western limb; but nothing could be seen. Weeks passed, but no comet! It was evident that one of two things must have happened: either the great body had plunged headlong into the sun, or it was in process of flight so directly in a straight line from the sun to the earth as to be totally obscured by the sun's rays. Opinions were divided. If the latter supposition were true, the time of its nearest approach to the earth had been calculated from its known velocity; and the majority of the best mathematicians were of the opinion that its second advent could only mean the world's destruction. Under these circumstances, it was natural that the world's inhabitants should be oppressed by a grievous doubt, and stirred by the strongest possible incentive to religious fervor. Expectations were not wholly disappointed. It did reappear, and in a position very nearly in a direct line from the sun, but the divergence was sufficient to prevent the catastrophe feared. The rush of its dreadful presence as it fled past our affrighted globe was by far the most appalling spectacle that humanity ever had an opportunity to look upon. As a matter of fact, no eyes actually looked upon it as it passed, — it was more blinding than the sun."

"Is it expected that to-night's visitation will resemble that which you have just described?"

"Yes, in most features; but it will be all the more brilliant for the reason that it comes at night. Its course is not precisely the same, and it will probably not approach as near; but it is just at this point that authorities differ; and, as I have told you, its appearance at this hour puts to confusion the theories I have occupied years in developing. At present, I have no more idea what to expect than you have, but it is only fair to you to confess that the course and time-table it is now following point to the correctness of my opponents' theories, who have prophesied the worst. The God who made us now holds us in his hand!"

With this ejaculation, the Professor returned to his wife's side, and his children gathered closely around him. Paul remained alone, till

Smudge crept to his side, trembling violently. He felt a sudden chill. There was no further need of examining the approaching visitor through the telescope, which now stood idle, casting its dark line like a bar sinister across the sky. Dimmer and dimmer grew the lights in the streets and along the terraces, until they — and with them, all the people — paled into complete obscurity. Brighter and brighter grew the heavens, and nearer and nearer swept the glowing fire-sphere, till it became a sun — till its heat grew scorching — till the world's enveloping atmosphere burst into a crackling sheet of flame — till all things crashed about the trembling spectator — till all was blackness — till, till —

PART VI.

CONCLUSION.

CHAPTER XXXII.

A Ray of Moonlight.

THE very chamber, with the eye of its night-lamp shaded, yet alert, had a look of expectancy about it. It was in the small hours of the night. Now and then a white face peered between the curtains of the doorway. From the bed came the sound of regular breathing, then a sigh, a gentle movement; and the one who lay there awoke by slow degrees, and looked vaguely about him. At last his eyes fell on a square of moonlight that lit with pale flame the otherwise obscure pattern of the carpet. His attention became gradually fixed upon it.

"Why, what does that mean?" he murmured. "To-morrow is Christmas, and the moon fulled on the first day of the month. She is now in the middle of her last quarter, and ought not to be in the southwest until to-morrow."

Apparently the thought came to him that he might be dreaming; and, as if to still the doubt, he turned in the bed and whispered: "Mary, are you asleep?"

The curtains closing the adjoining room were quickly parted, and the pale face of the watcher drew near to his. "What is it, Paul?" The voice trembled with excitement, as well it might, for ten years had passed since he last called her by name.

"Mary, what is the meaning of that moonlight on the carpet?"

"Oh, I see, — the curtain is raised." And she walked to the window with the evident purpose of drawing the shade.

"No, no; that is not what I mean. Is n't to-morrow Christmas?"

"Yes."

"And did n't the moon full on the first? And, if so, how can it be shining from the southwest at this time of night? That 's what puzzles me."

"Paul, you know much more about such things than I do. But don't try to study it out to-night. Wait till morning, dear."

He closed his eyes, and said with a voice as if from afar: "Oh, I understand, Professor; they are the rays from the comet."

He became restless, and made several requests which Mary was unable to comprehend.

"Where is Smudge?" he asked abruptly.

The dog was called, and took his accustomed place on the bearskin rug that lay by the bedside; and Paul rested a hand on the shaggy neck.

"Smudge must be tired. I am. I only wish I could be sure whether that is the light of the moon or of the comet."

"To-morrow we will ask Dr. Clarkson about it," said Mary soothingly; and she stroked his forehead with her soft, cool hand until his measured breathing told that he was once more asleep. Then she slipped to her knees, raining tears upon his hand; and her whole heart went out in a fervent prayer that the moonlight, which had clearly penetrated into the long darkened chambers of his mind, might soon give place to the illumination of full day.

What a long mental sleep that had been from which this husband now seemed to be awakening — and oh, how sorrowful beyond human speech to the waiting wife! As she recognized that the happiest prophecies of the doctors seemed now about to be realized, she became filled with a growing excitement and joy that made action necessary, and for some minutes she paced rapidly up and down the hallway, with hands clenched — with tears streaming. Then she returned, and sat by his bedside until daybreak, stroking his forehead whenever he showed signs of restlessness, and reviewing again and again the events of the momentous ten years that were passed.

So much had happened, — so much that was disheartening, so little that was pleasant to recall! In the darkness of the nightwatch, the sad scenes presented themselves earliest and oftenest. She dwelt upon every incident of that far-away Christmas night when the accident happened, until it seemed like yesterday. Then, more or less connectedly, she followed the subsequent course of events.

She remembered how financial troubles had gradually compassed her about, till sympathizing Dr. Clarkson had lent a hand, and, among the invalid's papers, discovered certain patents which he pronounced worth a fortune to any one who had the skill and the means to develop them.

She remembered how Will Clarkson, the doctor's son, had then made one of those patent-papers the nucleus of his first law case; and how the suit against a railway company had dragged through the courts until on the point of failure from lack of further funds, when her brother Tom, from Brazil, had appeared on the scene, so tanned, bearded, and rotund that she scarcely recognized him as the slender youth who had kissed her good-by fifteen years before; but his brotherly love was past all mistaking. What a providence his return had proved! Backed by the ample capital and resolute business qualities that he and his partner, Tom Hamlin, had been able to lend to the undertaking, that initial lawsuit had been speedily pushed to a successful termination, carrying a hundred others in its wake; and wealth beyond her wildest hopes had wrought a change in her fortunes.

She remembered with special pleasure how she had lived over her own happy girlhood as she watched the courtship between her daughter and Will Clarkson. And now, joy of joys! if the promise of this night was not disappointed, Paul would be able to be an interested spectator at the approaching nuptials.

And gladdest of all, she recalled every incident of the recent Thanksgiving-Day gathering, when hope, though very faint at first, had reëntered her widowed heart. For the first time in many years, she had then converted her home into a house of merry-making. There were that day gathered at Paul's dinner-table all the friends who had contributed to the present fortunes of his family: Brother Tom and his wife and children, Mr. Hamlin and his family, Dr. Clarkson and Will. Paul was also present, and Mary could not help thinking that he also felt the genial influences of the cheerful company, though he never smiled or said a word. Shortly after the meal, Will had strolled into the library, where Paul lay upon the lounge, taking his usual after-dinner nap. He noticed that the sun poured full upon the head of the sleeping man, from which fever had recently stripped every vestige of hair, and he was about to shut out the sunlight, when his attention was attracted by an appearance of a deviation of the median line and a slight general depression on one side of it, which the sense of touch could scarcely be expected to detect, but which the strong sunlight, striking it at an angle, now threw into prominence. Will's powers of observation were naturally acute, and a single glance suggested a swift train of thought that was not unnatural to one who had been brought up in the constant companionship of a skilled physician.

"What a magnificent head he has! From that treasure-house have already proceeded mechanical wonders that lend might to the world's arm; and others no doubt still sleep there, only awaiting the wand of some magician. Father was never able to discover that the brain was injured, but is it not possible that suspension of mental activity might result from the apparently slight cause to which the sun now points the finger?"

He called his father to the room. A careful inspection that Dr. Clarkson then made resulted in his promptly calling a consultation of experts, and in the medical operation that had just now occurred. Would it be successful? This was the question in which the watcher by the bedside was now interested to a degree that almost paralyzed her power of thought. The incident of his awakening this night in what appeared full possession of his faculties was certainly a cheering harbinger. If its promise should hold true, what a change was in store for her! Life had shown to Mary Prognosis many glimpses of sunshine, but now — now all clouds seemed about to leave her sky. She had to restrain herself to keep from waking the sleeper and demanding of him: "Paul, Paul! tell me, — have you come back to me? — and have you come back to stay?" She did not again leave his bedside. She sat there, with his hand in hers, until the moonlight paled, the morning twilight began to cast aside its torpor of chill silence, and the red daybreak flashed into the room.

CHAPTER XXXIII.

Sunlight, and " Good-Morning!"

CHRISTMAS morning dawned crisp and bright. To Mary's ears came the distant jingle of sleigh-bells; and her weary eyes were greeted by a rosy glow that sparkled from the snowy roofs. Presently a church clock sounded. The bell gave the muffled note that told the presence of freshly fallen snow; but its summons evidently reached the senses of the sleeper, and he slowly awakened, raised himself up on an elbow, and said cheerfully: "Well, well! Good-morning! You 're up before me this time. A Merry Christmas to you, my dear!"

"The merriest of my life!" she said, as she bent down and kissed him.

"You deserve the merriest. And, by the way, I brought home for you yesterday a little present. You will find it in the cash-pocket of my blouse."

With a strange light in her eyes, Mary hastened to the store-room, flung open a camphor chest, and took from it the garment that had lain there unused all these years. In the pocket, as he had said, was a jeweler's box, wrapped in tissue paper and tied with a pink string. Returning to his bedside, she opened it in his presence, and with trembling fingers drew forth a ring set with a single diamond, that caught the glory of the morning and glittered like a star. With tear-dimmed eyes, she watched the look of intelligence and happiness with which Paul followed her every movement; then suddenly she lost control of her feelings, and knelt beside him without power to utter a word of thanks.

"Why," said Paul, "I really believe you are crying! Why should you?"

"For joy."

"You are so pleased with the ring?"

"Yes; but a thousand times more pleased because I now know that you are going to be well again."

"Have I been ill? Has anything been the matter with me? I do feel a little faint this morning, but I cannot think why. What is this bandage about my head? Have I been hurt?"

"You had a fall, you know."

"A fall? I seem to remember that there was some trouble last night, somewhere, about something. It was at the bridge. I begin to recall it now. Old Jake Cummings needed my help, and I tried to give it. Did I succeed? Is Jake all right now?"

"All right, my dear. But I don't think we had better talk any more now. Everything is all right. And your Christmas present is beautiful. I thank you, Paul."

When Dr. Clarkson entered the chamber an hour later, a single sweeping glance at the patient and the smiling watcher told him the story. He greeted Paul familiarly, felt his pulse, and merely recommended perfect quiet for a few days. "This is one of the cases, Mrs. Prognosis, where 'waiting will be the wisest speed.' He evidently thinks the accident happened last evening. The intervening ten years are a perfect blank to him. For the present, it is better that he should not be undeceived. Let the knowledge come gradually. Tell him nothing except in answer to direct questions. His eyes show clearly that his mind is unimpaired. The mental machinery is now again in running order, but it must be allowed to take up its tasks gradually."

In the evening, Paul asked to see his daughter, and in the dim light she came to his side.

"I am Patty. Do you remember me?"

"I remember a little girl who kissed me good-by when I left the house yesterday morning; but you, — why, you are Mary, just as she looked when she first came to this house as a bride, and made me the happiest man in Boston."

After this interview he seemed a little confused, and no one else was allowed to see him until New-Year's Day, when the doctor decided that he was strong enough to know more, and that fuller knowledge would assist rather than retard the working of his faculties. "You see," he explained to the family, "before Paul Prognosis takes up life again, there must necessarily be a long succession of shocks in his ideas, as he gradually adjusts these to the many altered conditions of life which he will discover. To reveal all at once would be enough to paralyze the faculties of a man in perfect health. We must let him slowly pick up for himself the scattered threads, only proffering information when we think it would assist him in arranging them."

One May morning the doctor entered, bearing a spray of apple blossoms, which, he noticed, seemed to strangely agitate his patient.

"Ah! that is the emblem of John Costor," said Paul.

"And who is John Costor?"

Paul looked abashed. "That belongs to my past." Then, taking the physician's hand in his, he suddenly added: "Doctor, I must tell some one, — let me tell you! I understand now that I have been ill for a long time, — for years; and that, during that time, I have lived in a dream-land. I seem now and then to flutter between that land and this. For instance, the sight of those apple blossoms, the sight of the diamond on my wife's finger — and like a flash I am transported to the dream city of Tone and to the civilization of John Costor."

"Tell me something about it," said the doctor kindly. And he allowed Paul to talk as long as he thought advisable.

"Prognosis," he then said, "some time I hope you will let me wander with you throughout your city of Tone. But now, it is best that you should think as little about it as you can. I will help you. You have now given me the key how to help you. I am going to confide to you some new things to think about." And he gave Paul a short sketch of some of the events that had happened in the world during the ten years' interim.

He carefully watched the effect of his announcements upon his attentive listener. There was no visible sign of any ill effect. They seemed rather to calm him.

The doctor continued: "And now, Prognosis, there is one further piece of news which I know will make you glad. As you have seen, your daughter Patty has grown meantime into a beautiful woman. I know a young man who has asked her to help him found a new home. That young man is my son Will. I want to ask you for Patty as a daughter-in-law. Have you any objections?"

"None; and I began to think, from the manner of the young people, that this was likely to come about."

"That shows progress. In a few days you will evidently be prepared to take a look at that electric engine of yours. Let me tell you now that your brother-in-law Glide and his partner, Hamlin, have got it going, and it's a world's wonder!"

"I knew it would be, and I had hopes that I should be able, some time, to open a factory for developing it. By the way, doctor, what are those great new works whose walls I see just across the square?"

"They constitute a city of Tone that your mind conceived, which has been wrought out in actual brick and mortar. Lean upon me, and come to the window. Can you read the sign that surmounts the roof?"

Under the influence of this skillful manner of introduction, Paul was able, without a tremor, to decipher the words, —

"PROGNOSIS ENGINE WORKS: 1876."

"You did n't imagine, did you," continued the doctor, "that we should wait all these years before getting your engine into running order? My dear Prognosis, we 've done some watching and waiting, but we 've done still more working. Now, all your friends ask is that you will rest a little while longer. It 's your turn to do some watching and waiting, so that you can do some working later on. You 'll find plenty to do, and you are going to be perfectly capable of doing it. For the present, don't ask too many questions — that 's the chief requisite. Is it a bargain?"

"It 's a bargain."

"And is it also agreed that Patty may be my daughter-in-law?"

"If the young people so elect."

"Oh, don't trouble yourself about that. I now give up my charge in favor of those who can better explain the particulars."

Mary came and took her seat beside him, while Patty and Will put their hands in his. Tears dimmed Paul's eyes so that he could not see their features distinctly, but he looked up with a smile and said very quietly: "My dear ones, this is indeed a glad day in the new year. May you in your lives realize every hope that is symbolized in this spray of apple blossoms and in the crystal button."

"The crystal button — what is that?" asked Patty.

"To explain that would be a long story. Some time I will tell it to you. Meanwhile, I want you and Will to each wear such a button for my sake. Later, I hope you will wear it for its own sake, — for what it means. Mother, please let me have two of those glass buttons which I saw in your work-basket the other day."

Before she handed them to him, she went to the bureau and unlocked a little jewel-case. "And here, Paul, is another such button, which you held in your hand when they brought you home to me after the accident. I think it must have slipped from old Jake's neck when you rescued him."

"Strange," said the doctor, "that a trifling incident like that could have exerted so powerful an influence over a brain that had apparently ceased all action! It seems that the death-clutch you gave that button, Prognosis, — probably the last fleeting impression you received before unconsciousness, — has never been relaxed in all these years."

"Will you wear one, too, doctor? — and you, Mary?"

When Mary's ready needle had attached each in its appropriate place, Paul added solemnly:

"I now ask you all to repeat with me these words. Are you ready?"

"We are ready, father."

"And I'm with you, Prognosis," added the doctor.

"'*I will try, from this moment henceforth, to be true and honest in my every act, word, and thought; and this crystal button I will wear while the spirit of truth abides with me.*'"

"In this same place of safe keeping," said Mary, "is the watch you wore that day. Will has had it put in order. Is n't this, Paul, a good opportunity to wind it and set it in motion?"

"Yes, dear. To-day, time begins for me once more. What is the hour?"

POSTSCRIPT.

I, Paul Prognosis, recently restored to health, have committed to paper, by dictation, the substance of the chapters that form this book. I have been led to do this partly in fulfillment of promises to my family, and partly in response to the oft-expressed wish of my friend, Dr. Clarkson, who has taken scientific interest in my occasional references to the world of fancy wherein I so long dwelt, and has earnestly requested that I furnish him with as full an account as possible of all my recollections, however vague and disconnected they may now appear.

He has particularly desired that I should endeavor to fix the duration of the period covered by these imaginings, and he has lent what assistance he could by suggesting correspondences with real events. Were these impressions conveyed to my mind by certain brief flashes, as in a dream or in the last semi-conscious moment of a drowning person, the remainder of my waking hours being passed in total mental oblivion? Or did I continue to be a part of these mind-pictures during the ten years of my mental aberration, leading a life among the scenes here described that had all the apparent reality of life in the material world? I am at a loss to determine this point. If the former were the case, the main dream would seem to have occurred soon after the accident and to have left a lasting impression, for the doctor tells me that nearly all my mutterings and answers to questions, from the very beginning of my illness, become perfectly coherent when applied to the conditions and surroundings indicated by this story of my inner life. On the other hand, I seem to recall the loss of my hair as among the earliest of my recollections, while, as a matter of fact, this occurred during the last half-year of my illness. After careful deliberation, I find myself unable to offer conclusive evidence on this point; and any one of my friends, acquainted with the incidents of my life, is as capable as I am of making a correct judgment.

One further fact, that has greatly interested Dr. Clarkson, may also appeal to the sympathies of those who have taken the trouble to hereby acquaint themselves with the dream city of Tone. Although I am now in perfect health, and happy in the active exercise of all my faculties, I have been accustomed, ever since my recovery, to spend all my sleeping hours in that same dream city, and among the same familiar scenes and faces, that I have here described. I consequently continue to lead two lives that are perfectly distinct; and in whichever city I find myself at the moment, whether Boston or Tone, that seems the real and the other the dream city. In spite of Dr. Clarkson's confident assurances to the contrary, I sometimes entertain a suspicion — it can hardly be called a fear, for it is not unpleasant — that the dual life I now lead may some day again melt into one, and that one the world of fancy. Mary always hastens to change the subject when I allude to it; but sometimes I cannot help whispering to myself that it may be a boon vouchsafed to me that, if entire mental rest should again become requisite, I may once more be permitted to spend some of my waking as well as sleeping hours amid the placid scenes of beauty and harmony that constitute Tone, the City of Truth, — my veritable heaven on earth. What then? Life has many experiences that are less to be desired; and what city of the after-life Death holds in his sacred keeping, I know not. Perchance — who shall say nay? — each one of us is now building his own, even as I have builded Tone.

Well, well! if so it should be, and if the society of my family should again be denied me,

I only hope that faithful Smudge may once more bear me company. His head rests on my knee as I now write, and the intelligent and affectionate look he gives me seems an unspoken promise that this wish shall be gratified, if it depends on efforts of which he is capable.

PAUL PROGNOSIS.

BOSTON, MASS., *February* 9, 1878.

Works of Fiction.

A List of Novels and Stories, selected from the Publications of Messrs. Houghton, Mifflin and Company, Boston and New York.

Thomas Bailey Aldrich.

The Story of a Bad Boy. Illustrated. 12mo, $1.25.

Marjorie Daw and Other People. Short Stories. With Frontispiece. 12mo, $1.50.

Marjorie Daw and Other Stories. In Riverside Aldine Series. 16mo, $1.00.

These volumes are not identical in contents.

Prudence Palfrey. With Frontispiece. 12mo, $1.50; paper, 50 cents.

The Queen of Sheba. 12mo, $1.50; paper, 50 cents.

The Stillwater Tragedy. 12mo, $1.50.

Lucia True Ames.

Memoirs of a Millionaire. 16mo, $1.25.

Hans Christian Andersen.

Works. First Complete Edition in English. In ten uniform volumes, 12mo, each $1.00; the set, $10.00; half calf, $25.00.

The Improvisatore; or, Life in Italy.
The Two Baronesses.
O. T.; or, Life in Denmark.
Only a Fiddler.

In Spain and Portugal.
A Poet's Bazaar. A Picturesque Tour.
Pictures of Travel
The Story of my Life. With Portrait.
Wonder Stories told for Children. Illustrated.
Stories and Tales. Illustrated.

Jane G. Austin.

A Nameless Nobleman. 16mo, $1.00; paper, 50 cents.

The Desmond Hundred. 16mo, $1.00; paper, 50 cents.

The strongest American novel that has been produced for many a year. — *The Churchman* (New York).

Standish of Standish. 16mo, $1.25.

Arlo Bates.

The Philistines. 16mo, $1.50.

It has many strong situations, much admirable dialogue, and we consider it decidedly the best thing Mr. Bates has yet done. — *New York Tribune.*

Patty's Perversities. 16mo, $1.00; paper, 50 cents.

The Pagans. 16mo, $1.00; paper, 50 cents.

Edward Bellamy.

Miss Ludington's Sister. 16mo, $1.25; paper, 50 cents.

Looking Backward: 2000–1887. 352nd Thousand. 12mo, $1.00; paper, 50 cents.

Ein Rückblick (Looking Backward). Translated into German by Rabbi Solomon Schindler. 16mo, paper, 50 cents.

"Looking Backward" is a well-made book, but it is more — a glowing prophecy and a gospel of peace. He who reads it expecting merely to be entertained, must, we should think, find himself unexpectedly haunted by visions of a golden age wherein all the world unites to do the world's work like members of one family, where labor and living are provided for each man, where toil and leisure alternate in happy proportions, where want and therefore greed and jealousy are unknown, where the pleasures of this world are free to all, to cheer, but not to enslave. — *The Nation* (New York).

Mr. Bellamy's wonderful book. — EDWARD EVERETT HALE.

William Henry Bishop.

Detmold: A Romance. 18mo, $1.25.

The House of a Merchant Prince. 12mo, $1.50.

Choy Susan, and other Stories. 16mo, $1.25.

The Golden Justice. 16mo, $1.25; paper, 50 cents.

Mr. W. D. Howells, in *Harper's Monthly*, praises this volume highly, saying: "As a study of a prosperous western city, this picture of Keewaydin is unique in our literature." He adds that "it is full of traits of mastery which cannot leave any critic doubtful of Mr. Bishop's power."

Björnstjerne Björnson.

Novels. American Edition. Translated by Prof. R. B. Anderson. Including Synnöve Solbakken, Arne, The Bridal March, A Happy Boy, The Fisher Maiden, Captain Mansana, and Magnhild. Illustrated. In 3 volumes, 12mo, $4.50.

The Bridal March, and other Stories. Illustrated. 16mo, $1.00.

Captain Mansana, and other Stories. 16mo, $1.00.

Magnhild. 16mo, $1.00.

Alice Brown.

Fools of Nature. 12mo, $1.50; paper, 50 cents.

Helen Dawes Brown.

Two College Girls. 12mo, $1.50; paper, 50 cents.

H. C. Bunner.

A Woman of Honor. 16mo, $1.25; paper, 50 cents.

Clara Louise Burnham.

Young Maids and Old. 12mo, $1.50.
Next Door. 12mo, $1.50; paper, 50 cents.
Dearly Bought. New Edition. 16mo, $1.25.
No Gentlemen. New Edition. 16mo, $1.25.
A Sane Lunatic. New Edition. 16mo, $1.25.
The Mistress of Beech Knoll. 16mo, $1.25.

Edwin Lassetter Bynner.

Agnes Surriage. 12mo, $1.50; paper, 50 cents.

We congratulate the author on a well-earned success, and the reader on an unusual pleasure. — T. B. ALDRICH.

Penelope's Suitors. 24mo, 50 cents.
Damen's Ghost. 16mo, $1.00; paper, 50 cents.

Helen Campbell.

Under Green Apple-Boughs. Illustrated. 16mo, paper, 50 cents.

Alice Cary.

Pictures of Country Life. Short Stories. 12mo, $1.50.

Mrs. L. W. Champney.

Rosemary and Rue. 16mo, $1.00.

Clara Erskine Clement.

Eleanor Maitland. 16mo, $1.25; paper, 50 cents.

Mary Clemmer.

His Two Wives. 12mo, $1.50; paper, 50 cents.

An absorbing love story — a portrayal of life held amenable to the lofty and poetic ideal. — *Boston Traveller.*

John Esten Cooke.

Fanchette. 16mo, $1.00.

My Lady Pokahontas. 16mo, gilt top, $1.25.

The narrative of Pokahontas has never been so deliciously presented. — *Quebec Chronicle.*

Rose Terry Cooke.

Somebody's Neighbors. Stories. 12mo, $1.50; half calf, $3.00.

Happy Dodd. 12mo, $1.50.

The Sphinx's Children. Stories. 12mo, $1.50.

Steadfast. 12mo, $1.50.

James Fenimore Cooper.

Works. New *Household Edition.* With Introductions to many of the volumes by Susan Fenimore Cooper, and Illustrations. In 32 volumes. Each, 16mo, $1.00; the set, $32.00; half calf, $64.00.

Precaution.
The Spy.
The Pioneers.
The Pathfinder.
Mercedes of Castile.
The Deerslayer.
The Red Skins.
The Chainbearer.
Satanstoe.
The Crater.
Afloat and Ashore.
The Prairie.
Wept of Wish-ton-Wish.
The Water-Witch.
The Bravo.
Red Rover.
Homeward Bound.
Home as Found.
The Heidenmauer.
The Headsman.
The Two Admirals.
The Pilot.
Lionel Lincoln.
Last of the Mohicans.

Wing and Wing.	Jack Tier.
Wyandotté.	The Sea Lions.
The Monikins.	Oak Openings.
Miles Wallingford.	Ways of the Hour.

New Edition. With Introductions by Susan Fenimore Cooper. In 32 vols. 16mo, $32.00. (*Sold only in sets.*)

Fireside Edition. With Portrait, Introductions, and 43 Illustrations. In 16 vols. 12mo, $20.00; half calf, $40.00. (*Sold only in sets.*)

Sea Tales. First Series. New *Household Edition.* With Introductions by Susan Fenimore Cooper. Illustrated. In 5 volumes, the set, 16mo, $5.00; half calf, $10.00.

Sea Tales. Second Series. New *Household Edition.* With Introductions by Susan Fenimore Cooper. Illustrated. In 5 volumes, the set, 16mo, $5.00; half calf, $10.00.

Leather Stocking Tales. New *Household Edition.* With Portrait, Introductions, and Illustrations. In 5 vols., the set, 16mo, $5.00; half calf, $10.00.

Cooper Stories. Narratives of Adventure selected from Cooper's Works. Illustrated. Stories of the Prairie. Stories of the Woods. Stories of the Sea. 3 vols. 16mo, $1.00 each; the set, $3.00.

The Spy. 16mo, paper, 50 cents.

Charles Egbert Craddock [Mary N. Murfree].

In the Tennessee Mountains. Short Stories. Eighteenth Edition. 16mo, $1.25.

Mr. Craddock is a master of the art of description. . . . The style is admirable. — *The Nation* (New York).

Down the Ravine. For Young People. Illustrated. 16mo, $1.00.

The Prophet of the Great Smoky Mountains. 14th Thousand. 16mo, $1.25.

In the Clouds. 16mo, $1.25.

The Story of Keedon Bluffs. 16mo, $1.00.

The Despot of Broomsedge Cove. 16mo, $1.25.

The essential part, the treatment of the human problem, is characterized by real power, — the power of divining motives and piercing through contradictions. Not the hero of "Where the Battle was Fought" is so intensely vital a study as Teck Jepson. The side-lights are not the least striking elements in Miss Murfree's art. — *Springfield Republican.*

Where the Battle was Fought. 12mo, $1.25.

Thomas Frederick Crane (translator).

Italian Popular Tales. With Introduction, Bibliography, Notes, etc. 8vo, gilt top, $2.50.

F. Marion Crawford.

To Leeward. 16mo, $1.25.

A Roman Singer. 16mo, $1.25; paper, 50 cents.

An American Politician. 16mo, $1.25.

Paul Patoff. Crown 8vo, $1.50.

Maria S. Cummins.

The Lamplighter. New *Popular Edition.* 12mo, $1.00; paper, 25 cents.

El Fureidîs. A Story of Palestine and Syria. 12mo, $1.50; paper, 50 cents.

Mabel Vaughan. 12mo, $1.50.

Czeika.

An Operetta in Profile. 16mo, $1.00.

Madeleine Vinton Dahlgren.

A Washington Winter. 12mo, $1.50.

The Lost Name. 16mo, $1.00.

Lights and Shadows of a Life. 12mo, $1.50.

Katharine Floyd Dana.

Our Phil, and other Stories. Illustrated. 16mo, $1.25.

All so true to life, so simple, touching, and so real, as to be as noteworthy from an artistic as well as from a human standpoint. — *New Haven Palladium.*

Parke Danforth.

Not in the Prospectus. 16mo, $1.25.

Charming in style, . . . and altogether as happy a story as we have read for a long time. — *New York Times.*

Daniel De Foe.

Robinson Crusoe. Illustrated. 12mo, $1.00.

Margaret Deland.

Sidney. A new novel. 12mo, $1.50.

John Ward, Preacher. 55th Thousand. 12mo, $1.50; paper, 50 cents.

There are pages in it which, in their power of insight and skill in minute delineation, remind us of Thackeray; while the pictures of country life constantly recall Mrs. Gaskell's fresh and charming tale of "Cranford." But "John Ward" is no mere fugitive story. Behind the story lie some of the deepest problems which beset our life. — ARCHDEACON FARRAR.

P. Deming.

Adirondack Stories. 18mo, 75 cents.

Tompkins, and other Folks. 18mo, $1.00.

There is a deep and wonderful art in these quiet little tales. — *The Critic* (New York).

Thomas De Quincey.

Romances and Extravaganzas. 12mo, $1.50.

Narrative and Miscellaneous Papers. 12mo, $1.50.

Charles Dickens.

Complete Works. *Illustrated Library Edition.* With Introductions, biographical and historical, by E. P. Whipple. Containing all the Illustrations that appeared in the English edition by Cruikshank, John Leech, and others, engraved on steel, and the designs of F. O. C. Darley and John Gilbert, in all over 550. In 29 volumes, each, 12mo, $1.50; the set, with Dickens Dictionary, 30 volumes, $45.00; half calf, $82.50.

Pickwick Papers, 2 vols.
Nicholas Nickleby, 2 vols.
Oliver Twist, 1 vol.
Old Curiosity Shop, and Reprinted Pieces, 2 vols.
Barnaby Rudge, and Hard Times, 2 vols.
Pictures from Italy, and American Notes, 1 vol.
Bleak House, 2 vols.
Little Dorrit, 2 vols.
David Copperfield, 2 vols.
Martin Chuzzlewit, 2 vols.
Our Mutual Friend, 2 vols.
The Uncommercial Traveller, 1 vol.
A Child's History of England, and other Pieces, 1 vol.
Christmas Books, 1 vol.
Dombey and Son, 2 vols.
Tale of Two Cities, 1 vol.
Great Expectations, 1 vol.
Mystery of Edwin Drood, Master Humphrey's Clock, and other Pieces, 1 vol.
Sketches by Boz, 1 vol.

A Christmas Carol. With thirty Illustrations. 8vo, full gilt, $2.50; fancy silk and vellum cloth, $2.50; morocco, $7.50. 32mo, 75 cents.

Christmas Books. Illustrated. 12mo, full gilt, $2.00; morocco, $4.50.

Charlotte Dunning.

A Step Aside. 16mo, $1.25; paper, 50 cents.

The *London Saturday Review* said of it: "Miss Dunning's name is new to English readers, but we hope it will not remain so long. She contrives to tell a very unobtrusive story with interest and charm."

Edgar Fawcett.

A Hopeless Case. 18mo, $1.25.

We know of no English novel of the last few years fit to be compared with it in its own line for simplicity, truth, and rational interest. — *London Times.*

A Gentleman of Leisure. 18mo, $1.00.

An Ambitious Woman. 12mo, $1.50; paper, 50 cents.

Olivia Delaplaine. 12mo, $1.50.

The Confessions of Claud. 12mo, $1.50; paper, 50 cents.

The House at High Bridge. 12mo, $1.50; paper, 50 cents.

The Adventures of a Widow. 12mo, $1.50; paper, 50 cents.

Tinkling Cymbals. 12mo, $1.50.

Social Silhouettes. 12mo, $1.50.

Mrs. James A. Field.

High-Lights. 16mo, $1.25.

The style and tone of the book quite lift the familiar material out of the ruts, and it is pleasant to record so refined a story. — *The Critic* (New York).

Harford Flemming.

A Carpet Knight. 16mo, $1.25.

Admirably written, with a dash of humor. — *Cleveland Leader.*

Mary Hallock Foote.

The Led-Horse Claim. Illustrated. 16mo, $1.25; paper, 50 cents.

John Bodewin's Testimony. 12mo, $1.50; paper, 50 cents.

The Last Assembly Ball, and The Fate of a Voice. 16mo, $1.25.

Baron de la Motte Fouqué.

Undine; Sintram and His Companions, etc. Illustrated. 32mo, 75 cents.

Undine, and other Tales. Illustrated. 16mo, $1.00.

Johann Wolfgang von Goethe.

Wilhelm Meister. Translated by Carlyle. With Portrait. 2 vols. crown 8vo, gilt top, $3.00.

The Tale, and Favorite Poems. Illustrated. 32mo, 75 cents.

Oliver Goldsmith.

The Vicar of Wakefield. Illustrated. 16mo, $1.00.

Handy-Volume Edition. 24mo, gilt top, $1.00.

Jeanie T. Gould [Mrs. Lincoln].

Marjorie's Quest. For Young People. Illustrated. 12mo, $1.50.

Her Washington Season. 12mo, $1.50.

Robert Grant.

An Average Man. 12mo, $1.50.

The Confessions of a Frivolous Girl. 12mo, $1.25; paper, 50 cents.

A screaming success. — *Saturday Review* (London).

The Knave of Hearts. 12mo, $1.25.

A Romantic Young Lady. 12mo, $1.50.

Henry Gréville.

Cleopatra. A Russian Romance. With Portrait of the author. 16mo, $1.25.

Dosia's Daughter. 16mo, $1.25.

Count Xavier. 16mo, $1.00.

Henry Gréville is idyllic, in the sense that most of her stories may be read with pleasure by the innocent maiden and the sophisticated man of the world; how many writers of fiction in these days have been able to attract so diverse an audience? — *Literary World* (Boston).

The Guardians.

16mo, $1.25.

It is an unusually clever book, every page of which is to be enjoyed, perhaps we may venture to say delighted in. The style is admirable, fresh, crisp, rapid. — *Boston Advertiser.*

Lucretia P. Hale and E. L. Bynner.

An Uncloseted Skeleton. 32mo, 50 cents.

Thomas Chandler Haliburton.

The Clockmaker; or, the Sayings and Doings of Samuel Slick of Slickville. Illustrated. 16mo, $1.00.

Kate W. Hamilton.

Rachel's Share of the Road. 16mo, $1.00.

Mrs. E. M. Hammond.

The Georgians. 16mo, $1.00.

Arthur Sherburne Hardy.

But Yet a Woman. 16mo, $1.25; paper, 50 cents.

The author's drawing of character is the drawing of a master. — *The Academy* (London).

The Wind of Destiny. 16mo, $1.25; paper, 50 cents.

No one that reads it will doubt for a moment that "The Wind of Destiny" is the work of a man of genius. — *London Spectator.*

Passe Rose. 16mo, $1.25.

Joel Chandler Harris.

Mingo, and other Sketches in Black and White. 16mo, $1.25; paper, 50 cents.

Nights with Uncle Remus. Illustrated. 12mo, $1.50 ; paper, 50 cents.

It is not a book; it is an epoch. — *The American.*

A wondrously amusing book. — *Chicago Inter-Ocean.*

Miriam Coles Harris.

Writings. New Edition, uniform. Each volume, 16mo, $1.25. The set, 10 vols, $12.00.

Rutledge.
The Sutherlands.
St. Philip's.
Happy-Go-Lucky.
A Perfect Adonis.
Frank Warrington.
Richard Vandermarck.
Missy.
Phœbe.

Louie's Last Term at St. Mary's (for Young People). 16mo, $1.00.

Bret Harte.

The Luck of Roaring Camp, and other Sketches. 16mo, $1.25.

The Luck of Roaring Camp, and other Stories. In Riverside Aldine Series. 16mo, $1.00.

These volumes are not identical in contents.

Mrs. Skaggs's Husbands, etc. 16mo, $1.25.

Tales of the Argonauts, etc. 16mo, $1.25.

Thankful Blossom. 18mo, $1.00.

Two Men of Sandy Bar. A Play. 18mo, $1.00.

The Story of a Mine. 18mo, $1.00.

Drift from Two Shores. 18mo, $1.00.

The Twins of Table Mountain. 18mo, $1.00.

Flip, and Found at Blazing Star. 18mo, $1.00.

In the Carquinez Woods. 18mo, $1.00.

On the Frontier. Stories. 18mo, $1.00.

Works. *Riverside Edition*, rearranged. With Portrait and Introduction. In 7 vols., crown 8vo, each $2.00. The set, $14.00 ; half calf, $21.00.

1. Poetical Works, Two Men of Sandy Bar, Introduction, and Portrait. 2. The Luck of Roaring Camp, and other Stories, a portion of the Tales of the Argonauts, etc. 3. Tales of the Argonauts and Eastern Sketches. 4. Gabriel Conroy. 5. Stories, and Condensed Novels. 6. Frontier Stories. 7. Camp and City Stories.

By Shore and Sedge. 18mo, $1.00.

Maruja. 18mo, $1.00.

Snow-Bound at Eagle's. 18mo, $1.00.

A Millionaire of Rough-and-Ready, and Devil's Ford. 18mo, $1.00.

The Crusade of the Excelsior. Illustrated. 16mo, $1.25.

A Phyllis of the Sierras, and Drift from Redwood Camp. 18mo, $1.00.

The Argonauts of North Liberty. 18mo, $1.00.

Novels and Tales. 17 vols., 18mo, in box, $12.00.

Cressy. 16mo, $1.25.

The Heritage of Dedlow Marsh, etc. 16mo, $1.25.

A Waif of the Plains. 18mo, $1.00.

Bret Harte moves like a master within the sphere of his special descriptions and characterizations. . . . The story before us maintains his power over his readers. It is cut with the well-known precision and naturalness. It glows with the old color. — *Public Opinion* (Washington).

A Ward of the Golden Gate. 16mo.

Wilhelm Hauff.

Arabian Days' Entertainments. Translated by Herbert Pelham Curtis. Illustrated by Hoppin. New Edition. 12mo, $1.50.

Julian Hawthorne.

Love — or a Name. 12mo, $1.50.

Fortune's Fool. 12mo, $1.50; paper, 50 cents.

Dust. 16mo, paper, 50 cents.

Nathaniel Hawthorne.

Works. *Little Classic Edition.* Each volume contains vignette Illustration. In 25 volumes (including Index), 18mo, each $1.00; the set, in box, $25.00; half calf, or half morocco, $50.00; tree calf, $75.00.

Twice-Told Tales. 2 vols.
The Snow-Image, and other Twice-Told Tales.
Mosses from an Old Manse. 2 vols.
The Scarlet Letter.
True Stories from History and Biography.
A Wonder-Book for Girls and Boys.
Tanglewood Tales.
American Note-Books. 2 vols.
English Note-Books. 2 vols.
The House of the Seven Gables.
The Blithedale Romance.
The Marble Faun. 2 vols
Our Old Home. English Sketches.
French and Italian Note-Books. 2 vols.
Septimius Felton.
Fanshawe, and other Pieces.
The Dolliver Romance, etc.
Sketches and Studies.
Index, and Sketch of Life.

Riverside Edition. With Introductory Notes by George P. Lathrop. With 12 original full-page Etchings and 13 vignette Woodcuts and Portrait. In 13 volumes. Crown 8vo, gilt top, $2.00 each; the set, $26.00; half calf, $39.00; half calf, gilt top, $40.50; half crushed levant, $52.00.

Twice-Told Tales.
Mosses from an Old Manse.
The House of the Seven Gables, and the Snow-Image.
A Wonder-Book, Tanglewood Tales, etc.
The Scarlet Letter, and The Blithedale Romance.
The Marble Faun.

Our Old Home, and English Note-Books. 2 vols.
American Note-Books.
French and Italian Note-Books.
The Dolliver Romance, Fanshawe, Septimius Felton, and, in an Appendix, The Ancestral Footstep.
Tales, Sketches, and other Papers. With Biographical Sketch by G. P. Lathrop, and Indexes.
Dr. Grimshaw's Secret.

Wayside Edition. With Portrait, twenty-four Etchings, and Notes by George P. Lathrop. In twenty-five volumes, 12mo, uncut, $37.50; half calf, $67.75; half calf, gilt top, $72.75; half levant, $88.50. (*Sold only in sets.*) The contents of this Edition are identical with those of the *Riverside Edition.*

Dr. Grimshawe's Secret. 12mo, $1.50. *Riverside Edition.* Crown 8vo, gilt top, $2.00.

The Scarlet Letter. *Holiday Edition.* Illustrated by Mary Hallock Foote. 8vo, full gilt, $3.00; levant, $7.50. *Popular Edition.* With Illustration. 12mo, $1.00; paper, 50 cents.

The Gray Champion, etc. In Riverside Aldine Series. 16mo, $1.00.

The Marble Faun. With fifty beautiful Photogravures of Localities, Paintings, Statuary, etc., mentioned in the novel. A Holiday Edition. 2 vols. crown 8vo, gilt top, $6.00; full polished calf, $12.00, *net;* full vellum, gilt top, in box, $12.00, *net.*

Twice-Told Tales. *School Edition.* 18mo, 60 cents.

Tales of the White Hills, and Legends of New England. Illustrated. 32mo, 75 cents. *School Edition*, 40 cents, *net.*

Legends of the Province House, and A Virtuoso's Collection. Illustrated. 32mo, 75 cents. *School Edition*, 40 cents, *net.*

Mosses from an Old Manse. 16mo, paper, 50 cents.

Isaac Henderson.

Agatha Page. A Parable. With Frontispiece by Felix Moscheles. 12mo, $1.50; paper, 50 cents.

The Prelate. 12mo, $1.50; paper, 50 cents.

Mrs. S. J. Higginson.

A Princess of Java. 12mo, $1.50.

Oliver Wendell Holmes.

Elsie Venner. Crown 8vo, gilt top, $2.00; paper, 50 cents.

The Guardian Angel. Crown 8vo, gilt top, $2.00; paper, 50 cents.

A Mortal Antipathy. First Opening of the New Portfolio. Crown 8vo, gilt top, $1.50.

My Hunt after "The Captain," etc. Illustrated. *School Edition.* 32mo, 40 cents, *net.*

The Story of Iris. Illustrated. 32mo, 75 cents.

Mark Hopkins, Jr.

The World's Verdict. 12mo, $1.50.

Augustus Hoppin.

Recollections of Auton House. Illustrated by the Author. Square 8vo, $1.25.

A Fashionable Sufferer. Illustrated by the Author. 12mo, $1.50.

Two Compton Boys. Illustrated by the Author. Square 8vo, $1.50.

Blanche Willis Howard.

The Open Door Crown 8vo, $1.50.

One Summer. New *Popular Edition.* Illustrated by Hoppin. 12mo, $1.25.

Aulnay Tower. 12mo, $1.50; paper, 50 cents.

A story which, for absorbing interest, brilliancy of style, charm of graphic character drawing, and even exquisite literary quality, will hold its rank among the best work in American fiction. — *Boston Traveller.*

Aunt Serena. 16mo, $1.25; paper, 50 cents.

Guenn. Illustrated. 12mo, $1.50; paper, 50 cents.

E. W. Howe.

A Man Story. 12mo, $1.50.

The Mystery of the Locks. New Edition. 16mo, $1.25.

The Story of a Country Town. 12mo, $1.50; paper, 50 cents.

A Moonlight Boy. With Portrait of the Author. 12mo, $1.50; paper, 50 cents.

Mr. Howe is the strongest man in fiction that the great West has yet produced. — *Boston Transcript.*

William Dean Howells.

Their Wedding Journey. Illustrated. New Edition, with additional chapter. 12mo, $1.50; 18mo, $1.00.

A Chance Acquaintance. Illustrated. 12mo, $1.50; 18mo, $1.00.

Suburban Sketches. Illustrated. 12mo, $1.50.

A Foregone Conclusion. 12mo, $1.50.

The Lady of the Aroostook. 12mo, $1.50; paper, 50 cents.

The Undiscovered Country. 12mo, $1.50.

A Day's Pleasure, etc. 32mo, 75 cents; *School Edition*, 40 cents, *net.*

The Minister's Charge. 12mo, $1.50; paper, 50 cents.

Indian Summer. 12mo, $1.50; paper, 50 cents.

The Rise of Silas Lapham. 12mo, $1.50; paper, 50 cents.

A Fearful Responsibility. 12mo, $1.50; paper, 50 cents.

A Modern Instance. 12mo, $1.50; paper, 50 cents.

A Woman's Reason. 12mo, $1.50; paper, 50 cents.

Dr. Breen's Practice. 12mo, $1.50; paper, 50 cents.

The Sleeping-Car, and other Farces. 12mo, $1.00.

The Elevator. 32mo, 50 cents.

The Sleeping-Car. 32mo, 50 cents.

The Parlor Car. 32mo, 50 cents.

The Register. 32mo, 50 cents.

A Counterfeit Presentment. A Comedy. 18mo, $1.25.

Out of the Question. A Comedy. 18mo, $1.25.

A Sea Change; or, Love's Stowaway. A Lyricated Farce. 18mo, $1.00.

Thomas Hughes.

Tom Brown's School Days at Rugby. New Edition. Illustrated. 16mo, $1.00.

Tom Brown at Oxford. 16mo, $1.25.

Henry James.

Watch and Ward. 18mo, $1.25.

A Passionate Pilgrim, and other Tales. 12mo, $2.00.

Roderick Hudson. 12mo, $2.00.

The American. 12mo, $2.00.

The Europeans. 12mo, $1.50.

Confidence. 12mo, $1.50; paper, 50 cents.

The Portrait of a Lady. 12mo, $2.00.

The Author of Beltraffio; Pandora; Georgina's Reasons; Four Meetings, etc. 12mo, $1.50.

The Siege of London; The Pension Beaurepas; and The Point of View. 12mo, $1.50.

Tales of Three Cities (The Impressions of a Cousin; Lady Barberina; A New-England Winter). 12mo, $1.50; paper, 50 cents.

Daisy Miller: A Comedy. 12mo, $1.50.

The Tragic Muse. 2 vols. 16mo, $2.50.

Anna Jameson.

Diary of an Ennuyée. 16mo, gilt top, $1.25.

Studies and Stories. 16mo, gilt top, $1.25.

Mrs. C. V. Jamison.

The Story of an Enthusiast. Told by Himself. 12mo, $1.50; paper, 50 cents.

Douglas Jerrold.

Mrs. Caudle's Curtain Lectures. Illustrated. 16mo, $1.00.

Sarah Orne Jewett.

The King of Folly Island, and other People. 16mo, $1.25.

Tales of New England. In Riverside Aldine Series. 16mo, $1.00. Uncut, paper label, $1.50.

A White Heron, and other Stories. 18mo, gilt top, $1.25.

A Marsh Island. 16mo, $1.25; paper, 50 cts.

A Country Doctor. 16mo, $1.25.

Deephaven. 18mo, gilt top, $1.25.

Old Friends and New. 18mo, gilt top, $1.25.

Country By-Ways. 18mo, gilt top, $1.25.

The Mate of the Daylight, and Friends Ashore. 18mo, gilt top, $1.25.

Betty Leicester. 18mo, gilt top, $1.25.

Rossiter Johnson (editor).

Little Classics. Each in one volume. New Edition, bound in new and artistic style. 18mo, each $1.00. The set, in box, $18.00; half calf, or half morocco, $35.00.

1. Exile.	7. Romance.	13. Narrative Poems.
2. Intellect.	8. Mystery.	14. Lyrical Poems.
3. Tragedy.	9. Comedy.	15. Minor Poems.
4. Life.	10. Childhood.	16. Nature.
5. Laughter.	11. Heroism.	17. Humanity.
6. Love.	12. Fortune.	18. Authors.

A list of the entire contents of the volumes of this Series will be sent free on application.

This series lays, for a very small sum, the cream of the best writers before the reader of ordinary means.—*Commercial Advertiser* (New York).

Virginia W. Johnson.

The House of the Musician. 16mo, paper, 50 cents.

Charles C. Jones, Jr.

Negro Myths from the Georgia Coast. 16mo, $1.00.

Edward King.

The Golden Spike. 12mo, $1.50.

Mr. King is a writer whom we shall look out for; and now that Tourguéneff is dead, it may fall to him to take up the mantle of the prophet. — *The Literary World* (London).

The Gentle Savage. 12mo, $2.00.

Ellen Olney Kirk.

Walford. (In Press.)

The Story of Margaret Kent. 16mo, $1.25; paper, 50 cents.

In "The Story of Margaret Kent" we have that rare thing in current literature, *a really good novel.* . . . Aside from the other merits which we have noted, this novel is to be praised for its artistic earnestness and sincerity. — *Boston Advertiser.*

Sons and Daughters. 12mo, $1.50; paper, 50 cents.

Queen Money. A Novel. New Edition. 16mo, $1.25; paper, 50 cents.

Better Times. Stories. 12mo, $1.50.

A Midsummer Madness. 16mo, $1.25.

A Lesson in Love. 16mo, $1.00; paper, 50 cents.

A Daughter of Eve. 12mo, $1.50; paper, 50 cents.

Joseph Kirkland.

Zury: The Meanest Man in Spring County. A Novel of Western Life. With Frontispiece. 12mo, $1.50; paper, 50 cents.

The McVeys. 16mo, $1.25.

"The McVeys," in its insight into Western life, both outer and inner, . . . deserves to take an exceptional high place in fiction. — *New York Tribune.*

Charles and Mary Lamb.

Tales from Shakespeare. 18mo, $1.00.

Handy-Volume Edition. 24mo, gilt top, $1.00.

The Same. Illustrated. 16mo, $1.00.

Mary Catherine Lee.

A Quaker Girl of Nantucket. 16mo, $1.25.

Henry Wadsworth Longfellow.

Hyperion. A Romance. 16mo, $1.50.

Popular Edition. 16mo, 40 cents; paper, 15 cents.

Outre-Mer. 16mo, $1.50.

Popular Edition. 16mo, 40 cents; paper, 15 cents.

Kavanagh. A Romance. 16mo, $1.50.

Hyperion, Outre-Mer, and Kavanagh. In 2 volumes, crown 8vo, $3.00.

Flora Haines Loughead.

The Man who was Guilty. 16mo, $1.25.

It is earnest, high-minded, and moving, lighted here and there by a demure drollery, interesting as a story, and provocative of serious thought. — *Overland Monthly* (San Francisco).

Madame Lucas.

16mo, $1.00; paper, 50 cents.

D. R. McAnally.

Irish Wonders: The Ghosts, Giants, Pookas, Demons, Leprechawns, Banshees, Fairies, Witches, Widows, Old Maids, and other Marvels of the Emerald Isle. Popular Tales as told by the People. Profusely illustrated. 8vo, $2.00.

Sure to achieve a success. . . . The Irish flavor, full, fresh, and delightful, constitutes the charm of the book. — *Philadelphia American.*

S. Weir Mitchell.

In War Time. 16mo, $1.25; paper, 50 cents.

Roland Blake. 16mo, $1.25.

Dr. Mitchell's book is indeed one to be grateful for. It is interpenetrated by fine and true shades of thought, and worked out with delicacy and artistic feeling. It contains striking, even brilliant incidents, yet its interest depends chiefly upon modifications of character. — *American* (Philadelphia).

Luigi Monti.

Leone. 16mo, $1.00; paper, 50 cents.

A story of Italian life written by an Italian, and shows an impressive fidelity to time and place. — *Boston Traveller.*

Henry L. Nelson.

John Rantoul. 12mo, $1.50.

Mrs. Oliphant and T. B. Aldrich.

The Second Son. Crown 8vo, $1.50; paper, 50 cents.

Peppermint Perkins.

The Familiar Letters of Peppermint Perkins. Illustrated. 16mo, $1.00; paper, 50 cents.

Nora Perry.

The Youngest Miss Lorton, and other Stories. Illustrated. 12mo, $1.50.

A Flock of Girls. Stories. Illustrated. 12mo, $1.50.

For a Woman. 16mo, $1.00.

A Book of Love Stories. 16mo, $1.00.

The Tragedy of the Unexpected. 18mo, $1.25.

Elizabeth Stuart Phelps [Mrs. Ward].

The Gates Ajar. 75th Thousand. 16mo, $1.50.

Beyond the Gates. 28th Edition. 16mo, $1.25.

The Gates Between. 16mo, $1.25.

The above three volumes, in box, $4.00.

Men, Women, and Ghosts. Stories. 16mo, $1.50.

Hedged In. 16mo, $1.50.

The Silent Partner. 16mo, $1.50.

The Story of Avis. 16mo, $1.50; paper, 50 cents.

Sealed Orders, and other Stories. 16mo, $1.50.

Friends: A Duet. 16mo, $1.25.

Doctor Zay. 16mo, $1.25; paper, 50 cents.

An Old Maid's Paradise, and Burglars in Paradise. 16mo, $1.25.

The Master of the Magicians. Collaborated by Elizabeth Stuart Phelps and Herbert D. Ward. 16mo, $1.25.

The above twelve volumes, $16.25.

Come Forth. Collaborated by Elizabeth Stuart Phelps and Herbert D. Ward. 16mo, $1.25.

The Madonna of the Tubs. With Illustrations. 12mo, full gilt, $1.50.

Jack the Fisherman. Illustrated. Square 12mo, ornamental boards, 50 cents.

Melville Philips:

The Devil's Hat. 16mo, $1.00.

Eça de Queiros.

Dragon's Teeth. Translated from the Portuguese by Mary J. Serrano. 12mo, $1.50.

Edmund Quincy.

The Haunted Adjutant; and other Stories. 12mo, $1.50.

Wensley; and other Stories. 12mo, $1.50.

J. P. Quincy.

The Peckster Professorship. 16mo, $1.25.

Opie P. Read.

Len Gansett. 12mo, $1.00; paper, 50 cents.

Marian C. L. Reeves and Emily Read.

Pilot Fortune. 16mo, $1.25.

A Reverend Idol.

A Novel. 12mo, $1.50; paper, 50 cents.

Riverside Paper Series.

A Continuation of Ticknor's Paper Series, appearing semi-monthly during the summer. Each, 16mo, paper, 50 cents.

1. John Ward, Preacher. By Margaret Deland.
2. The Scarlet Letter. By Nathaniel Hawthorne.
3. But Yet a Woman. By A. S. Hardy.
4. The Queen of Sheba. By T. B. Aldrich.
5. The Story of Avis. By Elizabeth Stuart Phelps.
6. The Feud of Oakfield Creek. By Josiah Royce.
7. Agatha Page. By Isaac Henderson.
8. The Guardian Angel. By Oliver Wendell Holmes.
9. A Step Aside. By Charlotte Dunning.
10. An Ambitious Woman. By Edgar Fawcett.
11. The Spy. By James Fenimore Cooper.
12. Emerson's Essays. First and Second Series.
13. In War Time. By Dr. S. Weir Mitchell.
14. Elsie Venner. By Dr. O. W. Holmes.
15. Agnes of Sorrento. By Harriet Beecher Stowe.
16. The Lady of the Aroostook. By W. D. Howells.
17. A Roman Singer. By F. Marion Crawford.
18. The Second Son. By Mrs. Oliphant and T. B. Aldrich.
19. A Daughter of Eve. By Ellen Olney Kirk.

20. A Marsh Island. By Sarah O. Jewett.
21. The Wind of Destiny. By A. S. Hardy.
22. A Lesson in Love. By Ellen Olney Kirk.
23. El Fureidîs. By Maria S. Cummins.
24. The Fate of Mansfield Humphreys. By Richard Grant White.
25. Prudence Palfrey. By T. B. Aldrich.
26. The Golden Justice. By W. H. Bishop.
27. Doctor Zay. By E. S. Phelps.
28. Zury. By Joseph Kirkland.
29. Confidence. By Henry James.

Extra Number *A*. Mosses from an Old Manse. By Nathaniel Hawthorne.

Extra Number *B*. Looking Backward, 2000–1887. By Edward Bellamy. New Edition. 347th Thousand.

Extra Number 3. Ein Rückblick. (Looking Backward.) Translated into German by Rabbi Solomon Schindler.

Other numbers to be announced later.

Edith Robinson.

Forced Acquaintances. 12mo, $1.50; paper, 50 cents.

Round-Robin Series.

Each volume, 16mo, $1.00; paper, 50 cents.

Damen's Ghost.
Madame Lucas.
Leone.
Doctor Ben.
The Strike in the B—— Mill.
Rosemary and Rue.
Fanchette.
Dorothea.

N. B. *The last three can be had in cloth only.*

Josiah Royce.

The Feud of Oakfield Creek. A Novel of California. 16mo, $1.25; paper, 50 cents.

Joseph Xavier Boniface Saintine.

Picciola. Illustrated. 16mo, $1.00.

J. H. Bernardin de Saint-Pierre.

Paul and Virginia. Illustrated. 16mo, $1.00.

The Same, together with Undine and Sintram. Illustrated. 32mo, 40 cents.

Sir Walter Scott.

The Waverley Novels. *Illustrated Library Edition.* Illustrated with 100 Engravings by famous artists; and with Introductions, Illustrative Notes, Glossary, and Index of Characters. In 25 volumes, 12mo. Each, $1.00; the set, $25.00; half calf, $50.00.

Waverley.
Guy Mannering.
The Antiquary.
Rob Roy.
Old Mortality.
Black Dwarf, and The Legend of Montrose.
Heart of Mid-Lothian.
The Bride of Lammermoor.
Ivanhoe.
The Monastery.
The Abbot.
Kenilworth.
The Pirate.
The Fortunes of Nigel.
Peveril of the Peak.
Quentin Durward.
St. Ronan's Well.
Redgauntlet.
The Betrothed, and The Highland Widow.
The Talisman and other Tales.
Woodstock.
The Fair Maid of Perth.
Anne of Geierstein.
Count Robert of Paris.
The Surgeon's Daughter, and Castle Dangerous.

Horace E. Scudder.

The Dwellers in Five-Sisters' Court. 16mo, $1.25.

Stories and Romances. 16mo, $1.25.

Mark Sibley Severance.

Hammersmith; His Harvard Days. 12mo, $1.50.

We do not recall any other book which so well deserves to be associated with the "Tom Brown" stories. — *Boston Journal.*

J. Emerson Smith.

Oakridge: An Old-Time Story of Maine. 12mo, $2.00.

Mary A. Sprague.

An Earnest Trifler. 16mo, $1.25.

Willis Steell.

Isidra. A Mexican Novel. 12mo, $1.25.

A. Stirling.

At Daybreak. 16mo, $1.25.

Louise Stockton.

Dorothea. 16mo, $1.00.

William W. Story.

Fiammetta: A Summer Idyl. 16mo, $1.25.

Harriet Beecher Stowe.

Uncle Tom's Cabin. A Story of Slavery. Illustrated. 12mo, $2.00.

Illustrated Holiday Edition. With Introduction and Bibliography and over 100 Illustrations. 8vo, full gilt, $3.00; half calf, $5.00; morocco, or tree calf, $6.00.

New *Popular Edition*, from new plates. With Account of the writing of this Story by Mrs. Stowe, and Frontispiece. 12mo, $1.00.

"Uncle Tom's Cabin" . . . must always remain one of the monuments of literature.—*New York Evening Post.*

Agnes of Sorrento. 12mo, $1.50; paper, 50 cents.

The Pearl of Orr's Island. 12mo, $1.50.

The Minister's Wooing. 12mo, $1.50.

My Wife and I. Illustrated. 12mo, $1.50.

We and our Neighbors. A Sequel to My Wife and I. New Edition. Illustrated. 12mo, $1.50.

Poganuc People. Illustrated. 12mo, $1.50.

The May-Flower, and other Sketches. 12mo, $1.50.

Dred. (Nina Gordon.) New Edition. 12mo, $1.50.

Oldtown Folks. 12mo, $1.50.

Sam Lawson's Fireside Stories. Illustrated. New Edition, enlarged. 12mo, $1.50.

The above eleven 12mo volumes, in box, $16.00.

Strike in the B—— Mill (The).

16mo, $1.00; paper, 50 cents.

Mary P. Thacher.

Sea-shore and Prairie. Stories and Sketches. 18mo, $1.00.

Octave Thanet.

Knitters in the Sun. 16mo, $1.25.

The best collection of short stories we have read for many a day. R. H. STODDARD in *New York Mail and Express.*

Frederick Thickstun.

A Mexican Girl. 12mo, $1.25; paper, 50 cents.

The sketches of scenery are as true as they are telling, and the character painting is strong and life-like. The racy writing and the abundant flow of humor that constitute so large a part of the charm of the Pacific-coast literature are at high tide in Mr. Thickstun's story. — *Literary World* (London).

William Makepeace Thackeray.

Complete Works. *Illustrated Library Edi-*

tion. Including two newly compiled volumes, containing material not hitherto collected in any American or English Edition. With Biographical and Bibliographical Introductions, Portrait, and over 1600 Illustrations. 22 vols. crown 8vo, each, $1.50. The set, $33.00; half calf, $60.50; half levant, $77.00.

1. Vanity Fair. I.
2. Vanity Fair. II.; Lovel the Widower.
3. Pendennis. I.
4. Pendennis. II.
5. Memoirs of Yellowplush.
6. Burlesques, etc.
7. History of Samuel Titmarsh, etc.
8. Barry Lyndon and Denis Duval.
9. The Newcomes. I.
10. The Newcomes. II.
11. Paris Sketch Book, etc.
12. Irish Sketch Book, etc.
13. The Four Georges, etc.
14. Henry Esmond.
15. The Virginians. I.
16. The Virginians. II.
17. Philip. I.
18. Philip. II.; Catherine.
19. Roundabout Papers, etc.
20. Christmas Stories, etc.
21. Contributions to Punch, etc.
22. Miscellaneous Essays.

The Introductory Notes are a new feature of great value in this library edition. . . . These notes are meant to give every interesting detail about the origin and fortunes of separate works that can be gathered from the literature about Thackeray. The introduction to *Vanity Fair* is thoroughly done; it brings together the needful bibliographical details, and adds to them delightful *ana* pertaining to the novel from Thackeray himself, James Payn, Mr. Hannay, Mr. Rideing, and others. — *Literary World* (Boston).

Maurice Thompson.

A Tallahassee Girl. 16mo, $1.00; paper, 50 cents.

Among the very best of recent American stories, and very far ahead of any of the many novels of Southern life. — *Philadelphia Times.*

Ticknor's Paper Series.

For Leisure-Hour and Railroad Reading. Each volume, 16mo, paper, 50 cents.

1. The Story of Margaret Kent. By Ellen Olney Kirk.
2. Guenn. By Blanche Willis Howard.
4. A Reverend Idol. A Massachusetts Coast Romance.
5. A Nameless Nobleman. By Jane G. Austin.
6. The Prelate. A Roman Story. By Isaac Henderson.
7. Eleanor Maitland. By Clara Erskine Clement.
8. The House of the Musician. By Virginia W. Johnson.
9. Geraldine. A Metrical Romance of the St. Lawrence.
10. The Duchess Emilia. By Barrett Wendell.
11. Dr. Breen's Practice. By W. D. Howells.
12. Tales of Three Cities. By Henry James.
13. The House at High Bridge. By Edgar Fawcett.
14. The Story of a Country Town. By E. W. Howe.
15. The Confessions of a Frivolous Girl. By Robert Grant.
16. Culture's Garland. By Eugene Field.
17. Patty's Perversities. By Arlo Bates.
18. A Modern Instance. By W. D. Howells.
19. Miss Ludington's Sister. By Edward Bellamy.
20. Aunt Serena. By Blanche Willis Howard.
21. Damen's Ghost. By Edwin Lassetter Bynner.
22. A Woman's Reason. By W. D. Howells.
23. Nights with Uncle Remus. By Joel Chandler Harris.
24. Mingo. By Joel Chandler Harris.
25. A Tallahassee Girl. By Maurice Thompson.
27. A Fearful Responsibility. By W. D. Howells.
28. Homoselle. By Mary S. Tiernan.
29. A Moonlight Boy. By E. W. Howe.
30. Adventures of a Widow. By Edgar Fawcett.
31. Indian Summer. By W. D. Howells.
32. The Led-Horse Claim. By Mary Hallock Foote.
33. Len Gansett. By Opie P. Read.
34. Next Door. By Clara Louise Burnham.

35. The Minister's Charge. By W. D. Howells.
36. Sons and Daughters. By Ellen Olney Kirk.
37. Agnes Surriage. By Edwin Lassetter Bynner.
39. Two College Girls. By Helen Dawes Brown.
40. The Rise of Silas Lapham. By W. D. Howells.
41. A Mexican Girl. By Frederick Thickstun.
42. Aulnay Tower. By Blanche Willis Howard.
43. The Pagans. By Arlo Bates.
44. Fortune's Fool. By Julian Hawthorne.
45. Doctor Ben. By Orlando Witherspoon.
46. John Bodewin's Testimony. By Mary Hallock Foote.
47. Rachel Armstrong; or, Love and Theology. By Celia Parker Woolley.
48. Two Gentlemen of Boston.
49. The Confessions of Claud. By Edgar Fawcett.
50. His Two Wives. By Mary Clemmer.
51. The Desmond Hundred. By Jane G. Austin.
52. A Woman of Honor. By H. C. Bunner.
53. Forced Acquaintances. By Edith Robinson.
54. Under Green Apple-Boughs. By Helen Campbell.
55. Fools of Nature. By Alice Brown.
56. Dust. By Julian Hawthorne.
57. The Story of an Enthusiast. By Mrs. C. V. Jamison.
58. Queen Money. By Ellen Olney Kirk.

There is not a poor novel in the series. I have been asked to give a list of good reading in fiction such as one about to go away can buy. I have no hesitation in naming most of the numbers in this series. —*Boston Advertiser.*

Mary S. Tiernan.

Homoselle. 16mo, $1.00; paper, 50 cents.

Jack Horner. 16mo, $1.25.

Mary Agnes Tincker.

Two Coronets. 12mo, $1.50.

Two Gentlemen of Boston.

12mo, $1.50; paper, 50 cents.

The writer has three of the best gifts of the novelist — imagination, perception, and humor. — *New York Tribune.*

Gen. Lew Wallace.

The Fair God; or, The Last of the 'Tzins. A Tale of the Conquest of Mexico. 77th Thousand. 12mo, $1.50.

We do not hesitate to say that the "Fair God" is one of the most powerful historical novels we have ever read. The scene where in the sunrise Montezuma reads his fate, the dance-scene, and the entry of the Spaniards to the capital, are drawn in a style of which we think few living writers capable; and the battles are Homeric in their grandeur. — *London Athenæum.*

Henry Watterson (editor).

Oddities in Southern Life and Character. With Illustrations by W. L. Sheppard and F. S. Church. 16mo, $1.50.

Kate Gannett Wells.

Miss Curtis. 12mo, $1.25.

As nobody knows Boston social life better than Mrs. Wells, the book is full of deliciously felicitous touches of social satire and wisdom. — ARLO BATES, in *The Book Buyer.*

Barrett Wendell.

Rankell's Remains. 16mo, $1.00.

The Duchess Emilia. 16mo, $1.00; paper, 50 cents.

One of the most striking features of this romance of metempsychosis is the delicate poetic feeling with which he has invested it. — *Springfield Republican.*

Richard Grant White.

The Fate of Mansfield Humphreys, with the Episode of Mr. Washington Adams in England. 16mo, $1.25; paper, 50 cents.

Bright, full of character, a little satirical, and thoroughly amusing. — *Christian Advocate* (New York).

Mrs. A. D. T. Whitney.

Ascutney Street. 12mo, $1.50.

Faith Gartney's Girlhood. Illustrated. 12mo, $1.50.

Hitherto. 12mo, $1.50.

Patience Strong's Outings. 12mo, $1.50.

The Gayworthys. 12mo, $1.50.

A Summer in Leslie Goldthwaite's Life. Illustrated. 12mo, $1.50.

We Girls. Illustrated. 12mo, $1.50.

Real Folks. Illustrated. 12mo, $1.50.

The Other Girls. Illustrated. 12mo, $1.50.

Sights and Insights. 2 vols. 12mo, $3.00.

Odd or Even? 12mo, $1.50.

Bonnyborough. 12mo, $1.50.

Homespun Yarns. Stories. 12mo, $1.50.

John Greenleaf Whittier.

Margaret Smith's Journal, Tales, and Sketches. *Riverside Edition.* Crown 8vo, $1.50.

Kate Douglas Wiggin.

Timothy's Quest.

The Birds' Christmas Carol. With Illustrations. Square 16mo, boards, 50 cents.

The only fault of this charming little book is that there is not enough of it. — *New Haven Palladium.*

The Story of Patsy. Illustrated. Square 16mo, boards, 60 cents.

A Summer in a Cañon. Illustrated. Crown 8vo, $1.50.

Justin Winsor.

Was Shakespeare Shapleigh? 16mo, rubricated parchment-paper covers, 75 cents.

Orlando Witherspoon.

Doctor Ben. 16mo, $1.00; paper, 50 cents.

Celia Parker Woolley.

Rachel Armstrong; or, Love and Theology. 12mo, $1.50; paper, 50 cents.

A Girl Graduate. 12mo, $1.50.

A. H. Wratislaw (translator).

Sixty Folk-Tales. From exclusively Slavonic Sources. Crown 8vo, gilt top, $2.00.

Lillie Chace Wyman.

Poverty Grass. Short Stories. 16mo, $1.25.

"Poverty Grass" is much more than a story book: it is a moral deed. Let those who think our social system perfect pause and read. — *Boston Beacon.*
